D & V Lovers

with love and passion

I0652489

Cover design by Getcovers Ukraine.

ISBN: 978-1-7640923-1-9

about

D & V - With Love and Passion, the first installment in a trilogy of erotic romantic adventures, is a thrilling blend of desire and suspense. As you turn each page, you'll be immersed in a world of lust, luxurious lifestyles, and adventure. Prepare to be aroused—you have been warned!

Set against a backdrop of tantalizing encounters and electric chemistry, the book draws readers into a whirlwind of emotion, seduction, and intrigue.

The writing pulses with sensual energy, making each scene *a vivid exploration of erotic and sexual connection.* The protagonists are raw and compelling, their every move charged with consequence and allure.

This is not merely erotica or a thriller; it's a captivating dance between intimacy and intensity.
D & V.-.With Love and Passion is perfect for readers of any gender who crave erotic intensity with depth. It's the first of a three-series that is certain to *arouse your interest.*

dedication

Dedicated to V,

You were not merely my muse, but my destiny.
Words began as whispers across digital space,
Each message a thread connecting us
When time and distance conspired against us.
What started has blossomed
Into the love story these pages can only echo.
For the woman who inspired every word,
Long before I understood what we could become…
You were V before I knew it,
And I was D waiting to discover myself.
Passion is not simply written, but lived.

With love across and beyond words, D

prologue

D had a passion for adventure...

V had for passion for love...

Fate entwined their paths,
teaching them both that true passion
is the greatest adventure of all

Love is one thing

Love with passion is another

When love and passion collide in a perfect
storm of desire
prepare to be transformed...

trains

I cannot understand the fascination with trains, V thought to herself as she gazed out the window of her day cabin aboard the trans-Pacific railroad bound for San Francisco. *Sure, the scenery was occasionally pleasant, but enough with the endless cows and farmyard barns. It was boring, a mobile prison cell that mocked her with its tedious scenery, mirroring the boredom in her life.*

At least she had the cabin to herself, she thought. *At least she would not have to entertain boring fellow travelers with equally boring and dull stories of their journeys.*

She turned her attention back to the book she was reading. It was an early 19th-century novel of romantic characters with an erotic element that helped her fill the void of excitement in her life.

She was halfway through a particularly steamy scene where the head of the manor was tantalizingly close to fucking the kitchen maid in the scullery when the door to her cabin slammed open abruptly.

She gazed up in annoyance at the interruption, preparing to scold the conductor for his intrusion when she saw *him*.

He was breathtakingly handsome, well-dressed, and clean-shaven.

"Pardon me," he said, as he sat opposite her, "it seems that wild children have overrun my cabin, and the conductor suggested that it would be a quieter journey here. Do you mind?"

His voice melted her resolve like heat on silk.

"Not at all," she responded, her previous objections dissolved by his raw sensuality.

"My name is D, by the way," he added.

They engaged in a conversation about tourist matters for a while. V, who had hoped to avoid this exact conversation, momentarily forgot about the boring cows and the barns as she listened attentively to his questions about her destination, her hometown, and her reasons for traveling alone.

Normally, she would be outraged by the last question, but something about how he asked it loosened her opposition to such a personal probing from a stranger.

He was gentle, *she thought.* Unusually so. It made her want to tell him everything.

Then came the silence. Not awkward—but weighted. She glanced down at his hand and noticed the wedding ring.

It surprised her, and before she had time to decide whether the question was appropriate, it slipped out as she tried to fill the void.

"You're wearing a wedding ring. Why isn't your wife traveling with you?"

V was embarrassed by the silence this caused in him. He appeared deep in thought, and she guessed he was thinking up some lie to explain away the ring.

Before she could apologize for such an invasive question, he looked her straight in the eyes and said with conviction of lived experience, "My wife was killed in a terrorist attack eight years ago; I just cannot bring myself to take the ring off."

Sadness softened his features as he spoke, and any suspicion she'd held melted in its warmth.

The next hour was spent discussing personal likes and interests, her work, and his work. But progressively, the conversation became more intimate.

There was evident chemistry between them, and he was definitely flirting with her because, at one point, D commented that she reminded him of someone but could not remember whom. V laughed and suggested that perhaps she had a familiar face.

D charmingly responded that her face could not be so common as beauty like hers was rare.

His travel was taking him in a completely different direction when they hit the west coast, but the depth of his feelings intrigued her. He was sensitive as well as manly.

The flirting soon became physical, slowly at first, as he touched her hand when she laughed at his joke about the punctuality of trains. Still, he brushed his hand against hers more frequently as he moved closer to her in intense conversation. Each touch sparked a profound sensation in the pit of her stomach and, increasingly, deep within her groin.

Embarrassed, she realized how wet she was becoming. It was almost as if he knew, though that was impossible.

They were laughing when he finally moved close toward her face.

She stopped laughing and stared into his eyes.

Yes, she thought, hoping he would read the signal and continue to the kiss she had been thinking about for thirty minutes.

He moved closer, and their lips met, soft at first, just a hint of his open mouth, soft and sensual.

Something shifted in V as they parted, catching her breath. She'd expected physical release from this encounter, nothing more—just a diversion from tedium. Yet there was a disquieting sense that this stranger had somehow seen past her carefully constructed facade, connecting with something vulnerable she'd thought well-hidden. The sensation was both thrilling and unsettling.

D was patient, as if waiting for direction, awaiting the next step in the dance.

V responded with a gentle thrust of her tongue, and he replied in kind, before they fell into a deep, passionate kiss, a potent promise of what could follow.

V could not remember how long they kissed; she was lost in the sensation as he moved from her lips to her neck, causing her nipples to tingle and become erect from the surge of endorphins. All she knew was that she wanted him, and her wetness grew with every kiss.

She was suddenly brought back to the present when she realized the train had pulled into a station and that the waiting platform passengers were staring through the window at them.

D was just as oblivious as he was when he looked up and saw the same faces staring back at them.

They quickly sat up like two teenagers caught in the act on the couch of their parents' house.

V looked down to ensure her clothes were adjusted correctly, only to notice that her nipples were so large that they threatened to tear out her blouse. D saw as well, and a small smile appeared slowly on his face and a cute redness on his cheeks. *He was blushing*, she thought, *how endearing*.

She wanted him more than she had wanted any man.

Passengers wandered up and down the train corridors, and V hoped, no prayed, that no one else would enter their cabin.

D then said, "I need to visit the boys' room" and left her alone, her breath still deep from the passion of their kisses.

You are no boy, she thought as she noticed his trousers held the imprint of a large erection that, like her nipples, was attempting to tear itself from its frustrated confinement.

The internal muscles in her groin tightened, and she almost had an orgasm on the spot.

How could I make this happen? It's too public, she thought. *What if someone joins them and ends this passion before it can reach the heights she intuitively knew it could?*

The train started pulling out of the station just as D returned. Her eyes immediately went to his groin to check if he had settled. *Had they missed their moment?* she thought to herself.

Then she saw that they had not.

V was surprised when he took her hand and said, "Come with me."

She was even more surprised by her immediate compliance with his request.

He excited her, and this only added to her excitement.

She stood and followed him out of the carriage, the train gently swaying from side to side as it picked up speed again.

They headed toward the back of the train, past many crowded carriages and through the bar carriage near the rear of the train. She wanted to stop and get a drink—her mind spun with excitement and thought that might help it settle, but he sped through.

Finally, they came to what must have been the last carriage.

The conductor stood at the end of the corridor, quietly nodding at D as he walked up to him and turned to the compartment door he was guarding. V noticed the sign said 'Staff Only'.

As D opened the door, she looked back at the conductor and understood.

V could see the tip of a $100 bill (*perhaps two*) poking out of the conductor's top jacket pocket.

Nice touch, she thought as she slipped into the room, and D closed the door behind them.

As her eyes adjusted to the dim lights of the room, she first noticed the bed. *This must be for the conductors as they swapped shifts during the long journey*, she thought.

There was a small table where a bottle of champagne and two glasses were placed.

Very nice touch, she chuckled to herself. *Very nice indeed*, as she noted it was Veuve Clicquot, her favorite.

D turned to her and quietly whispered, "I hope you don't think I'm assuming too much, but we only have this moment to bring this passion to the place it deserves."

V whispered back that she wanted him and was pleased that he had found them a private place.

V moved toward the bed, sat on the edge, and undid D's belt slowly, unzip his fly, and place her hands carefully into his undergarments to release his growing erection from its prison.

D moaned as she then placed her lips on the tip of his penis, showing she had hit the spot. Then, as she engulfed his penis deeper into her mouth, D began to almost sob with the unmistakable sound of ecstasy.

D's penis was large, not overly long, but thick at the top in a way she had not seen before; she wondered what this would be like inside her.

Her vaginal muscles twitched as she imagined his thick cock sliding inside her.

Then, almost as suddenly as she had started sucking on his cock, he pulled himself back and said, "Slowly, my love, it's been a long time, and you are so beautiful and sexy."

D knelt and kissed her again, a deep kiss that sparked an immediate rush in her pelvis, just like before in the carriage. He caressed her neck as he slowly unbuttoned the light, see-through blouse she had worn.

He dropped her blouse over her shoulder as he kneeled on the floor with V sitting on the side of the bed. He slowly moved down her neck, lingering at her shoulders briefly before he started caressing her breast with his mouth.

She could feel his strong hands supporting her back as she arched her spine toward him.

V's breathing quickened as her nipple rose to meet his lips. V was always surprised by the ability of her nipples to communicate with her vagina because, almost immediately, the sensation waved down her breast inside her body and into her pelvis. Her vagina began contracting, and her clitoris pulsed. V felt the wetness of her vagina beginning to build again.

He was taking this slow, she thought, *how wonderful.*

D played affectionately with her breasts as she slowly unbuttoned his shirt and revealed his shoulders and chest. He was not a well-built man but had a natural sensuality about him.

Then, as if sensing her desire to feel him naked against her skin, he slowly stood, pulled back the cover on the bed, slipped off his shoes and socks, and lowered his trousers to the floor before throwing them on the chair opposite.

Now he was naked, and in the dim light, the outline of his body stirred an almost primitive desire in her.

She wanted him inside her; she wanted him completely; she wanted him like no other man before.

As if reading her thoughts, D smiled as he silently helped her lie down on the fresh sheets. He unclasped the hook in her skirt and slowly lowered it as she raised her hips toward him. He moved closer toward her, sitting on the side of the bed as he placed his hands around her hips. She could see his erection in silhouette in the dim light and the unmistakable glistening of his pre-cum at the tip of his manhood.

She stirred again.

D slowly started to slip her panties down her hips.

V was suddenly embarrassed as she remembered that the last hours of their flirting and clothed foreplay had left her undergarments very wet with her passion juices.

D slid her pants under her bottom and over her knees in one swift movement until he had them in his hands. D paused for a moment as he felt the wetness of her panties.

Her embarrassment quickly faded as she noticed the significant firming of his erection as he slowly became aware that the moisture signified her intense desire for him.

D moved straight toward her and kissed her deeply on the mouth. She could feel his warm skin across her body, breasts, and hips as he slid slowly beside her in their bed.

V became aware of the train's movement again as it swayed from side to side in its forward motion to its destination.

She lifted her leg to cradle him more as they kissed again and again. V was now ecstatic, her body alive as it had never been, her desire so intense she thought she would explode soon.

And that moment rapidly approached as his kisses moved slowly down her aching body. She wanted to get there; she wanted to cum. Still, simultaneously, she tried to delay, build the intensity, and savor every sweet torture.

Every kiss took her closer to her destination.

D was now back at her breasts. Her pert breasts were engorged with desire now. Her nipples felt as firm and erect as ever, and were tingling in harmony with the rest of her body. She arched her hips in an involuntary demand for more. D was now moving his lips over her flat tummy; it was taut with the electric desire the anticipation was producing.

Yes, she thought, *go there, please*, as she moaned aloud to signal he was heading in the right direction. She could feel her wetness oozing down the small curved bits of her buttocks; it was flowing now, a testament to her desire for him.

He took it slowly, and she suspected he was tormenting her, but she wanted, needed the torment, and the orgasm building deep inside her.

She reached to grab his penis and felt its firmness and girth. Now she also wanted this deep inside her.

As she fantasized about his penis being thrust deep inside her vagina, D reached for her peach-shaped Flower, gently produced the tip of his tongue, and slid it slowly across the outside of her labia.

She arched again, demanding more as she moaned so loudly she was glad that the clatter of the train would hide their passion from those outside.

D deftly used his finger to gently part her lips as he took the end of his tongue and slowly began to circle the base of her clitoris. He skillfully avoided the most sensitive and responsive spot. This delay kept her intense feeling from turning into explosive pleasure.

He is good, she thought, *tormenting me in a way he knew instinctively I want.*

V desperately wanted to cum, but she also wanted to delay. Not too long, but long enough to ensure the final climax would be fantastic.

Sensing her thoughts and the rising pace of her breath, D moved from her clitoris to penetrate her vagina with his tongue.

It felt good, a further tease in the long line of teases that had been their lovemaking so far.

He used his tongue in various ways, slowly, fast, soft, then firmer, on the surface and in her depths before he suddenly moved back to her clitoris and started a slow, firm, rhythmic movement that V knew would be irresistible.

The intense feeling in her belly, in her being, began to rise.

That was the signal that the point of no return was close.

V could take it no more; she wanted this now and arched her hips to push firmly toward him so that the pressure he provided would intensify.

"Yes; yes," she said, "yes," as her breath deepened and quickened until she screamed out as the release of sexual energy pulsated deep within her and across her entire body. She pulsed for a short time as D tactically retreated, knowing that, at this point, the pleasure was all hers and that his contact could turn her focus from the sensation and pleasure of her climax.

V rode each orgasmic wave, breath catching, body suspended in afterglow.

D was patient and slowly rose from between her legs and moved carefully toward her face. He paused there for a while, watching the ecstasy in her face and the joy in her eyes.

V could see that he was a man that cared for her pleasure as much as his own. Likewise, she could see that her pleasure was as much his as hers.

As she slowly drifted back to the moment, her contractions subsiding, V smiled, and he responded with a small smile, almost like a small boy's smile when he had done something right. *He was pleased with his performance,* she thought.

D kissed her again, first on the cheek, then her forehead, before V moved toward him in an obvious demand for more. They kissed deeply again, slowly, then passionately.

V started to move her hips again; she was enticing him.

He was hard, and she wanted him inside her. His movements matched the rhythmic movements of her hips; he wanted her now too. With one deft move, D guided her from her back onto her stomach and began to kiss her neck.

She was unable to move freely from here.

She wanted to move; so she could entice him inside her.

No, she thought, no more; *I don't want kisses*; *I want you to fuck me*.

D's kisses moved down her back as he rose to his knees. He kissed her back more as he reached his hands under her.

Now she understood; she rose to her knees in response as his arms closed around her hips.

Yes, she thought, *deep this way, god, I want this deep*.

He maneuvered himself gently behind her and slowly moved the shaft of his penis up and down near the lips of her vagina, searching for its inviting opening.

Finally, he found her entrance and slowly penetrated her in one smooth movement that sent the very breath from her.

Then it started in earnest.

She smiled, relaxed her muscles, and let him take her— slowly at first. Then deeper as she pushed back with her hips and listened to the rhythm of his thighs against her bottom match the endless rhythm of the train, thrusting ever so relentlessly to its inevitable destination.

The rhythm drove her higher—closer—her body begging to break when she heard his slow and tormented moans. *He was close too*, she thought; *he was about to cum*.

That was enough for her; it tipped her over into the endless pulses deep within her body that were her climax. He kept thrusting, and she kept pulsing as the electric feeling spread throughout her in an explosion of orgasm of the kind she had never had before.

He slowed; he had not cum yet, and she felt a little cheated until she realized he was ready for more.

He kissed her back, helped her to roll over, and as he lay on top of her, he kissed her deeply as she regained her strength and desire for more.

V was satisfied with her desire being sated by their passionate lovemaking.

Yet, as she kissed him, her passion began to rise again.

D was quiet and patient as she slowly roused again. His manhood had rested slightly, surrendering from his constant excitement and then suppression to delay his climax for her.

She moved him over to his side and slid down the bed to take his cock into her mouth again. It was her turn to take the lead. He responded almost immediately as his cock hardened in her moist mouth.

The instant response excited her even more, and she felt the familiar sexual desire rising in her pelvis. She could feel her nipples and her clitoris harden in sympathy.

D moaned; *he likes this*, she thought as she slowly engulfed his cock with a slow sucking motion.

It was more than D could take. He pushed her over and mounted her; the strength of his movement took V by surprise, but it also excited her.

She opened her legs to him and caressed his penis in her hands, guiding him home to her Flower. Slowly, he entered her. This was a different sensation from his earlier penetration; he felt fuller and harder, and she gasped for joy as he entered her completely.

They started the rhythm of their lovemaking, thrusting in sync, her pelvis moving in to meet his thrusts and out again to lengthen the sensation before the next long thrust.

They moved in sync faster and faster.

She could see the joy on his face, in his eyes as she gazed at his face. He was half-raised, and the dim light was enough to show his expressions. She liked seeing his joy; it made her feel good and excited to see him respond to her skill. She clasped him with her internal muscles as he withdrew each stroke, and he enjoyed this.

V started to feel the inevitable build-up of her climax again. Her initial surprise gave way to longing, her breath catching in its race toward ecstasy.

V began to thrust under him. *Yes*, she thought, *another, but this time I would draw his semen into me. I want his seed inside me. I want him to cum with me.*

He responded by increasing his pace. Their eyes met, and as if their thoughts were in their vision, he lifted her legs over his arms and tilted her pelvis.

Suddenly, he was much deeper than she thought possible. Still, the inward thrust from this angle tugged repeatedly on her clit, creating a second sensation that raised the building tension that brought her toward another climax.

He thrust. She moaned. She moaned louder, and as V got close, she started to scream, "Fuck me, fuck me, cum with me, babe!"

That was enough to tip her over.

The beginning of her orgasm was clear, and all D needed to tip him over the edge of his orgasm. He thrust as his penis and pelvis pulsated continually, ejecting all the pent-up energy inside along with his love juices, squirting in bursts deep inside her.

V clasped her vagina in response, wanting to hold every pulse of his release as her own electric pulses continued to bring her ecstatic pleasure.

Slowly, they came to a standstill, with periodic small thrusts as their passion tried to keep going, not wanting the climax to end. Spent and entangled, they lay in silence—yet something between them had only just begun.

They held each other. His weight on top of her felt comforting. His hips on hers. His legs between hers as they kissed again. Not a word was spoken or needed.

They lay together exhausted and slowly began to fall asleep.

The light woke V first; she slowly took in her situation, remembering what had happened the night before.

The light filled the cabin, and she looked at the clock on the wall. They were three hours away from the end of their journey, the end of this intimate encounter. She tried to move, but his arm was across her chest and his hand upon her breast. The thought aroused her again, and when she noticed he had a morning erection in his deep sleep, she smiled.

She reached down to slowly stroke his cock; he stirred slowly, his cock was tantalizingly firm. D began to wake and realize where he was.

V told D they only had an hour before they needed to get ready for the train's arrival.

They spent the next hour bringing each other to a climax.

In the light, he was very handsome and visibly excited by her body. She wanted to have him deep inside her again and again. She was turned on when they were back-to-side with his legs under hers, entering her sideways.

His hand took hers and moved it to her Flower, indicating that he wanted her to touch herself; she liked that.

V masturbated regularly and enjoyed the control she had over how it was done. She responded even more when it was clear he was excited by her skill.

V came fast and deep, and he lost control, cuming deep inside her as her muscles clasped his penis in pulsating contractions.

She lay beside him, breathless, but not just from pleasure—from possibility.

As her breathing steadied, V studied D's face in the dim light. Beyond the obvious satisfaction, she glimpsed vulnerability in his eyes—a flash of something genuine that contradicted his polished exterior. For just a moment, she wondered about the tragedy that had taken his wife, what kind of man he'd been before that loss, and who he might become with the right person by his side.

Then her thoughts turned to the impending end of their passionate embrace.

They could not delay any longer; they had to dress and move back to the carriage where it all started.

V was somewhat surprised and slightly annoyed when D took the seat opposite her in the carriage. But then, she was devastated when he took out his *iPad* and started using it.

Well, she thought, *all that passion then....this! How can he turn it off like that?*

V was still going over every second of their lovemaking, desperate to prolong the experience she now knew was over. His gentle touch, his generosity, his patience, his unbelievable control. Her orgasms were simply the best she had ever had.

She couldn't explain it—she'd known skilled lovers, but none had touched her like this.

She looked across at him, *hmmp*, she thought, *still working*.

It was getting close to when they would pull into the station and part. Sure, they had exchanged contacts, but she suspected from his behavior this was it.

He glanced up at her at this point in her thoughts and threw a small, cute smile toward her as if to say, *here, this should tide you* over, then he went back to work.

She was getting angry now.

Finally, D packed up his *iPad* and moved to her side of the carriage.

V attempted to feign aloofness to punish him, but soon found herself engaged in chit-chat with him, and before long, they were holding hands. They did not have long now; the countryside scenery had given way to housing and was now becoming dense as their train moved closer to the city center where the train would stop, where they would stop.

She turned to kiss him one more time. D responded with a deep, passionate kiss that stirred her desires immediately.

She wanted him again, but there was no time and no opportunity.

Soon enough, the train pulled into the station.

This was it.

D helped her with her bags and lodged them onto a trolley. He had to get a connecting train to the suburbs and his meeting, so he said farewell then and there with a friendly, comfortable kiss devoid of the passion from the night before.

She watched him walk away, too stunned to move from her spot next to the train that stole her passion.

He disappeared up the escalator, and she turned to the train again.

It was different now; she had not understood why people enjoyed train travel, but now she had a different experience.

She would never forget this journey; she would remember the passion, the depths of her feelings, and the excitement of their secretive encounter in the conductors' sleeping quarters. But she would remember him most of all: his smell, tenderness, and gorgeous body.

And yet, now, she will also not forget how he walked out of her life with no more thought than he had when he stumbled into her carriage when they met.

Trains, she thought…

Tears started to well up in her eyes just as her *iPhone* beeped, bringing her back to reality.

She had a message. It was from D, and there was an attachment. V opened it to reveal a first-class ticket for the Orient Express next month. An invitation for her to join him on another train journey…

Trains, she thought, *I LOVE trains.*

depth

V was daydreaming as she slowly unpacked her luggage in the hotel.

It was now three hours since D left her at the station in a mix of emotions. V was saddened by the cursory way he left her on the platform and joyous at the surprise invitation she received from him soon after he left.

She loved a good plan, and this was the best of all. She had never been to Paris before, and now in twenty-four days, she would be there, ready to board the romantic Orient Express.

One night in Paris with D before they left was enough for her, given the long journey they would take in a first-class suite on the train across Europe to Istanbul.

As she started to undress and shower, she realized that she had not washed since they last made love only hours ago.

She could still smell him on her, and his scent mingled with her own familiar sex odor. It roused her, and she felt her wetness with her fingers, drawing them up to her face. *Yes*, she thought; *I can still smell his semen on me*. She contemplated delaying the shower to prolong the experience but soon changed her mind.

Nice shower, she thought as the water gushed over her, and her thoughts returned to the night before as D mounted her from behind, thrusting his manhood inside her. It was thick, she recalled, thicker than any man she had known. It was surprising to her that she effortlessly took his cock, but she reasoned that he had made her so aroused that she simply felt the fullness of his cock filling her completely.

It felt wonderful.

Her desire stirred again, and soon she had the hand shower between her legs, the water pulsating against her clitoris. Her nipples hardened as she clasped them between her soapy fingers, giving them gentle tugs as the sexual tension in her pelvis rose.

She visualized D, his face between her legs, imagining his tongue gently circling her Button, gently at first, but as she started to get closer, much firmer. The water gushed against her as she climaxed, her thighs clasping her groin to intensify the sensation. *I will have to do more of this over the coming days*, she thought; she smiled...

It's been a while since I felt this sexual, she thought. *Life is good.*

It was nearly a week before D finally texted her.

She had not expected them to have contact outside their planned meeting but was happy to connect with him again. He was working, he said, and had been away again, but this time he could not call anyone. She realized that in their small chit-chat, he had not told her anything about what he had done for work.

She knew he traveled a lot, meetings here and there, but what did he do, and whom did he work for?

The text chat slowly got flirty, and this excited V; they traded innuendo after innuendo, with overt references to their encounter, his thick cock, her body, and their orgasms.

He was now in Australia on some assignment he did not explain or was unwilling to discuss.

She did not press him.

He would be in Paris in just over two weeks, and then they would meet again.

She wanted him again; she had wanted him constantly since they parted and spent her evenings reliving their lovemaking.

This had led to more than the occasional session of masturbation, and her vibrator had been working overtime since they parted. Her showers became more frequent and far less about hygiene than she cared to admit.

The next time they texted, V suggested they should have an oral chat: another innuendo designed to entice D to call her and talk instead of texting.

It worked.

Soon V was on her bed, talking to D about the night they made love and how good a lover he was. She was a little surprised at how frank she was with him and somewhat turned on by the sweet things he said about her, her body, and her sexuality.

She loved the sound of his voice, which brought back memories, images, and the scent of that night. She had unconsciously moved her hand into her underwear. Before she realized it, she was stoking her clitoris and feeling her wetness. D had stopped talking, and she suddenly realized that she had too.

Finally, D broke the silence and said, "I can hear that your breathing has become deeper. Are you aroused, my love?"

She had to admit she was, and he confessed the same, indicating they should let this go where it goes.

As D spoke softly about what he wanted to do to her, she became intensely aroused. He said his image of her was with his head between her legs, looking at her sweet cherry blossom Flower and her slowly engorging Button.

She liked that and started to stroke her clitoris more determinedly.

D imagined her stroking his cock just as he was doing at that moment. His erection was now full, and his pre-cum glistened at its tip. He started to moan.

V stepped up the rhythm of her masturbation and asked D to do the same. She imagined him in front of her, stoking his hard, thick cock, his face filled with ecstasy. She could hear his breathing getting faster, and she could hear him pumping his cock.

V picked up her pace; the image and sound of him intensified the tension in her groin; she was close now.

She moaned.

D moaned. "Yes, babe," he said, "yes, cum for me –" and then she lost it.

Over the top, she went screaming as she heard D cum as well. She imagined his semen spurting over her breast as he knelt before her. She arched her hips and came again.

D gasped with joy as she did.

They slowly rested, hardly talking; as they had burned their passion energy completely even though they were thousands of miles apart.

When they disconnected, V sat motionless, staring at the blank screen. The intensity of their virtual connection troubled her. This wasn't merely physical desire—there was an undercurrent of something deeper forming, a bridge being built between their lives despite the distance. She wondered if he felt it too, or if she was simply projecting meaning onto something that was, for him, just a pleasant diversion.

It was not long before V and D were texting each other regularly.

She would text him when something reminded her of him or she thought or saw something he would like or find funny. Occasionally, she would text comments about his sexuality, thick cock, or make other flirty innuendos. This inevitably led to a flurry of increasingly sexual texts back and forth, ending with V being very wet and masturbating.

D was also excited by these exchanges and had indicated on a number of occasions that he was also masturbating.

V found it particularly sensual when he texted that he had just cum.

While this sexting excited V, she quickly became frustrated by the lack of physical contact and not hearing D's voice.

Several times a week, they managed a phone call (V saucily called these 'their oral').

These were always very hot and sexual and ended up in either mutual masturbation, so they came together, or each taking turns so they could focus on themselves.

V loved to hear his voice; she found it sexy. She particularly liked the image she held of him pumping his cock as she listened to his increasing moans, faster breathing, and the mix of noises he made as he went through the stages of his orgasm. She sometimes held her hand over the phone so she could masturbate and cum without his knowing, even when it was his turn...

By the end of the second week, V could not stand it any longer. D had previously suggested that they could FaceTime to see each other. But the thought of their text or oral sessions being played out on video that might be kept or shared was too much for her.

She had told D that she could not FaceTime because her internet connection would not cope.

Her will was breaking as her mental image of D began to fade, so the next time they talked, V said that she had upgraded her internet and they could FaceTime.

D suggested that they do so that evening so they could 'have a date'.

V liked the idea and excitedly dressed for the occasion that evening.

When D called and the video started streaming, V was pleased by what she saw.

D was dressed in a funky, casual shirt that showed he cared for his clothes. He had his dinner before him and drank an expensive Shiraz.

He liked playing games, she thought, and V relaxed into a date role that helped her overcome her shyness to the point that she almost forgot she was on video.

D felt natural, and he was certainly something to look at. She remembered him as handsome, but when he spoke, how he talked, and what he said all contributed to his attraction.

That evening, V lost her shyness and forgot her inhibitions as D slowly seduced her with his wit, innuendo, flirting, and suggestive talk. As he told V that he wanted to remove her blouse, button by button, slowly...

V found herself undoing each button as he spoke, as if his every description was a command she could not resist.

Step by step, he virtually removed her top, skirt, bra, and panties.

V complied willingly, as if in a trance.

She was wet, hot, and wanted him badly. As he described how he would mount her from behind, V found herself on all fours, with her tight buttocks presented to the camera as D knelt facing his screen with his thick cock in his hand and making a pumping motion as if to fuck her.

V was wetter than she had ever been; his detailed description of his kisses, caresses, and sexual acts had been so erotic that she had forgotten he was not physically there.

V masturbated her clit while on her knees, fingers moving with a rising rhythm, she gave in to the heat he ignited in her; her rising orgasm was building strong and fast.

Then, as D started to pump his cock faster, she tipped over into one of her best orgasms in a long time.

D loved this and came in a quick burst shortly after she did. He ejaculated so forcefully that it splashed across the screen of his phone.

D had also forgotten that was the barrier that separated them.

They fucked like this twice a day until the last week of the wait until they met in Paris.

V felt a familiar twinge between her thighs as she eventually boarded the Eurostar from London to Paris. *Trains will never be the same*, she thought as she walked down to her First Class compartment for the journey.

In four hours, she would be in Paris, and an hour later: checking into the George V hotel and dressing for her evening with D. He had arranged it all: the journey from London, the accommodation in Paris at the George V Hotel, and dinner at the Eiffel Tower's famous Jules Verne Restaurant.

He was a good planner, and he certainly understood what she liked.

And then they would take the Orient Express from Paris to Venice, with a two-day stay over at the Luna Baglioni

Hotel before rejoining the Orient Express for its journey to Istanbul.

D's plans for the next part of the journey remained a secret – he only told her she needed three weeks from when they arrived and had not given her a return ticket to London.

Her excitement grew… as did the nerves gnawing in the pit of her stomach.

V was ordinarily shy, although their love tryst on the train to San Francisco would have indicated otherwise; that was different then.

D saw her as a stranger then; there was no expectation, no commitment.

Now she faced the prospect of meeting him again after a few weeks of passionate flirting, virtual sex, and discussions. They were intimate and profound, and D just seemed to get her. He understood her deepest desires, the depth of her love, and what turned her on.

The train moved onward.

V daydreamed about her train experience, how D made her feel, and was amazed that she had almost been continually wet ever since.

She started to panic…

The nervousness that knotted her stomach wasn't just anticipation of pleasure, but fear of disappointment. Over these weeks, D had become something beyond a lover in her mind—a possibility, a future that took shape in her quiet moments. What if the reality couldn't possibly live up to what they'd created in their shared imagination?

Would he still like her?

Would their lovemaking be as passionate?

Would she still desire him?

It all swirled through her mind as she fell into a deep sleep nurtured by the comforting movement of the train.

V was in a room; it was half-lit, and she could tell she was not alone. She was not alarmed because there was a familiar smell of someone in the room. She did not know who it was, but it somehow comforted her. She could not make out who was there with her in the poor light, so she started calling out for the person to identify themselves, even though she knew it was D in her heart.

V was trying to find the light when something grabbed her on the arm, saying, "Madame, Madame, we have arrived."

As she woke, she realized the train had stopped, and the conductor was trying to wake her. She looked out the window to see that she was in Paris. She jumped up and started to prepare herself to disembark, and as she did, she reflected on her dream.

She understood what she had to do now. Even though they had been together physically, D had been a shadow in her life, never entirely with her, completely, never fully revealed, and she had been the same with him. V decided to completely put herself into their relationship with D on this journey. She could not tell where that would lead; but whatever happened, she needed to be true to her feelings. It may hurt her, he might hurt her, but she loved him, and he had to know her truth.

V was greeted by a traditional chauffeur when she exited the train. The driver knew just what carriage she was on.

D's planning skills were impeccable and even started to rival her own.

She wasn't used to such indulgence—but oh, how she reveled in it.

The drive to the George V was a little hair-raising and even exciting. V had heard about the infamous Paris traffic and their hectic drivers, but nothing prepared her for this.

Fortunately, her driver was skilled, and they soon arrived safely at the hotel.

The hotel was breathtaking, like something out of a romantic French novel.

V allowed the doorman to open her door and assist her from the car.

"Bonjour Madame V," he said, as if she had just returned from a shopping trip.

He thinks of everything, she smiled.

The lobby was spectacular, and as she approached reception, the hotel manager said confidently, "Welcome, Madame V. I have your key, and I will personally escort you to your room. Your bags are being sent to your suite as we speak."

Mademoiselle Begie moved around the desk and took her to the elevators. Once there, she turned a key and pressed an unmarked button. A broad smile on the manager's face indicated she knew a secret.

As the door to the elevator opened into a private lobby, V understood that they were entering what must be one of their best suites. The manager opened the door to the enormous suite, and V was stunned by the room's incredible furniture and exquisite décor.

Very French, she thought.

V could already see the Eiffel Tower through the balcony window across the room.

"The George V Penthouse, Madame," she said, "one of our finest suites. I will have our maid assist you in unpacking; here is your key. Should you need anything, press these buttons: number one for the maid, two for the butler, and three for prompt personal attention from me."

V looked at the manager; she was very French, beautiful, and petite. V thought for a second. *I would not mind a little personal attention from her,* but thanked her instead and turned to take in the view.

After the manager left, V scurried around from room to room, excitedly looking at the opulent fittings in the bathroom and an adorable bath.

We will certainly enjoy that, she thought. Finally, V moved to the bedroom, with its beautiful bed, dressing room, and view of Paris from the large windows.

V imagined making love to D with Paris in the backdrop.

Soon the maid arrived, and V started to choose what she would wear for their meeting and dinner that evening. She had brought several outfits but had not decided which to wear. The dress would also determine the underwear; all sets equally sexy, all sets designed to ensure D was as impressed as he had been when they first met.

She chose the black velvet dress. It was perfect for the weather (a little cold in the evening), and V found the material particularly stimulating as she moved. She hoped D would feel the same as they caressed that evening.

To contrast, V would wear a beautiful ensemble of hot pink bra and panties – *'perfect'*, she thought, it *highlights my skin tones and attracts his attention to my warmth.*

V showered after the maid left; put on her makeup and slid into her velvet dress. She was nervous and had just decided to get a drink from the extensive bar in their dining room when the doorbell rang.

The butler entered with a bottle of Dom Perignon on ice and one crystal glass.

Perfect, V thought.

It was now seven thirty p.m. She was to meet V in the lobby in fifteen minutes, and she sat drinking the champagne, trying to rehearse what she would first say as she greeted him.

Should she play it cool to keep him keen and chasing her, or should she show how much she missed him and cared?

It was time.

V thought about being late but could no longer bear the suspense. She had to see him again and know if the love for this new man she had been with for just one day was real. Yes, she had spent the last month in a whirlwind virtual romance, but was that real or a fantasy?

She had to know…

As V rode the elevator to the lobby, her heart beat faster, her head spun a little from the champagne, and she still had not decided which way to greet D.

Eager or aloof.

Which was it to be?

The door opened, and she exited the elevator and walked to the main lobby. She scanned the room, suddenly realizing she might not recognize D. She checked again, but no one was familiar, no D.

Her heart sank.

The possibility that he would not be there or D would be late had not crossed her mind, so now she felt annoyed at herself for even thinking she should play with him and deliberately come late. It felt terrible for her, and she could not do that to him. Then, as she chastised herself, she heard her name spoken in a very familiar voice.

She turned, and there, walking up from behind her, was D.

She sighed, took him in with her eyes, took him in her arms, and took him into her heart: instantly.

D hugged her and kissed her gently, respectful of the lipstick she had carefully applied before leaving the suite. "How are you?" he said. "Are you happy with the room?"

V smiled and said, "Well played. I could not have planned this better myself. It's perfect."

"I have a room on the second floor," he responded. Then, as the smile and joy drained from V's face, he quickly added, "I'm just joking; of course, we are together."

V was annoyed that he could make light of their relationship but forgave him quickly.

"Shall we go?" D said as he took her hand and motioned toward the exit of the hotel.

Outside, there was another chauffeur with a beautiful Rolls-Royce Caprice. As they entered the car, V said, "You will run out of tricks if you use them all too soon."

D laughed knowingly, and V understood that this was her attempt at punishing him for his earlier, *'I'm in room on the second'* joke.

D secretly understood that he could never run out of tricks.

They took in the Paris scenery in the short drive to the Eiffel Tower, pulled up much closer than all the other tourists were allowed, and walked across the pavement to the priority entrance and straight up to the Jules Verne Restaurant.

It was a stage set for seduction—Paris alight, flavors dancing, and love hovering in the air all combining to create a perfect atmosphere for their first *actual* date.

They started with champagne cocktails, then he had a starter of mushrooms in French wine, and she had the most delicious oysters she had ever tasted.

She wanted him to try one, but he declined, and when she appeared hurt by this, D added, "This is our first real meal together, and the topic has not come up before, but I'm Jewish, and I do not eat pork, seafood, or shellfish. I'm not a religious Jew, but I still follow the dietary restrictions, as it is part of who I am."

V was shocked by this revelation; she had not even thought about his religious beliefs. V looked at D, a bit speechless, but eventually, she smiled and said, "I find it endearing that you honor your past in this way. I'm pleased that you do."

D responded with a smile, and V thought that he had been worried that this might have been an issue.

It was not.

His religion did not matter to her, and there was the bonus that he was circumcised. She loved the look of his circumcised flaccid penis and loved it even more when erect.

They talked about her past and background and ordered a Pinot Noir wine. As the waiter brought out their mains (his a French lamb dish, hers a traditional French-style fillet of fish), V realized it was time for her to ask more about what he did for a living.

V was a little perplexed why she was unsure how to ask him…

Finally, as they ordered dessert (he, profiteroles and her, a soufflé), V started to talk about her work. She had been nursing all her life and now cared for a small number of children at one of the most exclusive boarding schools in London. She was not so much a nurse now as a coach and friend to this small group, though if they ever hurt themselves, she was more than equipped to deal with them.

The parents were often away overseas on business or holidays. Still, when they were home, they welcomed her into their homes as a family member. They were all very wealthy, grateful for her help, and occasionally invited her on holidays. That was why she was in the US when she met D.

Sometimes they wanted her there as one of the only people who understood their children or knew how to control them. Still, she did not mind as it gave her many opportunities to travel.

D moved his chair closer next to V. She liked that.

They were in a very private corner of the room, so when D started to stroke her on the leg, she was perfectly at ease: and beginning to feel that familiar twinge in her pelvis, and the inevitable sensation of intimate moistness she had come to associate with D.

As if to hide her embarrassment from D, even though he could not possibly know the impact this was having on her at this stage, suddenly she blurted, "OK, enough about my work, tell me what you do for a living."

D took his hand off her leg, looked in the air as if to think, moved closer, looked her directly in the eyes, and said softly as if it mattered.

"If I tell you... "His voice dropped. "You can never repeat it. To anyone." He held her gaze. "Ever. It's not just my secret to keep."

V felt a chill run through her. His intensity was unsettling. Her mind raced—spy? Criminal? Drug lord?—as seconds stretched between them. What kind of secret demanded this level of discretion?

Finally, she looked at him and said sincerely, as she had already made up her mind, no matter what was to come next, that she wanted him more than ever…

"I promise."

He started slowly as if to emphasize the importance of his words;

"V, I work for the Simon Wiesenthal Center and the Israeli government," he said.

"The first is an international organization established to find those responsible for the Holocaust against the Jews, Gypsies, homosexuals, and people of color in World War II. The second, you know.

"I'm a Nazi hunter and have been for twenty-two years."

"I spend my time traveling the world, seeking out the most notorious Nazis, and my network helps get them back to Israel to face trial. There are few left, and they are all old. I have committed my life to ensure that those who perpetrated the crimes of the Holocaust are brought to justice."

V had not expected that, and she took a while to take it in. It did explain everything: his trips, the secretive nature of his work, and the sense that she had that he was much more profound than he let on. This depth attracted her in the first place, and now this.

She did not quite understand the history of the Holocaust, but what she had seen had disturbed her deeply. This was a cause she could accommodate; she could accept the long periods between their meetings. She had to ask one thing, though, which would be even more delicate. She took a deep breath and asked...

"Do you have to kill some of them?" she asked tentatively as if this could be a deal breaker.

She sat back and studied his expression.

He looked sad but said, "You understand that we seek out those who committed heinous crimes. They murdered and tortured people, women and children, but it's justice we seek, not revenge. If we were to kill them, we would be no better than them.

"No, my love, I use all but lethal force to capture them; sometimes, we drug them but never kill them. Once back in Israel, they are tried. We even provide them with their own defense attorneys.

"Those convicted are sentenced to prison, as Israel does not have the death penalty, although one was hung in 1961 when the pain of the Holocaust was still fresh. He was the worst of the worst: Adolf Eichmann, the man who organized the deportation of the Jews and established the extermination camps."

She was relieved but slightly embarrassed and ashamed of her private response to this statement... after she heard 'No,' the words that stirred her most were those two that followed: '*my love.*'

He had said it with such tenderness that she instantly connected to him.

Here was a man she could love, she thought, *tender, generous, one who had beliefs he worked for, and all this with a sexual skill she had longed for all her life.*

She now knew. She now understood and wanted D more than anything she ever wanted.

It was time to go. As she stood up to leave with him, she leaned over and whispered in his ear, "I promise your secret is safe with me, as is your heart."

She had not meant to add the last bit, but it just came out naturally as if it had to, and she could not stop it.

D smiled and said, "As is yours, my sweet."

glimmer

They were quiet on the trip back to the hotel, each deep in thought.

Silence stretched between them—not distance, but reflection.

V found herself reevaluating everything. His revelation about being a Nazi hunter cast their connection in a new light. This wasn't just a man who pleased her physically, but someone defined by a moral purpose, who had dedicated his life to justice. The complexity of him— tender lover and determined hunter—created a fullness that both attracted and intimidated her. What place could she hold in such a life?

She also thought about the last time they made love (not virtually); she was a little nervous that their sexting and FaceTime lovemaking may have built up his expectations of her and was worried about whether he would be satisfied with her again.

V did not have to worry for long because as they kissed in the car, she noticed that familiar thick cock rising underneath his trousers.

Yes, she thought, *we are going to have a fun night.*

Little did she know just how much!

As they drove toward the hotel, they stopped by the riverbank. D said the view was exceptional, so they got out of the car and walked over to the river's edge. He was right; they were near the Eiffel Tower, yet far enough to take it all in along with the rest of the Paris lights.

It could not get more romantic than this, she thought.

Then D whispered, "Happy birthday, my sexy Vixen."

The excitement of the trip, being in Paris and reuniting with D, had completely overshadowed her birthday.

"Of course, I hadn't even realized it; once I turned forty, I started to ignore that milestone," she admitted.

"You're in your prime, Janine," Steve said, as she blushed and discreetly appreciated the compliment.

"How did you know?" she insisted, trying to hide her embarrassment at the praise.

"If I can hunt down Nazis across the world, do you think it would be hard for me to find out your birthday?" he replied as he took a small box out of his pocket and handed it to her.

The box was well-wrapped, small, with white paper and a little pink ribbon.

V looked at him, and he smiled. "Just a small token for your birthday. I want you to remember this night," he said, affectionately.

"Of course, I will remember this night with or without your small token. It's been exceptional so far," she added.

She slowly started to open the small package until she saw the unmistakable box.
Whatever it was, it was from Tiffany's. She slowly opened the box to find two gorgeous platinum and diamond earrings.

The earrings glittered in the lamplight, beautiful but hardly extravagant. V appreciated his restraint—the gift acknowledged their connection without presuming too much. It balanced perfectly on the edge of meaningful and appropriate, showing a thoughtfulness that touched her more deeply than any diamond necklace could have. He understood nuance, timing, the language of gestures. This, perhaps even more than their physical compatibility, made her heart quicken.

He had chosen well. At this point in their relationship, a very expensive gift would have been an overstatement. He had, after all, paid for this incredible trip, so she would not have expected anything even if she had mentioned her birthday.

I will remember my birthday now she, thought with a smile in her heart.

"They are lovely," she said, and kissed him deeply.

As they drove back to the hotel, V discreetly admired the way the earrings glistened in the Parisian lights. Despite not hinting at her birthday, she was delighted that he had taken the effort to discover it, let alone plan to make this one of the most memorable nights of her life.

And the night was still young…

They started earnestly in the lounge of their hotel suite, with D kissing her passionately on the lips and neck. She could feel the velvet dress sliding on her skin, accentuating her rising sensations.

In his embrace, a quiet certainty settled over V. This wasn't just chemistry or compatibility—it was recognition. Each touch carried the weight of understanding, as if they were remembering each other rather than learning. She'd never believed in such things, had prided herself on practicality, yet here she was, falling into something that felt remarkably like fate.

He was also a good kisser, and sometimes she would passively let him kiss her, enjoying the feeling and reveling in his passion for her.

It was not long before her hands were in his trousers, seeking out that familiar, firm, thick cock of his. She had only seen it in real life in dim light on the train, but she knew it well; she had every curve, every shape embedded in her mind, the sense of it entering her, the feeling as his thickness passed a certain point in her vagina, and that unbelievable feeling of him filling her completely when it finally found its home.

These memories had been overlaid with images he sent in texts and the video from their FaceTime sessions, so she knew his cock intimately and liked what she saw.

V undid his trousers to release him completely, and as she saw his glistening manhood appear, she knelt and took him into her mouth. Gently at first, savoring his smell and taste, slowly building her pace and the depth of her oral strokes down the shaft of his thick penis.

D was clearly enjoying this as his moans became more audible and deep.

He now had his hand between her thighs, stoking the soft bits at the top of her legs; she enjoyed that; it was a tease.

She wanted him to touch her vulva but did not at the same time.

D seemed to understand this as he alternated his touch from her thighs to moving, almost, to her mons and her Button, still held captive under her panties.

V started to realize that D was breathing faster and started to worry; she loved sucking his cock but was unwilling to have him cum in her mouth. She began to slow her pace again, and D responded accordingly; his breathing slowed, but undoubtedly, his enjoyment did not diminish.

He also likes to be teased, V thought.

D started to move away from her, and as her mouth slid away from his firm erection, she heard D sigh; he wanted this but was moving on.

D fell to his knees and deftly slid her panties down her legs over her hold-up stockings and black high-heel shoes.

She was reclining on the edge of the couch now, her legs astride, feet on the ottoman, knees bent, and D between her legs, looking longingly at her now exposed Flower. It was such a turn-on to V as she watched him take her in with his eyes.

When D inhaled her scent deeply, it was more than she could handle.

"Please," she said, "lick me, taste me, I want you," she cried, and D obeyed in good measure.

It was not long before V breathed heavily, thrusting her hips as she came closer toward her orgasm; the image of her lover's head between her, the shoes on her feet, and the stockings were all she needed; the oral sex was the cream.

She often masturbated in sexy underwear and nice shoes but seldom had the chance to combine the two.

Then she lost it as she tipped over into the most incredible orgasm she had ever had; it pulsed through her, sending that familiar release sensation throughout her pelvis and her entire body. Her nipples were already electric, and they had not even managed to get released from her bra.

Yet…

As V slowly recovered from her ecstasy, D stood up and ran a bath.

The bath was lit from inside by a blue light that seemed to come from nowhere, and by the time V arrived in the bathroom, D had placed candles and two glasses of Dom on the edge of the bath.

He slowly and sexily helped V remove her dress. It was as if he was in slow motion, taking care at every step to ensure he brushed her ever so slightly with his hands in all the parts that exited her.

V helped him take off his clothes now, taking the cue from his. She also worked slowly, occasionally brushing him in places and once or twice, moving so close so she could touch his side with her face and smell him before he went into the bath and took on the scent of the bath salts he used.

He smelled good.

As they lowered themselves into the bath, end to end, they both smiled and felt the heat relax their muscles.

V could see the thick erection D still had through the bluish bath water; the refraction made it look even bigger. She involuntarily contracted the muscles in her vagina in response. V noticed new things about D now: his skin color and the slight imperfections that came with age and maturity. It made him whole to her, more real than the virtual D of the last few weeks.

She particularly liked how the waterline of the bath framed his nipples.

D soon moved toward her, lying above her in the water. It was a big bath and easily accommodated them in about any position. He kissed V's breasts slowly, taking her nipples into his mouth and using his tongue to make circular motions while gently tugging her nipples with his lips. V's nipples were large and constantly firm. They were even firmer when they received his attention, and D loved them.

As D started to caress her breast with his large hands while continuing to suck her nipples, V started to feel the sensations she usually reserved when her clitoris was being stimulated.

This was new, she thought, but sat back and went with the sensation.

As V savored the building tension, D stepped up the intensity of his nipple caresses, the pressure from his tugging lips and the firmness of his grasp as he massaged her whole breast.

That was enough, and V tipped over into an orgasm.

It was a different kind of pleasure—unexpected, slow-burning, profoundly intimate. It demonstrated to V for the first time what she knew instinctively; there was a direct connection between her nipples, her clitoris, and vagina.

She hadn't expected that pleasure. But now, she craved more. She whispered in D's ear, "I have never been nipple-fucked like that. Let's go to bed so you can take the rest of me…"

She moved to the bedroom first and put on a black negligee and very sexy French knickers. She wanted D to work for her again rather than take her naked.

D arrived still looking quite firm, although it was clear he needed to warm up a little more.

V enjoyed this as she got hot watching the impact she had on him, so as she cuddled up to him, she kept an eye on developments. She was not disappointed as he soon visibly hardened, lengthened, and thickened – the thickening made her the hottest, and she could feel the wetness rising inside her.

They kissed slowly.

D was a patient man.

He kissed her back and managed to caress her breast through the low-cut opening of her negligee. He did not attempt to remove it. This element of their lovemaking turned him on.

V moved her legs over him and pushed him over to his back; she wanted to control the next stage, slowly mounted him, and started to lean over and kiss his neck.

D responded in kind, and soon they passionately embraced and kissed deeply.

V could feel his cock pressing against her vulva through the material in her French knickers.

He was ready for her, but she wanted this to last.

Given his performance on their previous date, she thought *he could last quite well even when inside her.*

She was very hot and highly aroused and wanted him inside her already. She wanted to feel that thick penis push through that gasping barrier and fill her again.

Her desire had already changed her mind.

She reached down, slid the crotch of her knickers aside, and grasped his penis in her hand. It was rock hard, and she felt a sudden rush in her pelvis, and her vagina contracted in anticipation. Carefully, she guided him toward her vulva and started to probe gently for the wetness that would help his cock make the entry she so desired.

D was patient and let her take control. She loved that.

Gradually, she slid his penis up and down her wet vulva, using it to stimulate her clitoris as it started the build-up she knew so well.

Desire finally overruled restraint—she could wait no longer. She straightened her hips, leaned back, and gently slid down the shaft of his cock.

She felt the fullness as he entered her; gradually, it became fuller, thicker until she could almost not take it anymore and then… Just as he broke through the point of his thickness, she gasped and relaxed into the sensation of his cock slowly filling her.

D now responded with a grateful moan and slowly moved his hips with hers.

V was still in control of the pace, had a perfect view of D's face, and loved watching his expression as she varied the rhythm of her motion. She was building again, slowly but surely, toward her climax. V leant forward to kiss D; she found she could keep him inside her and maintain control of him this way, until…

D grasped her across her hips and buttocks and started to move her with him; he lifted his legs, so his knees were bent, and pushed forward using his legs' force.

In this angle, V's clitoris was forced down onto his pubic pad.

As D thrust upward, her clitoris was stimulated in a way she had not experienced before. His thrusts were deep, and his motion increased in pace.

This was like her favorite position, from behind but with the benefit of being close to him, seeing him enjoy her. It was deep, full, and very hot.

V was getting close now, and when D kissed her deeply as he thrust deeper and faster, she came quickly and kept cuming longer than her usual orgasm.

D kept his composure; clearly, he was excited but did not cum yet.

Instead, he was generous, wanted it to last, and wanted to please her.

They rested and chatted briefly while V recovered from her latest orgasm.

V was on her back now, and D had slowly positioned himself on his side with her legs over his; he was stirring again, and the thought of his desire was all she needed to stir again.

He entered her from this position, gently rose to his elbow, and started a slow movement that got deeper and faster; she could see his cock entering her, just at the top but enough to get the sense of the length his shaft pierced her; she had never really considered just how a penis disappeared inside her.

This image only increased her arousal even more.

D took her hand and motioned for her to masturbate her clitoris as they moved in unison.

She complied willingly as she was now very aroused.

She saw that D was also close and wanted to cum with him. As she got closer, she could see how much this excited D, and she knew now that he was very close.

She started to moan louder and called out to D to fuck her, to fuck her fast; he complied, "Cum with me, my love," she called out, "cum with me, baby."

He moved faster, and just as V was about to tip over the edge, she knew that D had also hit the point of no return. They were locked in, pushing and withdrawing as they exploded into their orgasms;

V was massaging her clitoris. Still, it was her vagina that led to this climax.

D's deep plunges had provided the perfect stimulation, and she cried out, "I'm cuming, babe; I'm cuming with you."

D responded, "Me too, babe," even though this was obvious. D started to push in and out slower as his semen filled her, as he pulsed to his orgasm.

Their bodies quieted together, still trembling from the storm they'd just weathered. D remained in her, and they slowly drifted to sleep, still locked together in this embrace…

V woke first.

D had moved from within her but lay close and had his hand over her. He was still sleeping and looked so peaceful.

Even though the sight of him was already starting to stir wetness deep in her, she gently slipped his hand from her breasts, slowly got out of bed, and placed her feet on the floor.

As she did, the duvet moved, revealing his lower body. He must have been dreaming of something erotic because he had an erection. She wanted to climb back in and take his cock into her mouth so he could wake to her slow seduction, but she needed to pee.

Reluctantly, she made her way to the bathroom, had a tinkle, and thought that she could masturbate but instead got up and put on the short teddy negligee she planned to wear the next night.

She wanted D to wake up with her looking sexy.

The suite was magnificent as the morning light poured through the windows, gilding every surface, warming her skin and memory alike. The Eiffel Tower stood framed in gold light—an icon, but now, merely a backdrop to her desire.

V, remembering the night before, checked that her diamond earrings were still there and pottered around the room.

She now had a coffee and moved to the desk, where she opened her *iPad* and began to write her secret thoughts in her journal.

V had kept a record of her encounters with D in this journal and was very aroused as she read some of her earlier entries. Finally, she stood up to recharge her *iPad* and had to reach over the desk to plug it in when it happened.

She did not hear him enter the room, but she felt him as he entered her, for D had been watching her from the bedroom door, his manhood getting firmer as he looked upon her beauty across the room.

The sunlight was streaming into the room, making her teddy almost invisible against her slender body.

It was too much for him as his lust for her escalated to a pure, animalistic state.

When she stood up and leaned across the desk, revealing her tight, well-proportioned buttocks and the hint of her vulva, he could take no more. He moved silently across the room and, without even a word, took her from behind across the desk.

V was speechless as this happened and drew a quick breath as his thick cock entered her and plunged past its thickness to fill her completely; she was wet already, and although his entry was forceful, she felt only pleasure and tingles through her pelvis.

He had one hand on her back and the other on her buttocks as he pushed and partially withdrew and pushed and withdrew, building to forceful thrusting as he took her against the desk. He was excited, and V could sense he was moving quickly to orgasm.

She was too.

The pure desire in D excited her more than she had imagined such forceful sex would.

The naked, animalistic way he was taking her raised her excitement rapidly, and she climaxed just as he did.

It was passionate, fast, and lustful and left V wanting more.

As D relaxed his hold on her, she turned over on the desk, placed her legs up, and looked at D directly. She said nothing, but he knew instinctively what she wanted.

He leaned over and placed his lips and tongue onto her vulva and slowly started to work her clitoris, her beautiful Button, with his tongue.

She responded to this instantly, her tension rising rapidly, and she came explosively; D's semen, still fresh within her, was expelled with the contractions of her orgasm, sending warm fluid down her vulva.

It was a strange sensation for V, but she liked it. They kissed deeply, and when V finally stood, he embraced her quietly for a long time.

D finally broke the silence by saying, "We have a train to catch in three hours. Are you ready for our next ride, babe?"

express

As V looked out the window of the limousine that was taking them to Gare de l'Est station to meet the Orient Express to Venice, she stared out at the sights of Paris, the most romantic city in the world.

Still, she could not shift her mind from the night before. She was thinking about the dinner, the diamonds, and the delicious sex that followed. Never before had her body responded this way—an orgasm drawn from nothing but the brush of lips, a tongue and the suction on her breasts—that glorious suction.

Orgasms had always been a part of her sex life; she usually had one. Occasionally, she could have multiple orgasms, though this was generally by her hand or sometimes through her vagina with secondary stimulation near her clitoris but never had orgasms without her clitoris being stimulated somehow.

This was different; D was different. First, he managed to give her almost continual orgasms. Now he brought her to orgasm purely but stimulating her breasts.

Deliciously unexpected—and wholly unforgettable! She recalled.

As they arrived at the station, a porter took their luggage ahead, and they ambled to the first-class carriage. They walked through the first-class dining car, all set up for lunch, which would be taken soon after leaving Paris. The porter took them through into the carriage with the cabins.

Their cabin had a lounge and sleeping area decorated with velvet, timbers, and time—every inch promised pleasure before Venice even arrived.

V turned to D and kissed him.

"It's lovely," she said, "much more luxurious than the last sleeper we had, but that will always be special in my mind."

D smiled, tipped the porter generously, and closed the door behind him.

After moving to the dining car, they took tea and enjoyed a refreshing meal of pasta and French cakes. V ordered a glass of champagne and D ordered a Black Russian.

They chatted about her work and the children she cared for. They laughed at the antics her wards had managed to get up to under her care.

"You certainly have a way with them," he remarked. "No wonder the children like you; I'm sure their parents would not be as indulgent," he quipped.

D talked about his early youth, how he went from relationship to relationship, never satisfied completely, never settling.

V was taken with his consideration and his insight into his past, though she had the feeling he was skipping over details.

He reflected on his life, and this showed he sought growth. He was also generous in giving compliments. He frequently stopped mid-sentence and remarked on her eyes, smile, beauty (and discretely, her figure and sexuality).

She liked this, and it made her feel appreciated and loved.

They finally moved back to the cabin. It was mid-afternoon, and they were now traveling through the wine districts of France.

V was tipsy from the champagne and started to get a little flirty with D again.

D loved this and joined in the game, exchanging innuendos about the benefits of wine on libido.

They kissed passionately as V enjoyed the train's gentle, rhythmic rocking. She became aroused again and started to feel the familiar wetness as she savored his kisses around her neck.

D was rising, too; she could see his thick cock firming in his pants and suggested they move to the small bed in their cabin.

D slowly undid the tight dress she was wearing, unzipping it in steps as he kissed her back and the nape of her neck. Soon he was on his knees, kissing the small of her back and tight buttock as she stepped out of the dress that was now on the floor.

"Breathtaking!" D said as he gazed upon her from behind in her dark green lace bra and panties. V turned around to face him, leaving D face to face with her stomach and his hands on her hips.

"Magnificent indeed," he added. "Your beauty leaves me breathless."

He slowly slipped down her panties with reverence, pressing a trail of kisses down her trembling belly as his hand guided her onto the small bed.

V leant back on the pillows on the bed, her legs still over the side, and D gazing upon her now naked and hairless vulva.

He stared intently and took her in; he did not touch her, he just looked, but his gaze aroused V. She could feel her wetness seeping out, and clearly, D could see this happening because he smiled and moved closer, took a deep breath, and took in her aroma.

V was now almost ready to demand he take her immediately or at least pay some attention to her Button.

Yet she waited; she knew this would build tension in her; she knew D understood what he was doing and how this affected her. She trusted him with her body more than any man she had been with.

D slowly lifted his hand and very gently parted the lips of her vulva, revealing the glistening wetness. He stared intently; his desire was clear, increasing V's desire for him. He slowly moved the small hood of skin over her Button, revealing her clitoris completely.

By this time, she was full and engorged; her clitoris was twice its usual size and visibly pulsating as if to call to him.

Finally, she could stand it no longer. "For god sake, lick me, kiss me, touch me," she said to D, pleading for his attention.

He smiled and then moved his lips to her womanhood, taking his tongue to taste her slowly before rhythmically circling her clitoris.

That was all she needed.

The entire prelude, without contact, was as stimulating to her as any touch had been. His pure desire for her, demonstrated by how he took her in with his eyes and breath, had excited her so much that it had placed her on the brink. The only trigger she needed now was the slightest touch with his tongue.

V came, moaned, and clasped her head in her thighs as she contracted, forcing D to place pressure on her mons as she did. She convulsed in pleasure.

D also moaned; he was enjoying her orgasm.

As V bathed in the afterglow of her last orgasm and D quietly rested with her, she thought, "*He was a patient man, and he understood her desire to enjoy the glow and not rush.*"

As she began to recover, V turned her attention to D.

Time for him to beg me, she thought.

She was lying on the bed, and D was beside her, lying on his back. The short rest meant that his thick cock was relaxing, but V could see he was not far from being erect. She sat up on her elbow and kissed him, and he responded with a deep kiss that stirred her deeply.

He tried to move up to her, but she pushed him back and indicated with her eyes that she wanted him just where he was.

She kissed his neck, his shoulders, and his chest.

He was not a hairy man, and she was grateful because it meant she could feel his soft skin as she kissed him.

Slowly, she moved to his stomach.

D was already responding with slow hip movements; he was getting into this.

By the time V reached his cock, he was already hard, and it was ready for her attention.

D had shaved or waxed recently, so he was totally bare and smooth.

This was new to her, but as she kissed the base of his penis, she realized why he had done this. It made him soft to kiss, no hair to avoid.

She teased him for a while, kissing him close and then back to his stomach before she finally took her tongue and slowly made her way up the shaft of his thick penis.

It was smooth and hard but soft in feel.

D was enjoying the attention.

As V worked her way up his cock, she used her tongue to stimulate him softly, with the tip of her tongue, sometimes kissing and sometimes taking the shaft of his cock between her wet lips sideways and sliding up and down the shaft.

He firmed in response.

Her previous lovers had always wanted her to suck them, and more often, it felt more like they were fucking her mouth, but she had an instinct that D was different.

She sensed that he was more into the sensation than the result.

She was right.

D was moving his hips, but he was not guiding her actions. Instead, he trusted her to take this where it should.

V kept moving her tongue around his shaft but had now started to focus on the tip of his penis. She loved the shape of his thick cock, the way it tapered up to a thick shaft, and the way its skin was tight when he was erect like this. His erections excited her because she knew that this meant she excited him.

V was now perched on top of D, and he was moaning as she started to take his cock into her mouth, just the tip at first, but slowly she began to take more into her mouth as she did. He was responding to this with heavier breathing. Finally, as she started to reach the thick part of his cock, she was surprised at just how much she could take in. As she withdrew each time, she used her tongue to stimulate him more.

Slowly, she built the momentum of her oral strokes on his cock and progressively increased the amount of sucking she did as she did.

D was now breathing heavily and moaning loudly, but he was not fucking her with his cock; she was fucking him with her mouth; it was different, pleasant, and very sexy.

D was now clearly close to cuming, and although she did not like the taste of semen in her mouth, she committed to bringing him to climax this way.

He was enjoying this, and she wanted to please him.

He was breathing very fast now, and she could see the signs, the movements, and the noises he made and readied herself for the pulsing of his orgasm.

D started to moan louder and then reached out and stopped her, placed his hand on her face, and slowly guided her off his cock.

"I want you, V," he said.

"I want to enter you slowly. I want to hear you gasp as I enter you. I want to fuck you deeply. I want my firm cock to feel the tightness of your Flower. I want you to call my name as you fuck me, and I want us to cum together."

V could hardly refuse such hospitality!

D moved toward V, taking his time to kiss her back, shoulders, and breasts.

V was trying to get D to linger on her breasts as she recalled the incredible orgasm she had when he breast-played her in the hotel.

D felt her urging, complied, and started to suck, lick, and tug at her pert nipples. He moved from breast to breast, each time letting V build her excitement, and as she rose, he stopped, moved to the other breast, and lingered long enough for her to subside just a little.

He did this for a while, and V was getting extremely wet and frustrated.

Her passion heightened when he finally settled on the right breast while gently massaging the left and tugging at her nipple.

V was close.

It was still a new sensation, but she was close and knew she would spill over into orgasm.

He continued; she moaned, writhed, begged with her body, and finally, as she was almost there, D stopped, mounted her, and slowly worked his thick penis into her wet Flower.

As he did, he lifted her legs onto his arms so her hips were raised and he could move deeper into her.

V felt his thickness and gasped as he entered her past the point of his greatest girth. She was so close to orgasm, even though the stimulation of her nipples had suddenly stopped.

D moved slowly. As he filled her with his cock, he withdrew slowly, then penetrated her deeply, in and out, building the rhythm as V moved her hips into him.

She could see his face; he was ecstatic, enjoying the feel of her tight, wet Flower.

This excited V even more, and she wanted him, wanted his semen, and she wanted him to explode inside her.

V cried out, "Fuck me, baby, fuck me fast, god I love you, I love you so much, cum with me, baby cum!"

As D started fucking her deep and fast, his pleasure was immense, his tension sublime, until he moaned that familiar moan V understood as his point of no return.

"Oh god," she cried, "I'm cuming babe" as she went over the top into her orgasm as he shot his load of semen into her, pulsating as he did.

V could feel his cum inside her and contracted her muscles as if to draw out every last drop of him.

D collapsed on top of her, his weight partially taken by his arms, his cock still inside her.

V liked the sensation of his body on hers.

He kissed her, he kissed her neck, and he kissed her cheek. Both were recovering slowly, and V was quietly reliving every moment of their last lovemaking session: his thick cock, his attention to her, her sucking his cock, and finally, his explosive orgasm.

This and her incredible orgasm, slow to build, teased out of her by D's stop-start build of her desire and then the explosive burst of ecstasy as she came with him, the intensity of his desire. Not to mention his explosive orgasm, the feeling of his cum inside her, the steady pulsing as her orgasm receded, and the afterglow as she recovered.

She stirred again.

D could feel her stirring and smiled.

"More, baby? Do you want more?" he asked. He needed no answer and slowly withdrew from her and moved to her side.

D helped move V's hand to her Flower, indicating she should stimulate herself.

He took his hand, slowly entered her Flower with his fingers, and withdrew, bringing a pool of his semen with his fingers.

D smeared his juices over V's Button, and she finally got the idea.

Mmmmmm, she thought, *a natural lubricant...*

She started to rub her Button rhythmically and firmly. V was not entirely sure she could manage to cum again so soon but got into the sensation; she liked that she was using D's cum to help her—it was sexy.

Her doubt was soon removed as she realized that D was also rubbing his cock and had now started to pull it in and out with his hand. He was still erect, not hard, but not flaccid either. He was enjoying himself and liked her doing the same.

That was enough for V as she rapidly started to build her orgasm.

He responded to her deep breathing and moaning by stroking faster.

They both moved closer to orgasm.

V broke first and started to cum, moaning as she did.

Then in response, D came and moaned her name as he did.

They lay there quietly, both on their backs, clearly exhausted.

Both were deep in thought. V re-lived the events of the last month: meeting D, their passionate first night, the texting, the video sex, Paris, and now this. She was wondering what D was thinking when he spoke.

"Did you mean it?" he said.

"Did I mean what?" V asked.

"You said you love me," he replied. "Do you love me, or was that just said in the passion of the moment?" he asked.

V rolled onto her side and placed her head on D's shoulders, her arm around his waist. She was reluctant to say what she felt. She feared the truth on her lips might break the fragile magic between them.

She started to answer, carefully probing his response to gauge the depth of danger such honesty would reveal.

"It's been a whirlwind romance," she said, and D agreed. "So much attention from you, the gifts, the holiday, the frequent contact, it's been very intense."

D agreed again.

"D—" She started, but he gently touched her lips.

"Wait, I need to say this." His eyes never left hers. "You've changed everything for me. Everything."

He took a deep breath. "I've loved you since that first day on the train. Can't explain it, but it was like—" he searched for words, "—like recognition. As if we'd known each other before, lost each other somehow, and finally found our way back." He drew her closer. "Being with you feels like coming home."

V was shocked! She had not expected this.

Sure, she knew he had courted her completely and lavished her with gifts and kind words, but love: this was more than she expected, more than she had dreamed of.

She had understood that the sex was fantastic, her body was more than beautiful, and she could feel that D was attracted to her sexually.

She began to understand and recognize the signs as she lay there silently, thinking about this. He was sensitive but guarded; he had been hurt and was only beginning to heal.

Suddenly she realized that she had not responded to him.

"I cannot begin to express my joy when I hear you say that, D," she said. "I, too, have felt the same connection. I cannot explain the depth of my feelings either, but I understand deep within my core that I truly love you and love you more than I have ever loved another."

They stared at each other and quietly smiled.

"Then it is clear to me," D said, "you have my heart and soul in your hands now. I know in my mind and heart that this love I feel will last, and if you want to share this journey with me through life, I want you to join me. I understand that you may not be able to make such a commitment so soon, and you need not state it now, but more than anything, I want you in my life."

V was shocked again; a commitment so soon. She was unsure she was ready to take such a risk with her heart. She had lovers before, even committed relationships, but this was scary. How could she be sure of his love? She was confident she loved him, and he made her feel wonderful. She vowed to herself that she would remain open to him, be true to her heart, and allow him into her heart. She would see where this goes, giving it her all, but for the moment, she would keep a little back just in case he hurt her—again.

V turned to D and explained. "I love you, but I'm scared; this sometimes feels like it could get out of control, and I might lose myself to you. Please understand that it's not that I don't love you; nothing could be further from the truth. I have built my life, work, home, and friendships in a different world to us, and what you propose is such a significant change that I fear it will sweep me away. I could lose everything, including you."

D was trying to understand her and asked if she wanted to change the nature of their relationship.

V said no.

She loved him and loved where they were; she was scared but understood where this could take her.

D thought for a while and caressed V gently as they lay on the bed.

Finally, he said, "V, you must take your time and take each step when you feel it's right. As long as you say you love me, I will be patient. We need not commit now. All I ask is that you search your heart and be true to your feelings, be honest about your love for me, and be here for me when we are together.

"In turn, I promise I will be here for you, help you with your fears, and if our love transforms into what I believe it could be, I will worship you for eternity. I can wait for commitment, as I know it will come when you recognize that your fear is only a fear of being completely in love. When that happens, the fear will disappear."

There was a sudden knock on the door, and the conductor called, "We arrive in Venice in forty-five minutes; tea and coffee are being served in the dining car."

revealed

V packed her small day bag slowly as D did the same. They were quiet as they did so and later chatted about insignificant matters over coffee as the Italian countryside landscape gave way to the beautiful city of Venice.

They were met at that station by another chauffeur-driven car and taken to their hotel. The excitement of being in Venice had allowed her to drift away from their earlier conversation about commitment, but V knew she would have to come back to this sometime, and sometime soon.

They checked into the hotel apartment, decided to see some of Venice before sunset, and went for a walk.

This was V's first time in the eternal city.

They passed small outdoor cafés and crafts stalls as they wound their way around the streets near the hotel, occasionally pausing as they walked across small and ancient bridges that crossed the canals.

V commented on the gondolas passing under them with couples clearly on holiday and soaking up the romance.

D joked with her about how they would likely break or overturn the gondola if they were to take a romantic ride in private.

Walking the streets, they chatted about their favorite music, foods, and movies.

They were struck by the similarities in their tastes, sometimes naming the same song or food. Both loved lemon meringue, both loved the same music, and they agreed that A Thousand Years should be their song, given they both had the sense that they had loved before. They talked about their work, past loves, and how they had always felt something was missing and sometimes sought more by taking lovers.

V confessed that she had several lovers when she met D but had decided that she no longer wanted to continue with this and that D would be her only lover from now on.

D explained that since his wife was killed, he had had many sexual relationships with women but never one like theirs. Now he only wanted her. They agreed that would be their first commitment. They would be exclusive lovers.

Later on their walk, they took coffee in a small café near the central canal and watched the passersby, commenting on each person and making up stories about their lives and relationships.

Some stories were tragic; lost and lonely people, devoid of love. Some were funny; couples who looked so unsuited were turned into co-conspirators in a lovers' tryst, and older couples were given passionate lives and took eternal lovers in their final years.

V laughed often and thought D was a romantic as he repeatedly tried to make happy stories for these strangers.

As they speculated on the lives of the others, V slowly became aware of just how special her relationship with D was. She had so much love for him, and he for her. She began to understand that she was lucky to have so much love from him and had so much love to give. So many people had little or no love in their lives. She decided then and there to do all she could to keep this love alive and cherish every moment she had with D.

It was a romantic spot, music played from a nearby street busker, and V had decided.

She quietly turned to D, took his hand, and said, "D, you must know I truly love you. You make me very happy; you are so generous with your time, affection, and lovemaking. You say you want a committed relationship. It scares me deeply, and I'm worried that this will get out of control and hurt me. I have to tell you now."

V took a deep breath and continued...

"The key to understanding how I feel about us, D, goes back many years to when I was young, seventeen to be exact. My story is familiar: a young girl meets a young man several years older than her and is swept away by him, her first true love. I was so much in love with him that I could not bear to tell him, as I feared rejection. Even though I gave myself to him so completely, he was unaware and did not understand the depth of my love. It broke my heart and left me with a scar so deep I could never love like that again.

"Sure, I have had relationships since and have loved others in a way but never as special as this first love. I loved him then, have always loved him, and still love him to this day, and part of me has always been reserved for him, sometimes consciously, most times unconsciously. I have not thought of him all the time, but my thoughts of him have never been far away. It was as if part of my heart had been locked away, reserved for him and could never be filled by any other love I felt for others.

"Now and then, I would think of him, wonder what he was doing, where he was. I tried to find him several times, but as time passed, I buried my love for him deep in my heart and got on with my life.

"I have had a great life, don't get me wrong, it's been fulfilling and exciting, and I would not change anything I have experienced as that makes me who I am."

D was looking perplexed; he had expected V to talk of her love for him, her desire for him, but instead, she was speaking of another love, and he was becoming sad and scared.

V continued her story…

"It was six months ago that I started thinking of him again, and I decided that even though it had been over thirty years since I saw him, I wanted to look for him again. It was then that I stumbled on a tiny bit of information that led me to find where he was. I could not find him all this time because following people in the pre-Internet world was near impossible. I found him by chance when I absentmindedly typed his name into LinkedIn, and there he was.

"I was excited but needed to figure out what to do next. We were both thirty years older. We both had a lifetime of experiences and who knows what relationships. I was sure I had to meet him again, but I needed to do this on my terms, in my time, and in a way that I could slip back into my life should he not be what I believed he was."

D listened patiently, carefully, and with dread, as he felt he was losing his V to another love, another life forged so many years before.

V continued her story…

"I eventually found out where he lived, in another country, another life. So I began to plan my approach to meeting him again, to see what he had become. I found out he was traveling and planned to meet him, simply bumping into him, but when we met, he did not recognize me. It was a shock initially, but I quickly recovered because we connected immediately despite him not remembering who I was.

"So I kept it secret; until now...

"You see, you and I first met thirty-three years ago. You did not recognize me on the train when we met again that day Steve, but my name is not V, my name is Janine, and you and I were lovers years ago. You ask me if I love you, well, I do; I have never stopped loving you deep in my heart all these years."

D was speechless, his cover was exposed and V knew his real name but what really stuck him was that they had met before the train. He frantically processed this revelation.

"Say something! she said.

"Please understand, I'm so sorry that I deceived you, but I did not lie to you; I just omitted to talk about my earlier life, our earlier life. I meant to tell you immediately, but I panicked when you did not recognize me."

"It's not that," Steve replied, "I'm simply stunned. I'm cross with myself for not realizing it was you."

"You remember me," Janine asked tentatively.

"Of course, I do, Janine, using her real name for the first time; although you certainly have changed a lot, you have blossomed as an beautiful and confident woman.

"I knew there was something very familiar about you, Janine.

When I first met you on the train, you reminded me of someone, sorry… I guess you reminded me of you, but I never said it because I thought it would be in bad taste to tell you that you reminded me of a girl I once loved and lost.

"But wait," he said, after thinking it through. "How would you have even known I would come to your carriage?"

Janine smiled, "That was easy; I paid the conductor handsomely to get you there; he arranged to move those children to your carriage and then kindly rescued you by sending you to the quiet of my carriage. It was the same conductor you tipped to access the bedroom compartment that day. It seems he made a tidy sum from us that day," she grinned.

Steve laughed now totally dismissing his concern about his professional cover name and continued to respond to her earlier story, "You never told me you loved me when we shared that time together. We certainly had a great time then, but I was at a stage when I was confused about relationships and love. I had been burnt badly and was in denial that love even existed. So I spent that time in and out of endless meaningless relationships."

"I remember that very well," she said. "You were a slut."

"Yes, I was, but I don't remember many women I slept with in those days—except you. I have always remembered you fondly, and now I understand why. We were souls that connected, we were real friends at that time, and that must be why I felt so close to you as soon as we met again. At the time, I could not understand why.

"As I said, being with you was like coming home to someone I always felt comfortable with. I felt we already knew each other, so we immediately went straight from the courting to intense love. It seemed so natural, but now I understand why."

"So you are not angry with me?" she asked.

"How could I be angry? What I feel for you has no place for anger. Over the last month, you have filled my heart with so much love that there is no room for anger. Instead, it would be best if you were angry with me as I mistreated you back then. If I had known you loved me at the time, I may have been more sensitive to you, and I may have even stayed in Perth and seen how our relationship developed. But that was then, and clearly, it was not our time—

"But how does this affect our relationship now," Steve asked, suddenly thinking this would significantly change their situation. "You must be angry with me for leaving you as I did. You were so young, and from what you say, I broke your heart."

Janine thought for a moment and then said: "Yes, you broke my heart, and yes, I have been angry with you from time to time, but I also played a part in our separation. I never told you that I loved you. Maybe I was not sure at the time or feared you would reject me, but you showed me that love was possible, deep, and something to cherish. I have loved others since, and my life has been good. This might not have been possible if you had not opened my heart to love.

"I'm sad that we missed our opportunity then, but at the same time, I also understand that what we have now is what it is because of what we had then and what we both experienced when we were apart.

"What is important now is that we have a second chance, and I hope my deception has not put that in danger. I have never stopped loving you, and I still do. I have often looked for you at periods of my life but could never find you. I could not believe it when I did. But, given your work, I now understand why it was so hard."

"You are right, of course, babe; what is important is now and what we feel."

Steve embraced Janine, and they kissed deeply; it was even more passionate than before.

The revelation hung between them, transforming everything yet changing nothing.

Janine had imagined countless scenarios for this moment, but never this quiet acceptance, this sense that the universe had simply been waiting for them to catch up to what it had always known. The years apart didn't feel wasted now, but necessary—each of them becoming the person who could truly recognize the other.

Somehow, knowing who Janine was intensified Steve's feelings and desire for her.

Janine intuitively understood this as she kissed him back, and she felt an inner glow in her heart that lifted her spirit.

She loved him more than she believed possible.

They kissed as if for the first time, and in a sense, this was true.

They were oblivious to the clutter as the Venetian waitpersons packed the dishes and tables around them until the waiter interrupted them and told them they were about to close for the night. They both realized that they had been at the café for over three hours and that the waitperson had discretely allowed them to continue their deep discussion even though Steve had only ordered one coffee each.

Only in Venice!

They stood up, paid for their coffee, and Steve tipped the waitperson what must have been enough for twenty coffees.

They walked silently back to their apartment, the full moon's light and the Venetian residents' sounds gently concluding their day.

"Did you mean it?" she finally asked.

"Mean what?" Steve asked.

"You said that when we met on the train, you thought it would be bad taste to tell me that I reminded you of a girl you once loved and lost: Did you mean it when you said that you loved me then?"

Steve stopped and took Janine into his arms.

He looked her into her eyes and said, "I may not have consciously known or understood it at the time, but it is clear to me now, perhaps even all this time: I have always loved you, Janine, I love you now, always did and always will. We are meant to be, and the universe knows it; it has conspired to make this happen, and it's just taken me a long time to realize it. The time is now. This is our time."

They entered the apartment in a frenzy; they were both extremely excited and aroused and wanted each other more than ever. They were wrapped in each other as they hit the bed, clothes flung across the room.

As Steve entered her now very wet Flower, she gasped and sighed simultaneously, for she was so wet that he filled her almost immediately. She came in seconds, as did Steve; it was quick, passionate, and intense.

Janine was overwhelmed with feelings of love.

He had taken her in passion, but she knew that even though he had cum, he would spend the next hour ensuring her pleasure was complete. She also knew that his desire for her would mean that before too long, he could make her gasp again...

She loved this man, and now she knew he loved her too.

Again.

Janine was correct, of course, because as Steve recovered his breath, he moved to kiss again. At first, he started with a passionate kiss on her lips.

She liked this; it showed her his attention was not always on her Flower or her breasts and that he cared for her enough to take the build-up slowly.

And build she did.

As Steve worked his way down her neck to her back, her excitement intensified, and she could feel her wetness growing again. She wondered how this was possible so often. She had never experienced this before, and she was in her early 50s when women were supposed to be *'drying up'*. Yet, it seemed to her it was not the women drying up but the lack of attention from the men in their lives.

Steve was kissing her buttocks affectionately and was taking in her beauty with his eyes, caressing her soft curves with his hands and driving her wild with desire; she wanted him inside her again.

He was not quite ready, though; it had only been ten minutes since they both exploded in an orgasm ripped from their bodies in a fit of quick passion, but he had been building slowly over the evening as they talked of their love and past relationship.

She was not to be disappointed, though, as Steve moved between her legs and gently inserted his finger inside her slowly but not deeply; it was strange to Janine as she was used to his thick cock, and she was about to protest that she wanted more when he started gently moving his fingers across an area toward her pubic bone.

It felt good.

He stared at her intently as he did this, seeking her reaction to what he was doing; as Steve moved his fingers and responded with a moan, he would do more of the same.

Janine was building and building fast.

She closed her eyes and fell back into the feeling, enjoying the new sensations this provided.

She wanted to move her hands to her clitoris to bring on her orgasm.

Steve stopped her.

She opened her eyes and glared at him, but he smiled and said, "Patience, sweet pea, go with it."

So she did, and go with it she did, because within two minutes, she was writhing to a lovely orgasm that was simultaneously both different and the same as the ones she usually obtained through clitoral stimulation or when fucking deeply.

It was very nice.

Janine was now even hornier; she wanted Steve's thick cock. She had to take matters into her own hands or mouth...

She moved quickly to reposition herself between his legs and slowly licked his now-firming cock; she took it into her mouth and gauged its state from how it felt.

She knew it well now and guessed he needed more. She started kissing the shaft of his cock while sliding her tongue along its length. She kissed the base and then caressed his balls with her lips.

He responded with a moan.

'He liked that', she thought, so she continued to use her lips and tongue to stimulate him there. He arched and raised his leg as if to ask for more, so she started using her tongue on the area between his balls and his anus.

More moans and a visible increase in the thickness of his cock.

She was fascinated with his response to this stimulation and started slowly using her fingers to stroke the outside of his anus.

More moaning.

Janine had not done this much before and was not particularly fond of this part of the anatomy, but she was drawn to this; it felt different, intimate, and right.
She reached for their lubricant and started applying some around Steve's perineum.

More moans and an instinctive rising of his legs.

She probed carefully around his small but pretty hole, slowly beginning to insert her finger into him.

She was surprised, not by his reaction, which was an increase in his breathing and bearing down to take more, but by hers. She found this erotic and could feel her vaginal contracting in pleasure as if the finger were in her.

She started to fuck him now, fuck him with her fingers; it was exciting; she felt in control and felt like she was fucking her man.

He was enjoying it, and Janine thought *'this was his time'*. As she watched herself enter him with her fingers, she decided he must have this moment.

She used her other hand to start stroking his thick cock, which was now hard, and even though she wanted this inside her so much, she resisted. She took his hand and placed it on his cock.

She wanted to focus on what she was doing, to watch herself fuck him and watch him bring himself to climax.

Steve did not know that this was what she wanted, nor did he know she was about to be so turned on by the sight of him pumping his cock. He got lost in the sensation he was building; he could sense his orgasm, and he started to slow, but Janine quickly said, "Don't stop, babe, this is exciting; I want to see you cum, I want to watch you pleasure yourself, it's so hot."

He was getting closer, and as he was close to exploding, She thrust her finger deep, and that was it.

Steve groaned louder and started to writhe as his orgasm commenced. Seconds later, his semen burst forth from the shaft of his thick cock, spilling over his stomach while he milked it all slowly from himself.

She gently withdrew her finger and discretely slipped out of the room to wash her hands.

Steve was resting on the bed when she returned, clearly glowing from their last act.

Janine slipped into the bed beside him, used her hand to collect the semen on his stomach, applied it to her clitoris and Flower, and began to stimulate herself rhythmically. It was not any different from the way she would generally masturbate, but somehow using Steve's semen as a lubricant was hotter, sexier, and very erotic. She found herself close several times within seconds but held back to build the intensity.

Steve was now very much present and was sitting up watching her with so much desire in his eyes that she almost came on the spot. *She loved that he desired her so much and watched her so intently. She loved that she loved him*, and with that thought, she spilled over into her orgasm.

She screamed this time, letting go of any concerns about noise or appearing too greedy; she just enjoyed it.

I want more of this, she thought as she slowly recovered, *and I want it now...*

She snuggled up to Steve, gently moving her hips and placing her leg over his legs, attempting to tantalize him into more amorous activity.

Steve was not slow on the uptake.

He was attuned to her needs and started to kiss her again. He was not erect anymore, but he was not tired either.

She was amazed at his ability to pay her so much attention when his body must be crying for rest and recovery.

Steve moved to her pert breasts and started to kiss her long nipples; they responded instantly as he began to gently suck her left nipple while using his tongue to tug and twist them.

They hardened.

Gradually she started to move her hips as if her nipples were connected to them; she began to move her hips faster; she was groaning now and was trying to fuck a cock that was not inside her but was exciting her.

Except that the only stimulation was on her nipples.

Steve sensed her rising passion and started to exert a gentle sucking motion to her nipples, not hard but just enough to make her rising orgasm get closer to the surface.

She moaned and started breathing faster and deeper.

Steve picked up the pace, his lips, his tongue, and the sucking, all combining to create a sensation she remembered from the train.

She loved his breast playing and let go, exploding in an orgasm that rivaled the earlier one when she had masturbated with his semen.

Janine turned to Steve, about to thank him for his attention, when she saw the pure joy on his face. It was clear he loved making her cum; *he is so proud of himself,* she thought. It was like she was giving him pleasure by cuming for him.

It was all she needed, so while she was about to thank him seconds before, instead, she looked at him directly and said, "More, please."

She was about to apologize for her sudden greed when Steve smiled and said, "As you command, my mistress."

Then, she fell back on the bed and lay there waiting for his next move.

And what a move it was.

As Steve moved his kisses down her belly and onto her bare pubic mound, she was already wet again. The anticipation of his silver tongue made her hot beyond measure. As his lips reached her vulva and his tongue probed the entrance, tasting her juices, she was already writhing with pleasure. His hands now reached around her buttocks and lifted the folds on her pubic area to reveal her Button, her favorite body part.

She braced for the ecstasy.

But instead, he took his time, teasing her with little kisses around the vulva and the curved bits at the edge of his thighs.

While dying for his tongue on her Button, she also liked the anticipation.

Then it started gently as he took the tip of his tongue and circled her Button at its edges; it was a beautiful sensation but begged for more.

Then his tongue started to flick softly across her Button as he pressed his lips to surround her Button; she drew a quick breath; she knew what was next, his special technique.

Next, Steve started a light sucking motion as he engulfed her now engorged clitoris with his lips, using his tongue to stimulate her at the same time; she groaned, heaved her chest, and then her hips as he sucked harder and faster, putting more pressure on her Button as she pushed forward against him. She had cum several times already, but she knew there was one deeper inside of her, and this was the one way it could be teased out.

She pushed harder, and he responded, with a movement of his tongue and lips in a rhythm that she knew too well.

Yes, she thought, "Yes," she cried, "YES," she screamed as she called out to him,

"Yes, I'm cuming babe," and then she exploded again, and again in a double orgasm that she had not experienced before.

Was it one orgasm or two simultaneously, or was it one which peaked, ebbed, and then peaked again? She was unsure, but she loved it nonetheless; she loved that she was so alive sexually, and most of all, she loved the man that woke her womanhood over thirty years ago and had woken her once again...

They lay entwined, sweat cooling on their skin, the weight of revelation settling around them like a comfortable blanket. She realized that her long search hadn't been about reclaiming the past, but discovering who they could be together now—two people shaped by separate journeys, finally converging again with wisdom their younger selves had lacked. The path ahead wasn't certain, but for the first time in thirty-three years, it felt right.

Later, as moonlight filtered through the window, she traced idle patterns on Steve's chest, wondering at how quickly her world had realigned around his presence. Only weeks ago, he'd been a stranger on a train. Now she struggled to remember what her life had felt like before him. The speed of it all should terrify her, yet instead, it felt like correcting a long-standing mistake.

urgency

Janine woke first in the morning, as was her way.

She was always up early to greet each day with enthusiasm and joy. This day was no less so, and as she looked across at Steve, she smiled and understood that this day would be even more special.

She lay there looking at him sleeping; he was not still, and his eyes indicated that he might be dreaming. She wondered what he was dreaming about.

Steve had told her he dreamed a lot and recounted many dreams when they chatted in the mornings they were together. His dreams seemed to have a sexual theme and usually involved her—*well, at least the ones he tells me about*, she thought.

She suddenly had an idea, slowly reaching over and gently lifting the sheet covering his body and revealing his manhood.

Her suspicion was correct; he was having an erotic dream and was erect. She wondered if she could influence his dream and slowly slid down the bed and positioned herself for some fun.

Steve was on his side, so as she lay on her side, she had easy access to his thick, hard cock.

She started to take his cock into her mouth, ever so gently so that she did not wake him.

Steve stirred slightly but did not wake. Instead, his hips began to move as she sucked on his cock.

She was surprised that this antic had a very erotic effect on her, and she was starting to feel her wetness rising deep within her. She wondered just how far she could go without waking him and continued to stimulate his cock with her mouth and sucking deeper, faster, and using her tongue to add to the sensations she was giving him.

His breathing increased, and he stirred again. He slowly started to groan as his excitement grew.

She felt he was close; she wanted to continue, to see if she could make him cum while he was asleep.

Steve stirred more and then spoke gently, "Babe, what a way to wake up; you are so sexy and so exciting."

Janine stopped so she could talk and thanked him for his praise; she liked hearing him say she was sexy and that she excited him.

They kissed a passionate morning kiss.

She wanted him again; her vagina twitched as they kissed, and Steve was aroused. She turned around and moved her hips back toward him, indicating by this movement that she wanted him to take her from behind.

He did not need convincing as he grasped his thick cock in his hand and started to probe her Flower, searching for the wetness that marked the entry to the depths of her passion.

As he slid his cock across her vulva, she could feel the pre-cum on his cock; it was plentiful and lubricated the sensation.

Then, he moved his cock up toward her Button and, with the combined wetness of her juices and his pre-cum, started to stimulate her clit with firm circular movements.

It drove Janine wild; she was already very horny from sucking his cock while he slept, so this stimulation rapidly brought her to orgasm.

However, this time, just as she came, Steve plunged his cock into her. He was already close to cuming from the stimulation of the end of his cock on her clit, and he wanted to cum as he pumped his cock deep inside her.

She was so excited at his primal passion, the way he took her and the orgasm she just had, that when he started to cum, she also tipped over in a second orgasm.

She pushed back against him as she did; she wanted him, she wanted him deep, and she longed for his cum inside her. She loved her lover cuming, especially as she did. It intensified her orgasm and made her feel attractive, sexy, and, most of all, desired.

She felt very desired now.

They ate a light breakfast from room service while she ran a bath. She loved her baths even more when Steve was opposite her.

They sat in the large tub and chatted about life, their past, and memories of when they were young lovers.

Janine chastised him for his insensitive sexual encounters with other women when she shared a house with him. She was half teasing, but part of her wanted him to understand how much he had hurt her young heart.

Steve was suitably humbled, so she assured him that she had forgiven him.

They talked about their recent reunion and the excitement of their encounter on the train, and he was firming up again despite it only being one hour since he last came. The sight of his thick cock rising in desire for her was exciting her again.

Steve looked at her with a smile and said, "Bath sex? Apart from that very sexy breast play in Paris, we have yet to try full sex in the bath."

Janine was so excited that she moved quickly to her knees. She knew just how she wanted this. She leaned over the edge of the large tub, presenting her rear to him.

Steve reached over to the vanity from the bath and grabbed their spare bottle of play lube. He was aware that the water would dilute her natural lubricant. He poured a generous amount into his hands, spread some on his now very firm, thick cock, and another generous amount over her vulva. As he did, his finger slid over her anal region, and as he did, she felt a twinge deep inside her.

She started to contemplate a different experience.

Steve moved behind Janine and probed her vulva for its hidden entrance; with her wetness and the play lube, it was easy for him to bring his thick cock home, and as he did, she caught her breath.

She still had not gotten used to the girth of his cock, and the sensation was both uncomfortable and exciting. It was always followed by a glorious sensation of him filling her and, of course, the feeling of him as he moved in and out. But, most of all, she loved the pressure against her Button.

The bath water was moving to their thrusting. Again, Steve was very excited, and this time he came quickly. Whether it was because of the situation or the impact of the water on the friction of his cock inside her, she did not know, but he was apologizing for his quick end.

She looked at him from over the side of the bath and said, "It's okay; I'm excited that you lost control with me. It tells me you are excited by me. It does not matter who cums first when we are always cuming. Anyway, I'm always happy to bring myself to orgasm, and I know you like to watch me."

She was already reaching down to touch herself but then stopped. She reached up, took Steve's hand, and moved it to her buttock.

She guided her fingers to her little hole and gestured that he should enter her rear with his finger.

Steve quickly picked up on this, added more play lube to his fingers and her anal region, and started stimulating Janine around her entry.

She was excited by this and started to rub her Button again, moaning as she did.

As she began to build her desire and excitement, Steve slowly entered her with one finger.

She moaned again. She liked this; it was different and exciting and felt right with him.

She was now getting close, and Steve moved in and out of her, progressively going deeper as he did.

She was there now; she started to cum, and as she did, Steve went deeper in a way that intensified her orgasm.

Finally, she cried out, "Fuck me, fuck me" as she came, and he did just that...

He fucked her little hole with his finger and was excited by what she wanted him to do.

Janine was pleasantly surprised by just how much she liked this. She originally wanted him to do this because she knew he would like it, but now, she thought, *I will add this to my list of likes...*

As they were off to meet the Orient Express again for the afternoon trip to Istanbul, they finished their bath, dried off, and got ready for the day.

Two days on the world's most romantic train with the world's most romantic man, she thought, *perfect!*

They laughed as they took the limo to the train station; She was teasing Steve about the fact that he had not recognized her. She should have been annoyed, but she was reassured that she had developed as a woman over the years.

When they pulled into the station, they had stopped laughing and were kissing passionately in the back seat, and the driver had to interrupt them to tell them they were there.

They laughed again.

The train glistened in the sun as they walked down the platform. The porter behind them with their cases. They were headed for the first-class section, and she felt a little glow as the other passengers realized they were '*special passengers*'. There were only a few first-class cabins, and they were taken directly to the first-class dining car for refreshments while the train valet took their bags to their cabin.

A glass of Verve Champagne awaited them.

When they picked up their glasses, Steve proposed a toast to their reunion, saying, "May the time we have together now be longer than the time we had apart."

She was touched by his romanticism and added, "To love rekindled and passion re-ignited."

Janine was slightly tipsy when they walked back toward their cabin. She had already had two glasses of Verve, and while this would not usually have made her so, she was also lightheaded by the atmosphere of the day.

Steve opened the cabin door and gestured for Janine to enter before him.

Ever the gentleman, she thought, as she stepped into the cabin.

She was unsure which hit her first, the perfume or the visual impact, but their cabin was filled with beautiful red roses (she estimated around three dozen).

They were magnificent, and she was surprised; she turned to look at Steve and saw the joy on his face.

He is very proud of himself, she thought. She walked up to him, kissed him on the cheek, and said, "Thank you, they are beautiful; you are so romantic and thoughtful."

She thought *it could not get better.*

It did.

Steve looked at her and said, "Thirty-three roses for my Janine, one for every year we were apart. I cannot replace that time, but I can at least acknowledge the loss with a rose for each year we were apart. I can also promise to dedicate myself to you every year for the rest of my life."

She could not contain herself anymore, and tears began to fall down her cheeks. She was happy, sad, delighted, loved, and honored at the same time.

"I love you, Steve, I always have. Yes, we missed those years, but I'm not sad about that. On the contrary, I'm pleased that I found you now and at a time when we both can appreciate what each has to offer.

"I have no regrets, only love that is deeper than ever it was, and if thirty-three years apart is the price I pay to feel what I feel now, then I'm happy to have paid it."

They kissed again and embraced on the bed as their passion rose with a different intensity. There was sexual desire and raw passion, but there was also a passion for love, their love of each other that intensified their mutual desire. Finally, the train pulled out of the station, and the gentle rocking of the carriage helped take their desire to new heights.

Trains, she thought as Steve entered her. *I just love trains…*

She shuddered with delight as he reached deep inside her, and she took his full manhood. She loved to engulf him, and the way his face showed every second of his desire for her. He kissed her as he plunged deeper and faster, gradually building his passion for her in a way that built hers at the same time. Cum with me," she screamed as she felt her orgasm rising to the surface. "Please, Steve, I want you and I want you to cum inside me now."

It was enough to tip him over the edge. As she came, he also came, both gasping with pleasure as they pulsated to their orgasms that appeared to merge into one orgasm that engulfed them.

"Vous me remplir mon amour, je ne pouvais pas demander plus à la vie," Steve whispered in her ear as he lay on top of her. His weight comforting Janine in a way that felt familiar.

"Was that French?" she said in response. "I did not know you spoke French."

"Did I speak in French?" Steve said. "I'm sorry, I did not realize. My job requires me to travel across the world and take on false identities, but sometimes I need to remember which language to speak, especially in moments like this."

"I'm not complaining, my love," she said; "I was just surprised. I had no idea you spoke French and have no idea what you just said. I only understood amour, the French word for love, so I assume it was a romantic comment."

"I'm not clear exactly what I said, sweet pea; but it roughly translates to: *You complete me, my love. I could not ask for more in life.*"

This brought a tear to Janine's eyes as she had never had such a more romantic comment. It showed her the depth of Steve's love for her.

"I feel the same, Steve," she said, "I cannot even say why, but I feel as if we have known each other for a thousand years, as if I have loved you all that time! And that I could love you for a thousand more."

They kissed deeply.

Janine and Steve chatted for the next hour. They discussed music, movies, food, and even their favorite time and place to live. They were surprised to learn they both had a passion for Paris in the 1930s and joked about sitting in a French café discussing philosophy and art with historical figures of that time.

Janine joked about being his French mistress, sitting in the café with a low-cut dress and suspenders showing, distracting him from his serious conversation about the nature of existence with Jean-Paul Sartre and how they would slip away in the afternoon for a bath prepared by their maid at their French villa in the Left Bank.

They joked about how their maids would be beautiful to look at but how they, both of them, only enjoyed their beauty visually.

The playful conversation aroused both of them, and they soon kissed again. She was wet and writhing under him as they embraced!

She was ready for more...

Steve rose to his knees and gently probed her Flower with just one finger. He had not done this before, and she was unsure what he was proposing. She was even more surprised when he placed his other hand over her pubic area and gently pushed down just below where her bladder lay. He was softly propping the upper part of her vagina wall.

She then understood he was attempting to find her G-Spot. She did not say anything. She let him play. She was skeptical about the existence of this spot; she had tried to find it before, but both she and her past lovers had failed to find it.

She let him probe her out of deference to him until she felt a sudden sensation.

Steve watched her intently and immediately noticed her expression as he found this spot. He asked if it felt good, and she said yes. So he made the pressure firmer, and she responded as an erotic but strange sensation spread from where he was stimulating her.

"It makes me feel like I might pee!" she said.

"That's a good sign," Steve said! "It shows we are on your G-Spot. But, of course, you won't pee," he said, "just let go and don't worry."

She was hesitant, but in the hands of her lover, she surrendered herself to the sensation.

Soon, she could feel an orgasm building rapidly deep inside her. She resisted for a while, but with Steve's reassurance and the desire to experience more of this sensation, she finally decided to bear down and let it happen.

And happen it did, for her orgasm was different, deep, and very satisfying.

She was delighted; after all these years, she had finally experienced a G-Spot orgasm.

Steve was also clearly pleased with himself, and she felt great pleasure from his response. But, of course, she was delighted for him as well.

"Well, that was interesting," she said finally, "I hope we can do more of that soon."

"Of course!" Steve said, "Was that your first?" he asked.

"Yes," Janine admitted as if she feared disappointing him.

Steve thought for a second, then said, "Well, your first is always the most difficult to find; next time, it will be easier and better. So, of course, we will do this again.

There is much for us to explore with each other, and I feel so comfortable exploring with you. I feel you trust me and that there is no pressure. It's natural."

"I feel the same," she said with a smile that made him feel loved and appreciated.

Steve woke up to the regular click-clack of the train moving across the landscape toward Istanbul. Half unconscious, he instinctively reached over to touch Janine as he had done over the last days they had been together in Paris and Venice.

She was gone.

He bolted upright; something was wrong—he could feel it.

Where was she?

It was still dark.

As he started to wake up and adjusted his eyes, he heard the sound of a toilet flushing and turned toward the en-suite bathroom off their cabin. He heard the tap run and the soft sound of her drying her hands and realized she was in the bathroom.

The door to the bathroom opened, and the light pierced his eyes, but almost instantly, they adjusted so he could see the silhouette of her naked body against the light. *She was magnificent,* he thought, as his cock reacted to the sight by doubling its size almost instantly. He was now aroused and turned to greet her amorously as she returned to their bed.

She stopped him in his tracks.

"I can't," she said, with sadness in her voice.

"What's wrong?" Steve asked. "Are you tired?"

"I'm unwell," Janine replied. "I have been to the toilet three times in the last hour," she moaned. "I think I have a bad urinary tract infection. We have been fucking so much over the last week that it looks like I have honeymoon cystitis, even though we are not on our honeymoon… I'm afraid my little Flower will have to rest for a while. She needs to recover."

Steve asked Janine if she had any treatments with her, but she did not. So he made Janine a cup of herbal tea, helped dress her in light clothes, kissed her, and said he would be back shortly.

He was gone for about thirty minutes (two visits to the toilet in her time) and returned with a triumphant look.

He pulled out two packets from his pocket and proudly announced, "Antibiotics and Ural—preferred treatment for cystitis. It took several interruptions, but I figured there must have been a doctor on board or at least a honeymoon couple. So the antibiotics are from the doctor three carriages down and the Ural is from a French couple on the last days of their honeymoon!"

He poured Janine some water, helped her take the antibiotics, and she drank the Ural. Janine was hot to the touch and had a temperature, so Steve wet a flannel from the bathroom and helped cool her by holding it on her forehead and neck.

She was touched by the love and care that he provided her over the next few hours, making her tea, getting some light breakfast, helping reduce her temperature, and comforting her after her frequent trips to the bathroom.

He was patient and loving, she thought, and even though she was suffering, she was comforted by his care and attention.

Gradually the frequency abated, and she started to feel better, so by the time it was around midday, she felt up to taking some lunch in the dining car.

Steve helped her get ready.

She was feeling weak, so he helped her shower, washing her back and hair affectionately and helping dry her and get dressed.

Had she not been so unwell, she would have found the experience erotic, but her Flower was on mandatory sick leave.

As they walked to the dining car, Janine stopped and turned to Steve. "Thank you," she said, "Thank you for taking care of me; you have shown me how much you care about me."

Steve smiled and said, "I'm sure if I were sick, you would do the same, besides it was nice to have you depend on me for this short time."

As they arrived at the dining car, they noticed it was nearly full and had a bustle of excitement. They found a table for two, and as they sat down,

He helped Janine with her chair. She was impressed.

He has traditional manners, she thought, as he passed her a menu. She was not very hungry because of her illness and turned the menu to look at the wine list.

Steve said, "Probably not a good idea, the antibiotics remember."

She had forgotten and was sad because she felt like a glass of champagne. They ordered a small meal and some juice (he had the decency not to order alcohol) and settled to talk again.

Janine looked at the table opposite and acknowledged the older couple looking at them. "That's the doctor who gave me the antibiotics," Steve whispered.

She was embarrassed because the doctor would realize she had a UTI because they had been having frequent sex. She wondered if he had told his wife because she kept gazing over at her now and then and quietly saying something to her doctor husband. *Probably all dried up,* she thought in an attempt to dismiss her from her mind. *She's just envious*.

A young couple stopped at their table as they were eating their salad.

The woman looked straight at Janine and said, "How are you feeling now? Better, I hope; I hate UTIs; I trust the Ural helped."

Janine wanted to disappear, as others in the dining car must have heard, but quietly said, "Much better, thank you, I appreciate your help."

As they walked away, Janine looked at Steve. They stared for a second, then both of them burst out laughing. They joked about what happened and played a game making up stories for each couple or group in the dining car, speculating who they were and why they were there. Each story got more fantastical until they finally had the Italian man at the table two tables down pegged as a mafia boss whose partner was a runaway nun from the Vatican.

As they talked, the conversation moved to past relationships, and Steve shared stories of his failed early relationships.

Janine was curious about his life and listened intently, weighing up how his past life might provide clues to how she could ensure this relationship worked. Steve's openness about his life and how he did not seem to hold back on details that might have given other women concern moved Janine.

He trusted her, her judgement, and her acute ability to understand him.

She liked that he made her comfortable when she talked about her life, her desires, and the tragedy that had happened to her family. He seemed genuinely moved when she told him about the tragic death of her nephew.

They talked about her childhood and her parents' hobby of breeding bulldogs and how she missed the companionship these dogs provided in her youth. Her work and travels had made owning a pet difficult. He noted the regret in her voice.

Steve, likewise, was amazed at how he could talk to her.

Janine had not studied at university but had a real grasp of human behavior and a depth of knowledge that showed her high emotional intelligence.

He liked that.

So many of his friends were academically brilliant, but they could not hold meaningful conversations about things that truly matter in life. *She was an impressive woman*, he thought.

They realized it was late, and as they were due to arrive in Istanbul at five a.m., they decided to go to bed. When they returned to the cabin and started to undress, Janine noticed that his cock was already half erect. She felt a familiar twinge, but her condition blunted the normal reaction she would have at the sight of his lovely, thick cock.

Once in bed, Steve was cuddling her but was not amorous in a way that suggested he wanted to take her. She appreciated this as it showed his concern for her.

She thought, then turned to him and said, "As you know, my Flower is in rehab, but my mind and eyes are not. I can see that firm erection you have, and I don't think we should waste it... I would like to see you pull your cock and cum. I would find it very sexy."

Steve was excited by the knowledge that his self-gratification in front of her would make her aroused.

She was already helping him get ready as her hand glided up and down his thick shaft, making him groan as she did; he fell back onto the bed and pulled the sheet entirely away so she had a full view of his next moves.

Steve took his hand and slowly started to slide his hand up and down his cock. At first, he slid it over the skin, but gradually he closed his grip so that he was moving the skin on his cock over his penis; he was holding tight and starting to breathe heavier.

Despite her condition, she felt her Flower getting wetter. She still could not contemplate sex but liked the excitement this was providing.

Finally, Steve groaned, and Janine's Flower twinged again.

As he started to pump his cock faster, his breathing got deeper. He was clearly getting closer, and her excitement grew; she now wanted him, but she wanted to see him cum; she wanted to see his face show every bit of pleasure he was getting from this.

She could see it in his face and writhing body as he moved faster and faster toward his orgasm.

Then it happened; Steve moved his other hand to his groin as if to squeeze out his orgasm and groaned very loudly, almost screaming as he came. It took a few seconds after his visible pulsation of orgasm before his cum appeared, shooting out of his cock and onto his belly. It was beautiful to her to see his ecstasy, manhood, and virility so starkly—all the while knowing he was doing this for her, to please her, to excite her.

This act of masturbation, of self-pleasure, was turned into a beautiful sexual show between them. It was as much an act *with* her as she could have imagined, and at that point, she understood the fascination and excitement that he expressed when she masturbated in front of him.

She knew then that the next time she did, she would no longer feel self-conscious at being observed but would feel connected to him in a mutual pleasuring that would take it to a new level.

I cannot wait till Flower is discharged from rehab, she thought as she drifted off to sleep.

east

The train arrived at Istanbul's central station around the time the sun rose, so they were unaware of the changes in scenery and architecture as they traveled through the Turkish countryside.

They were now fascinated by the difference as they rode in the chauffeured car to the hotel. They really were in the Near East now!

The early morning bustle of the locals setting up market stalls and the sound of early morning Islamic prayers filled the air as they entered the hotel. The staff were dressed in traditional clothes, which added to the atmosphere.

They checked into their suite and were blown away by its décor and size.

The balcony faced the port, so they had a view of the ships and yachts sailing into the large port that was framed with the silhouette of Istanbul's eastern profile.

The bathroom took their breath away as they entered the en-suite like children looking for Christmas presents.

It was blue, tiled from floor to ceiling, and had a sizable sunken Turkish bath.

On either end, the built-in waterproof pillows were made of a soft material. The bath was already full and had a soothing whisper of steam rising from the surface.

Large candles around the bath added to the atmosphere, and the perfume or salts used permeated the room.

Janine and Steve turned to look at each other and smiled. Steve said immediately, "I'll get the champagne" as she started to disrobe and pull out her phone to put on some music—their music.

As they lowered themselves into the Turkish bath, you could visibly see the tension from the day disappear and their muscles relax.

They toasted to the East as they sipped their champagne. They were both tired because they had not slept well, and she was recovering from her illness. They sat and soaked in the bath, knowing that any thoughts of amorous sexual activity would have to wait.

Janine still felt twinges from her Flower as she looked at him across the bath.

He was always half erect whenever he was in her presence, but now sight of her naked body ensured that he became fully erect.

They talked about life, their favorite holidays, family, and their time in Paris.

Steve seemed interested in her life over the last thirty years they had been apart. She had been married, she said, but even though she had loved her husband, something was always missing from her life. She said it was just too comfortable, too routine, and she somehow lost the excitement she wanted from life. So it ended slowly and amicably as they drifted off into other relationships. Since then, she has had several relationships, but none made her feel passionate or loved.

Janine said she had always hoped that her life would have been complete and that her life partner would have loved and adored her, and she would feel the same.

She was about to say to Steve that she had this once but lost it when he said, "It's a love I have always felt was missing in my life too, a love that I feel right now. I'm not sure how you feel, babe, but if you still loved me after so many years, loved me that much that you sought to find me, I suspect that it's the love we have both yearned for all our lives."

She looked at him and said, "I hope so, my love, but it feels right, complete, and like I am where I belong. I have always yearned for this feeling and thought it was possible, and now I feel it; I know it is exactly what I want."

They smiled at each other; they both knew what this meant and moved together to embrace in the bath.

They kissed deeply and held each other, softly whispering as they continued to talk and joke about what they liked and what annoyed them.

It was an hour before they noticed that they were getting wrinkled. The water in the bath had not cooled. It must have been heated continually, so they had lost their sense of time.

They rose from the bath, dried off, and retired to the large, oversized bed with curtains all around it. Steve commented that he felt like they were the sultan and his wife.

"His only wife!" she joked as she remembered that a sultan would likely have a harem. As Flower was still in rehab, they embraced and slept deeper than had ever before.

The heat of the bath or the comfort of the enormous bed certainly helped.

Still, both understood that their peaceful sleep was more about the contentment they felt about their life, their love, and the pure gratitude they had found each other, had found their true love after all these years apart.

They woke to the sound of early morning Islamic prayers, and Steve was in his usual state. She cuddled up to him and started to caress his engorged erection. Her Flower was beginning to wake, but the urgency of a pee soon took over, and she resigned herself to the fact that she was not entirely out of rehab yet.

Disappointed, she went to the bathroom and returned to their bed for a quiet time with Steve while he slowly woke. They discussed what they would do that day and decided to visit the famous spice markets and one of the palaces. Then, they would lunch in the bazaar to soak up the local atmosphere and spend the afternoon on the beach.

All that activity would keep their minds off the fact that they needed to respect Flower's recovery time.

They had breakfast in bed, then spent thirty minutes in their Turkish bath and slowly got ready for the day.

They periodically embraced, kissed, and joked about their forced celibacy, even though it drove them both crazy with frustration.

They were soon on their way to the spice market in a hotel taxi car and were amazed at the sights and sounds as they drove in the heavy traffic. It was slow going, but they were okay with it as they each pointed out different attractions and activities in the streets around them.

The spice market was enormous, and the colors and smells were spectacular.

They weaved in and out of the stalls, looking at spices they had never seen before and chatting with the stall owners about the uses of each spice. Many of the vendors tried to sell them a particular spice that they claimed had aphrodisiac properties—it was obvious to all that saw or met them that they were passionately in love. *An aphrodisiac was the last thing they needed,* thought Janine, *even if they did work.*

Both hung close to each other, and their frequent exchanges showed they were captivated by each other.

They could have bought fifteen carpets from the Turkish carpet stalls dotted throughout the market, each seemingly a bargain, only to find the same for half the price at the next stall they encountered.

Next, they had coffee in the small café at the edge of the market and sat and watched as the locals and tourists paraded by for their entertainment.

They arrived at the Topkapi Palace at eleven a.m. and were stunned at the sheer opulence of the lifestyle the Ottoman sultans must have lived with for the 400 years this was the home of the empire's royalty.

The grounds were stunning, and she loved the renowned tulip gardens. The views across Istanbul were spectacular, with the colors of the houses and streets contrasting with the blue of the Sea of Marmara. They wandered around the palace buildings, saw the harem quarters, and joked about Steve being a sultan and how he could efficiently serve more wives than the sultans.

Janine was frustrated because she wanted to make passionate love with him but was also pleased they had the chance to be together and chat as they wandered around the city. She felt that she had gotten to know him much better (other than sexually) and liked what she saw.

She also wondered how he felt about her as he began to spend more time with her in this way.

They had lunch late at one of the food outlets at the Palace and went down to the beach around three p.m. It was late afternoon, and the sun was hot. They changed at the bathing facility on the beach, which also had large Turkish baths. They spent the afternoon until six p.m. sun-baking on the beach, talking, and periodically swimming in the calm azure waters on the coast.

It was a relaxing time, and she felt her Flower rousing as she spoke and gazed upon Steve's now familiar body. Even though they were dressed modestly (she felt like she was in her grandmother's bathing suit), the sun often made her feel sexy, and now she felt like Flower might be ready for discharge.

She noticed through his bathing suit that the sun also affected him.

Or was it her? She hoped it was.

They arrived at the hotel late and immediately went to the large bath in their en-suite. They were salted from the sea, a little pink, and the bath beaconed.

Again, they soaked, talked, and caressed each other.

This time, Flower was much more aware, and she could feel her wetness rising inside her.

Steve was also clearly aroused, with his thick cock swelling with their caresses.

Janine decided, for better or worse, Flower was getting discharged from rehab as soon as they got out of the bath. She would take it easy, but she would have that impressive manhood deep inside, even if it killed her!

They dried off, and Janine slipped into some very sexy dark green panties and a small teddy that matched. She had it in her mind to seduce him, even though she knew no seduction was required. She sat on the armchair beside the bed and gazed across the room.

A flash of light attracted her attention.

It came from near the head of the bed, so she got up to investigate. She drew the curtains against the wall at the head of the bed where the light had come from and discovered a sizable wall-to-ceiling mirror on the wall behind the curtain.

There was no bedhead, only pillows, and with the curtains drawn, they had not noticed this last night.

That was it, she thought, *the perfect way to entice Flower out of rehab.*

She went to the wardrobe and took out a pair of high-heel shoes she had brought just for this purpose. They were also dark green. Steve had gone into the lounge room to get some champagne, so he had not seen this discovery. She lit the candles in the bedroom, lay on the bed seductively, and waited for her lover to return.

Steve had poured the champagne and entered the room, saying, "You know we really should think about going out to…" when he stopped mid-sentence.

"Wow," he said, staring at his beautiful Janine, lying on the bed before him in stunning dark green underwear. It was the sexiest sight he had ever seen, and his heart raced.

"You were saying?" she asked rhetorically.

Steve said he was about to suggest they go out to dinner, but obviously that was not about to happen. So instead, he handed Janine a glass of bubbles and proposed a toast.

"To beauty, whose name has been eclipsed by you, to sensuality, who pales under your vision, to love, which cannot begin to describe what I feel right now," he said proudly.

She sighed, put down the glass, drew him toward her, and kissed him deeply. "I want you," she whispered, "I want you now. It's been too long, and she craves your thick cock. Take me, Steve, take me now, love me, and never stop."

He rolled her over onto her back and mounted her; her Flower was so wet already that his gentle probing easily found its home. He slowly, patiently, and gently entered her until she uttered a soft cry. Then, he plunged deeper, completely into her, building the rhythm of his thrusts to a frenzied pace as she called out, "Yes, babe, fill me, fuck me deep, I want you, I need you."

She was so surprised that she was getting close to orgasm so soon.

She turned her head slightly to gasp some air and caught sight of the sexiest image she had ever seen.

It was them, her and her lover, fucking. She had forgotten the mirror in her lust for him, but now it was too much; the image of her in her green underwear (minus the panties) and her shoes took her breath away. She blurted out, "Oh god, babe, I'm cuming, cum with me, cum inside me. Fill me with your thick cock and hot semen."

She came explosively; she writhed as he thrust deep inside her, accentuating all the pleasure she had from her orgasm.

But Steve had held back.

Now he slowly withdrew, and as he did, she gave another gasp. *It was the same going out when he is hard*, she thought.

He slid down the bed, kissing her breasts and stomach, gradually working his way down to her Flower. He took it slow so she could recover, but she was ready for him when he arrived.

She loved the way he performed oral sex; she loved his skill, the way he understood what she needed when she needed it.

He did not disappoint her.

She stopped him about two minutes into a particularly arousing build-up as his tongue slid slowly around her Button.

He was a bit confused by this and asked if Flower was okay. He said if she was still unwell, he could stop.

"You dare," she blurted demandingly without thinking. "I just want to see," she said, as she nodded toward the mirror.

He had not even noticed the mirror earlier; his eyes had been on her magnificent beauty, adorned in dark green underwear and shoes.

He smiled and allowed Janine to reposition herself as his tongue hovered near her Flower.

Finally, she settled in a position that allowed them an erotic view of their passionate embrace. He resumed his attention on her Button. Janine's arousal level lifted as she gazed across the mirror and fully saw her lover devouring her womanhood.

As Steve began his special technique, Janine rapidly built until she tightened her thighs and came. It was intense and satisfying, but she wanted more. She loved orgasms from oral sex, especially his special.

Still, it also left her wanting to have him inside her.

So finally, she rose to her knees and demanded, "This time, you have to cum, babe; I want you to fuck me from behind, and I want to watch in the mirror. I want it deep, and I want it to drive you wild with desire."

He did not need any more encouragement as he mounted her and probed for her wetness.

Janine and Steve were transfixed by the mirror image of this primal act, the two entwined, his stomach on her buttocks, her rear presented upwards as she took him completely.

Their reflection in the mirror was all he needed as well.

He fucked her like this was the last time he would ever fuck, and the pure desire in his movement, the sounds of his groans and the way he held her to him, arms across her hips, drove Janine to orgasm rapidly.

But, it was her orgasm that, most of all, tipped him over into his orgasm, matching her moan by moan, scream by scream, stroke by pushback as they both sought to get every pulse, every electric spasm out of the mutual orgasm before they both collapsed on the bed.

He was lying there exhausted; Steve had given all he had to Janine and she to him.

Eventually, he turned to her, smiled, and said, "If we ever get a home together, promise me we will have full mirrors on at least one wall and the ceiling; that was so erotic."

"I was hoping you would say that," she said.

They cuddled close that night, with Janine on her side and Steve cradled against her back, hand upon her pert breasts. She did not usually sleep well, but she slept deeply with him. Indeed, she slept particularly well after passion. Still, she had a strong sense that her ability to sleep deeply and peacefully had more to do with her feeling of trust and safety with him. She felt at home, comfortable, and totally at peace with this man, her man.

They woke early and had breakfast on the balcony. They could see the busy port and ships coming and going. The sounds of the city grew louder and beckoned them as they finished breakfast. They resisted and withdrew back to their suite and headed for their large Turkish bath.

Their bath time was always precious, and Janine cherished it. It started as her method of avoiding UTIs but rapidly became a ritual between them and the place where they had some of their most meaningful conversations. But Janine still had to tell Steve a truth she had not revealed.

Slowly she said, "You know I never liked baths before I met you, Steve, but somehow we started this ritual, and now I love them."

He laughed, and she was a little taken aback by this.

"It's not funny," she said, "I was being romantic and honest."

"No," Steve said! "You have me wrong! I laughed because I rarely had baths before meeting you; I did not like them either. I just thought it was funny. We both believed the other always did this. I'm pleased this is a new ritual for us both; it makes it even more special to me. I love our bath time together."

They kissed and played around for a while, washing each other with too much attention to cleaning particular parts of each other's bodies.

The more they played, the more they both became excited, and it was not long before Steve was caressing her breasts with his mouth and tongue.

She was still shocked at how this made her feel, as she felt the electric connection from her breasts to her clitoris and deep into her pelvis. She lay back, fantasizing about Steve's cock being inside her as she let the sensation in her body overtake her, finally succumbing to an orgasm solely generated by his attention to her *twins*.

As she settled, she noticed that he was erect and ready for her.

She sat up, moved across to him, and helped him position so that his cock was out of the water and started to slowly run her tongue up and down the shaft of his cock.

He groaned and moved his hips to feel more, and she took this as her signal to take his cock into her mouth. It was large, and she was always unsure about stimulating him this way. Still, as she did, the sensuality of pleasing him this way and her excitement dissipated her concerns.

It was not long before she was taking the entire length of his cock into her mouth and was moving in and out as she sucked and used her tongue to excite him.

He was enjoying this and was starting to breathe faster, groaning and moving his hips in the water.

She knew he was close; if she continued, he would cum. She was unsure what to do and did not want to stop because he enjoyed this but was reluctant to continue.

She had almost decided to continue when he stopped her, kissed her, and said, "Time to dry off and go back to bed. My cock is about to explode, and I want to fill you with my semen."

It was less than two minutes before they were in bed, with Steve kissing Janine deeply and caressing her shoulders, back, and firm buttocks. He was patient, slowly building her desire again until she was ready. It did not take long. She pushed him onto his back, rose, and mounted him.

Sitting on her knees, she rose over his engorged erection and guided him to her wetness.

She liked this position as she could control the pace. She slowly lowered herself onto his cock, feeling her Flower expand as she did.

Gradually, the thickness of his cock filled her entry, and she readied herself for the pain/relief and then the pleasure that always accompanied his initial entry into her. She let her weight fall, gasped, and groaned almost simultaneously as he filled her Flower completely.

Janine started to move on top of him, watching his reaction as she did; she guided the movements according to his response, and before long, it was clear he was building to an orgasm.

He tried to move into her, but she stopped him. "I'm fucking you this time," she said, "Lie back and take like a man," she added.

Janine picked up the pace of her movements up and down on his cock and was surprised at how deep she could take his cock in this position. She was now building her orgasm and started to touch her Button as she moved.

This was an erotic image for Steve; now, he was very close to cuming.

They both tipped over around the same time, both realizing the other had started to cum. It was hard for them to even tell the difference between their orgasm and the ecstasy of the sensation from fucking this way. They both screamed out, groaned, and pumped each other with their passion.

She loved the feeling that she had fucked her lover until he came. *I must do this more often,* she thought as she stared down at her lover, his face displaying a pleasure that delighted her.

It was eleven a.m., and another bath before they finally emerged from the room.

Afterwards, they went to the beach and had lunch near the bazaar.

Janine was excited about seeing the city, but she thought it would not matter where she was; her excitement would be intense. It was fortunate that she felt that they were in such a fascinating city; otherwise, they would never get out of bed, and she would be very, very sore...

They spent the rest of the morning at the hotel's private beach; that way, they could get some sun without worrying about towels and the hordes of tourists on the public beach. The bazaar could wait, and they would be close to their private room, Turkish bath, and bed.

They chatted about their earlier time together, each trying to recall memories buried for many years. As she recounted events, He started to remember things as well, the house they shared in Perth and her visit to Melbourne when he was there.

He recalled the affection he held for her back then as he did. She was very young then and seemed infatuated, but He never understood that it was a genuine and deep love she felt.

This saddened him as he distinctly remembered their friendship and comfortable time together. He thought that if he had known how she felt, perhaps they would have made a life together.

Suddenly, He jumped up: "The photos!" he said.

Janine looked at him perplexed, and he realized she did not know what he had been thinking.

"I have photos from that time. I kept them, and when I went through my photos a while ago, I made digital copies of them. All my photos are synced to my phone, so I should have them here."

He pulled out his *iPhone*, searched his photos, and finally found them.

There were four in total, two with him and Janine, one of Janine having been doused with water in a prank with a friend, and one of Janine, her sister, and her mother.

He showed Janine one by one, and as she saw them, she began to cry. "I also had these photos and lost them."

"I never thought I'd see these again," she said, her voice catching. "Thank you, Steve. You have no idea what this means to me." She wiped her eyes. "Can you AirDrop them to me?"

She flicked through the photos, tears streaking her cheeks. "Look at us. We were so young, so cute." She looked up at him. "You shouldn't have left me, you know. It broke my heart."

"I'm sorry," Steve said, reaching for her hand. "If I'd known how you felt... but we're here now, aren't we? Older, wiser." He squeezed her fingers. "No more holding back. No more secrets about how we feel." His voice softened. "What we have, this connection—it's rare. We both know it. And I'm not letting go again."

Janine dried her eyes, promised to always cherish their love, and told Steve she understood how rare this was. They returned to their room and took a hot bath before making passionate love in their mirrored bed. The passion and intensity of their lovemaking were more intense than before as they both now understood how unconditional their love was.

She was now so convinced of Steve's love for her that she now completely relaxed with him. Until then, there was always a tiny part of her that held back. She had been burnt by this man before. But now she understood that he was not the immature man she knew then; he had grown, was clear about what he wanted, and wanted her.

It was at that moment that she surrendered to him completely.

Steve was smitten with Janine from the time he met her again, but he also had some doubts; he had loved in the past, had his heart broken, and had always been guarded in his relationships since then. He never loved completely for fear that his heart would be broken again. But now, after the last few weeks and today's events, it was different. Seeing the pure joy on Janine's face at the photos made him understand just how much she loved him! Just how much she still did. He felt safe with her now, and the passion of their lovemaking had reflected that feeling.

That day, he surrendered to his love for Janine.

He thought to himself, *this could not be better!* as he lay there next to his true love.

Neither could anticipate how much more passionate their lovemaking could be with such complete surrender.

They finally decided to get out of bed at three p.m.

flame

They wandered around the shops as she looked at clothes and jewelry. She was impressed with his patience and apparent enjoyment of shopping. She understood that only a few men enjoyed shopping, and they often were intolerant, wandered off, or sat somewhere and waited impatiently.

He was different, and she liked that in him. He showed interest in what she looked at and even pointed out items he thought she might like.

She then decided to try the ultimate test.

How would he react to her choosing clothes for him?

Again, she had experience with men who could not shop for clothes with her. They either never purchased them or tore through the shop, buying the same style they had always had, as if they were picking up the usual groceries from the supermarket and no more thought than their usual brand of toilet paper.

She suggested they look at the men's wear section of the vast up-market department store they were in.

"That would be nice," he said.

So far, so good, she thought.

As they arrived, she headed for the casual section. She had thought he would look sexy in a linen shirt, so she started to look in that section. She observed him as he looked through the racks. He stopped now and then to take out a particular shirt, hold it up against himself, and look in the mirror. Then, he would turn to her and ask if she liked what he was holding up.

Still good, she thought, *but could he commit*?

Janine finally found what she was looking for. She pulled out three linen shirts: a white, a black, and a beautiful deep dark green.

She moved toward him and asked if he liked them.

They were two different styles, but she could not choose which she liked best.

He smiled and said, "Linen, I should have thought of that. The perfect summer shirt, and they will be handy for the next part of our trip."

She was so excited that he liked her choice that she completely missed his comment about the next part of their trip, even though this was the first time he had mentioned what might come after Istanbul.

Steve took the shirts, looked at them closely to check their quality, then looked around for the fitting room. She had picked his size easily, and most men would have just accepted that a medium or large is what they wear without taking the time to try them. But not Steve. She was impressed.

He invited her over, saying, "I'll try each one but want to show you. I would value your opinion."

Now she was very impressed.

He appeared from the dressing room with the black linen shirt first. He had the sleeves partially rolled up (*good*, Janine said to herself, *he has class*), the shirt untucked and unbuttoned at the top three buttons.

Perfect, she thought. "Very sexy," she said to him, "It fits well and looks good on you. Black suits you."

He thanked her, then retreated to the fitting room and emerged several minutes later with the white shirt on. It was a different style, and the cut was unflattering. He looked uncomfortable in it and was not as pleased with this shirt. "No, I don't think so," she said diplomatically.

He smiled at her knowingly and said he was glad because he did not like the cut. He disappeared back into the fitting room, not even waiting until he was there before taking the shirt off.

Finally, he emerged with the green shirt on.

Janine took a deep breath as he walked up to her. It was a stunning color and suited him well. The cut was the same as the black, so there was no problem with that. She braced herself for the debate about which one he would buy, but instead he said,

"I have a white linen shirt already, so there is no need to find another white one; I'll get the black and green one then. They are both funky. I'm pleased you like them both."

This pleasantly surprised Janine, and she mentally awarded him a high distinction for his test.

They headed back to the hotel after coffee, shopping bags in tow. She had purchased a lovely red dress and some black shoes. He was attentive as she tried several dresses on, honest about what he liked on her, and ecstatic when she walked out with the red dress on. She loved it and hoped he did too.

He did not hesitate for a heartbeat and just said, "Wow."

She had found an attractive silver bracelet and tried it on, and when she went to pay for it, Steve stepped in and presented his card.

"Let me buy that for you," he said; "A woman should not have to buy her jewelry," he added. She was now in shopping heaven and impressed with her new shopping partner.

They arrived at the hotel room, unpacked the shopping, hung up the clothes, and retreated to the bath again. They talked about their shopping trip, and she thanked him for his patience in putting up with the time she spent looking around.

"Not at all," he said. "I enjoy seeing what you like and don't like; it helps me know you better. How could that possibly be unpleasant?"

Inevitably, they played around in the bath, so by the time they dried off, they were ready for bed again. They had completely forgotten about dinner, so they ordered some desserts from room service.

They were sharing strawberry mousse and a lemon tart and were semi-naked on the bed, so the temptation to play with the food was too much.

She started it first as she smeared strawberry mousse onto Steve's now-erect cock and sucked the flavors off slowly and tenderly. It was not long before Steve applied a generous amount of lemon tart filling over her Flower and took his time slowly tasting her and enjoying his dessert in this different way.

This particularly aroused Janine; it was not long before the food was forgotten.

Next, Steve focused his effort on her little erect Button. She soon exploded into an orgasm as he closed his mouth over her Button for his Special.

It was quick and intense and seemed to come from nowhere.

She was ready for him now; she wanted to feel him inside her again, but he had other ideas.

"We need to be careful," he said. "You know how sore you can get when we fuck as often as we do. I would like to please you, though, and we can do this without him being inside you. I'm turned on by you touching yourself, and I would very much like to watch you make yourself cum. I know that your orgasm would be good, and I want to see just how you do it.

"Just the thought of you pleasuring yourself makes me hot and hard," he added.

Even though she wanted him inside her, she was attracted to the idea of pleasuring herself in front of him and said, "OK, on one condition. I want you to do the same, so I can watch you as well. I love to watch you pump your cock, and it would make me so hot having both of us pleasuring ourselves for each other."

She rolled over onto her back, and Steve positioned himself between her legs and up on his knees to see her clearly as she looked at him. She moved her hands gently to her Flower as he looked intently at her and started to rub his cock with his right hand, holding it loosely at first. Next, he slid his hand up and down the shaft of his penis as he watched her gently probing herself for her wetness.

Then, carefully, she used her wetness to lubricate her Button and started to circle it with her fingers. The sight of Steve pumping his cock accentuated her desire and the intensity of the sensations she felt as she rubbed her Button progressively faster and firmer.

Her moans prompted him to pump harder, and his moans, in turn, moved her closer toward her building her orgasm.

She liked the control she had over her orgasm when she pleasured herself, and she was now grateful that he had suggested this. Her usual masturbation fantasies were discarded this time, as she had her latest fantasy right before her and as watched his building orgasm rise.

He was close now. She could sense it.

She had come to know the signs, the moans, the clenching of his thighs, the sweet expression on his face, the joy in his eyes.

She also felt her signs, the signs she knew so well; this was it, the point when Janine was about to explode, and to ensure he was with her, she called out, "I'm cuming babe, oh god, I'm cuming, cum with me, pump your semen onto me."

As she started to call out, Steve felt his tipping point; *God, this is hot*, he thought as he called out, "Yes, babe, I'm cuming with you, cum, babe, cum with me, you are so hot."

And they did; they came together, Janine writhing in ecstasy as she peaked with one of the best self-made orgasms in a long time. He leant forward, and allowed his semen to spurt out all over her Flower and fingers.

She felt the warmth hit her body like soft, warm rain. She was surprised by just how intense the sensation of it hitting her was. She opened her eyes to see Steve's pure joy as he gazed upon her, the desire in him and his lust for her more potent than ever.

What next, she thought? *What else does this man have to give me?*

She lay there, her fingers running absentmindedly through Steve's semen; it was all over her Flower and Button, and the sensation and knowledge that this was semen were erotic. Then, to her surprise, she felt that familiar sensation that heralded her desire to cum. *Alive already*, she thought, playing with her Button that was now sticky with Steve's juices. She let the sensation rise within her.

He was watching this remarkable recovery and seemed pleased with his part.

She circled her Button and rubbed firmer, tightening her thighs to squeeze one last orgasm out. It was elusive, and he could see she was having trouble peaking.

Eventually, he leaned over, took her nipple into his mouth, and started sucking.

"Yes, yes, yes," she said, "That helps; suck more," she demanded, now determined she would cum again.

He stepped up the pace; the sucking, the friction, and occasional tugs at her erect nipples were enough to complement her now frantic rubbing of semen across her Button.

She came with great relief; she wanted this, and even though it was a little one, she was delighted with herself and her lover.

They rested before heading for their bath. she was determined not to get another UTI. She drank her third glass of Ural for the day, downed another antibiotic, and sat in the bath, hoping that all three remedies would be enough to stop her from being punished for this wonderful indulgence.

As they sat in the bath, they talked.

Their conversation was sometimes fun, sometimes silly, often fantasy, and occasionally serious. This was a serious conversation. Janine spoke about how she had loved him since they first met and how this was very special to her.

He sat silent, then said: "I know that I was your first love, babe, and I would love to say that you were my first love also… but as you know, someone broke my heart before I met you. I have never been able to surrender to love since completely... Until now. I can, however, promise you are, and will be, my last true love."

She just stared. She was stunned. Finally, she said, "They are the most beautiful words you have said to me. I feel extremely grateful for your love and will always treat it accordingly."

The next few days were spent sightseeing, dining at many different restaurants (including one with Turkish belly dancers), sunning on the beach, returning to the hotel, making passionate love, having baths, and drinking an inordinate amount of champagne. They even managed to go to a 'club' one night for fun. It turned out to be quite a night, and they enjoyed it despite being a cross between a disco, a strip club, and a cabaret.

They had to have a 'rest' day for Flower's sake, as despite their best efforts not to overindulge, Janine got quite sore after four days of particularly frequent sex. Not that this meant she could not be satisfied because between Steve's exceptional oral, his ability to hit her G-Spot with one gentle finger, her breast orgasms, and her self-help method, she was pretty well served.

Penetration was simply off the menu—for a short time.

It soon came close to the time they were meant to leave. They had packed their bags the night before, but he had insisted they pack a small bag to go to the beach again before leaving. He still refused to reveal their next destination.

They had their usual lovemaking in the morning (if you could ever call their lovemaking usual), a bath, and breakfast. She put on her bathers and a cute little sun dress she had purchased locally. They left the bags in the room as Steve said he had organized a late checkout so they could return to their suite, have a bath, and dress for their next leg.

She attempted to find out where they were going and tried every excuse she could for him to tell her. "I need to know what to wear," she pleaded; "I might be too hot or too cold, I need to get my passport out, I will need local currency."

He simply said, "Nice try, what you are wearing is fine. I have all the other arrangements in place."

They took a hotel-chauffeured car to the beach, but halfway there, he said, "Let's go down to the Marina and have a look. I forgot to take you there, and there is a small café that serves the best coffee and ice cream in Europe."

"OK," Janine agreed; she was happy to linger in Istanbul as long as possible as it had been a wonderful time. The driver pulled up at the marina, and they alighted. They took their small day bag and he told the driver to pick them up in two hours. They had coffee and Turkish delight ice cream, which she had to agree was the best she had ever had.

They wandered along the jetties looking at the people and the boats, chatting about their time in Istanbul. Then, suddenly, Steve jumped up on the deck of one of the large sailboats and said, "Quick, take my hand and have a look."

"We can't," she said, "We will get in trouble; you can't just tour someone's private yacht!"

He smiled and said, "We can if you have chartered it for the next three weeks!"

Then, she noticed their luggage sitting on the yacht's foredeck. It was all a ruse: the late checkout, the driver returning, the coffee and ice cream, so he could have their luggage secretly stowed on the yacht. She took his hand and boarded.

It was an eighty-five-foot luxury yacht and was spectacular. "Where are we going?" she asked.

"First through the Mediterranean down to Tel Aviv in Israel, Monaco, Gibraltar, and through to Casablanca in Morocco. From there, we track the coast north to Lisbon before crossing to Bristol in England. Then we go up the coast to the yacht's homeport of Clydebank in Scotland. It's about forty kilometers from Glasgow up the Clyde River. The crew are from there but are currently re-provisioning in town and will be back in an hour."

"Crew," said Janine, "We have a crew."

"Of course," said Steve, "You cannot sail a boat like this with two people. We have a skipper, a spinnaker operator, and two deckhands. There is also a chef/valet. They are all Scottish nationals, so you better like the Scottish accent!"

They spent the next hour looking through the yacht. She was amazed at the luxury. She had been on boats often in her life, but none like this. The deck had every amenity possible; the sails were computer-operated with electric winches powered by solar rechargeable batteries. You could control every sail from the captain's bridge and they had every possible communication device, including an international satellite dish.

There was a large private sun deck at the rear and another at the front of the yacht with an outdoor eating area serviced by a dumb waiter from the galley below the sun deck.

As they went below, she was stunned by the spaciousness of the living area. A large circular lounge was positioned beside the bar across the yacht's width.

Janine noticed a bottle of Verve was in the ice bucket sitting on top of the bar.

The yacht sat high in the water and had three levels: the deck, the owner's living area, crew quarters, and the galley below. "We won't be disturbed by the crew unless we call for them," Steve explained. "Half will be working while the other half rests, two shifts of twelve hours each."

He took Janine through to the sleeping quarters, and she half expected to see bunks, but the room was also large and had a sizable king-sized bed. Behind the bed was the door to the toilet and shower. These were at the rear (stern) of the yacht. She looked into the room and noticed another door.

She opened it to find a large bathtub right up against the stern of the boat, and the window wrapped right around so that you could see around for nearly 180 degrees.

"Unless we are in port, no one can see in these windows; it's private, and we have a good tank for fresh water. One bath a day only, I'm afraid; I hope you don't mind roughing it for a while?"

She laughed and hugged Steve. "I had no idea you could have a bath on a boat; it's wonderful, romantic, and a total surprise. I have always wanted to go to Scotland and could not think of a better way to get there. And Casablanca is simply the most romantic place I could think of. What's the name of the yacht?"

"It's simply called QT; I have no idea why, probably some romantic story behind it and the owner, lost love, romance, a special place, or something. Anyway, we can stop anywhere you like actually. If you feel like a swim on the beach, we can simply find a place on the North African coast and weigh anchor."

They could hear some commotion on the wharf, and he turned to Janine and said, "Time to meet the crew; let's go on deck."

They made their way to the deck, as she stood close to him, affectionately toward this man who had pulled off a master stroke of surprise.

She was still focused on him as they reached the deck and turned to see the crew returning with several Turkish porters and many boxes.

She was speechless; she did not foresee this, but before her, dressed in smart white sailing uniforms, were five stunning young female sailors. "I may have omitted to tell you this is an all-female crew. I hope you don't mind," Steve explained sheepishly.

"They are all gorgeous," she said as she gazed upon the five women aged between twenty-five and forty-something, each sporting the bright flame-red hair that Scottish women are famous for.

"Of course, I don't mind, as long as your focus is on me," she added. She felt she had to say this, but as she did, she secretly thought it might be hard for her to focus totally on Steve with women like that on board.

As Steve introduced her to each crew member, she secretly thought, *this could be an enjoyable trip!*

temptation

It took the crew nearly three hours to ready the yacht and motor out off the coast, where they could hoist the sails for the first leg of their journey.

Steve and Janine had spent the time at the marina exploring the cabins, checking out the sound system, and, at one stage, going ashore for coffee at a quaint traditional Turkish coffee house on the marina.

They avoided discussing the all-female crew.

He was unsure how she would feel about having a group of beautiful women on their trip and was not prepared to test her view yet.

Janine was still considering the implications of this particular turn in their adventure. This development did not faze her, so he did not have to be concerned, but she was somewhat curious about his motivation and intentions.

They had discussed their sexual adventures earlier, and she confessed to a sexual encounter with her best girlfriend many years ago. He seemed to be particularly titillated by her tale. He had asked many questions about what she had done and what she liked, so she thought he might be trying to engineer some encounter.

They spent some time discussing the itinerary for the trip. Janine was excited by the route, and they discussed where they had both been before and where they had not. Neither had been to Egypt, so they added this to their itinerary. She was particularly interested in seeing the pyramids, so they asked the crew how far they could take the yacht up the Nile River.

As they started their journey, the captain, Jessie, gave them a safety briefing. Most of their time in the Mediterranean would be smooth sailing, and being on deck should be fine. "We should reach Tel Aviv by tomorrow evening if the winds hold," Jessie explained as she studied the navigation charts. "That gives us about twenty-six hours at sea."

That said, later in their trip, they would have to get clearance from her once they hit the Atlantic before going on deck, as the seas would get rough.

Janine giggled to herself as she thought, *I'm happy to spend quite a bit of time below with Steve, and he can spend as much time as he likes on me, down* below.

Jessie looked at her as she giggled and smiled a cute smile that almost made Janine feel like she had just read her mind.

They were both on deck when the crew raised the sails and cut the diesel motors. The difference in the feel of the yacht was palpable; the whole yacht took on a different persona, went quiet, and accelerated fast in the moderate breeze prevailing that day.

The full crew was all on deck, checking all the sails and the winches and listening to the various sounds now emanating from the boat. This was the traditional check when the yacht started its journey. From then on, only two or three were needed to sail the QT; though most of the action would be controlled from the bridge by Jessie or Angie, her first mate and acting captain when Jessie was off duty.

Janine watched these women with great admiration as they went about their work.

Perhaps a little too much admiration for Angie as she watched her closet than the others.

It was not so much her work that she admired but her striking figure and stunning red hair. She was the most tanned of these generally fair women and clearly worked out as her legs and buttocks were tight and lean. She was undoubtedly a stunning woman who had peaked in her mid-forties. Janine initially dismissed her interest, but she would occasionally catch Angie looking at her, which made *her wonder if Angie's* interest was just a little more than curiosity.

They were off to Israel, Tel Aviv to be precise, and it would take only the rest of the day, overnight, and the following morning. The yacht could sail fast, meaning their eventual full journey to Scotland would be a series of overnight sailing and some pleasant day sailing before exploring the many destinations they were about to discover. Most of the time, they planned to sleep on the yacht, but Janine and Steve would venture ashore to visit cities. On those occasions, they would stay in hotels.

As the sunset that first night, they ate a delicious meal cooked by Nadia and served by Irene, who was on valet duty for this first leg of their journey. Jessie, Angie, Nellie, and Evelyn were either off duty or on deck sailing the yacht. After the meal, Steve and Janine retired to their sleeping quarters and ran a bath.

They were now into the habit of having baths daily or even twice daily sometimes. It was a lovely ritual where they had learnt to converse and explore each other's lives.

It was also a very sexual experience for them both. It often was either foreplay to their lovemaking or, on occasion, outright lovemaking in the bath itself.

The bath was deliberately deep so the water would not spill.

The movement of the yacht as they sat in the bath was new. It was initially strange, but soon they adjusted and settled into their usual comfortable conversation.

Janine was telling Steve how incredible this experience would be and how amazed she was that he could secure such a mode of transport. While she spoke, he appeared somewhat distracted and was staring intently at Janine. It was not long before she worked out that this was a lustful fascination.

While the newness of the yacht was taking almost all of *her* attention, he was used to this and had more basic desires on his mind. As she began to understand this, his passion for her made her wet, deep inside her Flower.

Finally, Steve moved closer and kissed her, and their first sexual experience on an ocean-going yacht began...

The water in the bath was warm, not hot, but comfortable for the Mediterranean summer.

He kissed Janine on the lips and slowly moved to the nape of her neck, occasionally nibbling at her earlobes. The diamond studs in her ears glistened in the candlelight of the cozy bathroom, and they could see the stars through the window.

It was a very romantic scene.

The designers had even included a built-in ice bucket and glass holders in expectation that this bath would hold two lovers.

As Steve kissed the nape of her neck, he slowly massaged her shoulders. It was relaxing and sensual, and she felt her passion rising. She was cradled between his legs, her back against his front, and she could sense his growing manhood against the cheek of her left buttock as they sat in the bath together.

He now moved his attention to her breasts as he used the soap to slide his fingers over their pert shape and intermittently tugged at her nipples as he did. Soon his total focus was on her nipples as he slid his fingers around them.

Janine needed more!

She lifted herself just enough to turn around to face Steve, lay back in the bath, and beckoned him over to her.

He complied.

He kissed her on the lips, then moved straight to her twins, taking the nipple of her left breast into his mouth and began to flick it with his tongue. He knew exactly what she wanted.

As her excitement rose, Steve increased the suction he applied and periodically tugged her nipple with his lips. Finally, as she started to moan audibly, he took her whole breast into his mouth and sucked deeper still.

He was adept at creating this full suction and, at the same time, flicking her nipple with his tongue.

She swore he must have fingers on his tongue because he could do things with it no man she had met could ever do! It was enough for Janine, and she came in a shudder, her orgasm appearing to come from nowhere and yet being the inevitable result of his ability to almost suck out her orgasm from her clitoris and through her breast.

She smiled at him slyly as she recovered.

"I want you," she said, "I want that thick cock in me, and I want it now. Let's test out the bed; I have had enough of a bath tonight."

If records were ever kept, history would record the time it took for these two lovers to exit the bath, dry off, and hit the bed as a world record, even if they were not completely dry and she was very wet in places.

It was quick and passionate as it had ever been as he embraced her, taking her in his arms, kissing her deeply, and rolling over to place his weight on her. His cock pressed firmly against her pubic bone, sandwiching her clitoris between the two and providing her with a pleasurable sensation every time he moved one millimeter.

She was unsure if this was pure chance or part of his technique, but she was grateful nonetheless.

Finally, she could take it no longer.

She lifted her leg just high enough to get her hand between the two of them, grabbed his cock, and started to move it around her vulva to find her entrance. She found it faster than he ever did, but she had the advantage of feeling both ways.

She slid his cock in a bit to get some of her wetness all over the tip and moved it up and down across her Button to lubricate her. It was very erotic and took her impending orgasm closer to the surface. She almost stopped there and used his cock as a clitoral stimulator.

Then she remembered his thickness, the filling of her Flower, the fullness of that sensation, and the orgasms that followed, so she moved his cock back to the entrance and tilted her pelvis as if to say, *'come in, baby,'* because her tilt resulted in his cock penetrating half an inch into her wet and warm Flower.

It was all he needed to know; she was ready for him, and he was ready for her. So he slowly probed further until he reached that point.

She inhaled sharply as he pushed on and in to fill her completely. She moaned as she knew it was always the harbinger of her favorite orgasms… the ones where they both came together.

Almost immediately, the pleasure turned to ecstasy as he pushed through to the point where his thickness filled her internally. It was a fullness that provided a sensation of being merged with him.

Seconds later, he partially withdrew and pushed in again so that his fullness made the nerves inside her come alive. As he pushed, the pressure on her Button added to the sensation, and the tug of his partial withdrawal added another.

With each movement, she could feel her climax building.

It was an all-encompassing experience for her. The sensations swirling within her, the weight of Steve on top, the openness she felt with her legs draped over his shoulder, and the pleasure she was giving her lover by surrendering herself completely to him all contributed to her delight. The sounds he made, the expression on his face, and the primal manner in which he entered her and established the rhythm of his thrusts all further enhanced her pleasure.

Now as he was building his climax, she felt closer to him.

Somehow this act of love, of total union, left her with a complete experience of pleasure that no previous sexual experience had ever given her. She knew why. Indeed, he was an experienced lover, caring and generous, but her love for him and his love for her took their lovemaking to this special place.

She was breathing deeply now and could feel her climax building, but she knew it would take a little more; the icing on the cake, she called out to her lover.

"Deeper," she said, "fuck me deeper".

It was her way of controlling the rise of her orgasm, bringing it a bit higher and more intense.

It was also her way of bringing him to his climax!

She knew he loved to hear that she was close. It excited him that she wanted him to cum with her.

"Fuck me, baby, I'm cuming, cum with me; I want you," she moaned.

He stepped up the pace of his thrusts and pushed deeper.

Finally, Steve's pubic pad pressed against her engorged Button. It was all she needed to tip her over. "Oh god, I'm cuming," she cried, and his excitement peaked as she did.

He loved to know when she came; it was the sexiest part of their lovemaking, and he lost control.

"I'm cuming too!" he responded, though he needed not say and came, deep inside her pushing firm and deep inside her as his semen filled her in pulses of ecstasy.

She was halfway through her climax when he came, and the excitement of his orgasm pushed her up again into an extended orgasm. *Or was it a second orgasm*, she thought—she was unsure which, but it was wonderful.

They embraced; Janine was exhausted but complete; she was still full of him, his cock, his love, and she cried.

She was unsure why she cried but understood that this was a mix of the rush of her orgasm, her love for Steve, and the pure joy she felt from finally being with this man completely. She had loved and wanted him all her adult life, and now her desire was fulfilled.

He became aware that she had tears in her eyes and asked if he had hurt her.

"No!" she said. "It was amazing. I'm crying because I'm happy."

He had hurt her, she thought, *all those years ago, but all that had been forgiven, even understood, as she knew that neither of them was ready.*

"No, you did not hurt me," she said. "I could not be happier; I love you, Steve, I love you more than you know."

"I love you too, baby," Steve replied. "You must know that by now. I cannot explain why; I cannot even understand it myself, but I feel the most incredible love for you, and I always have. Thank you for finding me and bringing me back home to you."

They rested briefly, cuddled, and kissed, bathing in the warmth of their love. She was stirring again, and he moved his kisses from her neck to her breasts. She stirred more, and so he moved his kisses to her stomach. She stirred even more and was now moving her hips to direct his attention lower.

He complied.

He moved his kisses to her mons and repositioned himself between her legs. He placed his tongue on her lips, tasted her wetness, and inhaled her erotic fragrance.

"Yes!" she said. "Yes!" she begged. "The special Steve, I want the special; I need the special."

He complied.

He placed his mouth over her Button, almost engulfing her mons as he began to suck her upper Flower. In this position, he managed to use his tongue to stimulate her now engorged Button, sucking and flicking, biting her with his lips, eating her with a ravenous sound that lifted her excitement further.

"Yes, yes!" she cried. "I'm cuming, yes, yes, god, I love your special," she said, as she exploded into her climax, tightening her thighs and squeezing her lover between her legs.

They cuddled again, joked about the volume of their lovemaking, and wondered what the girls would think.

She knew what they would think.

Envy, who would not envy what she had, and who would not envy what he had, she thought proudly.

The gentle rocking of the yacht lulled Janine toward sleep, Steve's arm a comfortable weight across her waist. This floating cocoon seemed to exist outside normal time and space—a perfect bubble where only they existed. She wondered if real life could ever feel this seamless, this right, or if they were simply experiencing the heightened reality of vacation romance. The thought troubled her more than she wanted to admit.

Eventually, they both drifted off into a restless sleep...

exposed

They woke to the sound of knocking on their cabin door.

"Breakfast is ready, you two; it's nine a.m.," someone said. Janine recognized the voice as the broad Scottish accent of Angie and sat up as Steve stirred.

"It's breakfast," she said. "Come on, I'm starving."

They had slept soundly to the constant rocking of the yacht.

Janine had not slept so soundly for years, particularly with a man in her bed.

They both threw on light clothes and emerged into the lounge, where Angie had pulled out the hidden table and set up their breakfast.

"We have coffee, croissants, muesli, fruit, and tea or coffee," Angie pointed to the table. They sat down, and Angie served their tea and coffee from pots on the table.

Angie leaned over near Janine; her naked left breast was visible through the top of her loose shirt.

A little too convenient, thought she; *I wonder if she is flirting with Steve or me*?

Her breast was firm, slightly larger than hers, and she had erect red nipples. Janine felt a slight stirring in her loins, but her hunger forced her back to the table fare that lay before her.

"Is that all," said Angie, throwing a cute smile toward Janine that could have indicated that she knew her flirtation had the desired result.

"Thanks," said Steve. "How far did we sail?

"Jessie will be down shortly," she said. "She will fill you in on the night's sail and our current position."

Janine and Steve chatted over their breakfast, fed each other croissants, and talked about their passionate night. They had both slept well and were surprised they had slept in so late.

Jessie arrived and informed them they had made good time. They were about fifty nautical miles off the Lebanese coast, past Beirut, and about a hundred nautical miles from Israeli territorial waters. In five hours, they should be able to turn inland and enter the main harbor in Tel Aviv.

They showered, wanting to save their bath for after lunch. They then dressed in their swimming costumes so that they could both sun-bake on deck.

Janine planned to sun-bake naked as she hated tan lines, but she always wore her bathers until she got to lie down.

It was one thing to sun-bake nude and another to parade naked around the boat.

She had not broached the subject of nude bathing with him. Still, she was confident he would not have an issue with her being naked as there were no other men around, but she was curious to see if he would do the same given the all-female crew.

She would wait and see.

She lay down on the sun lounge on the fore deck. It was secured with bolts, so while she could not move it, she could be confident she would not be tossed over the side should the yacht suddenly roll.

Steve sat on the lounge right next to her.

She took off her top, asked him to rub some sunscreen on her shoulders and back, and did the same to him. When she removed the bottoms of her bathers, Steve smiled.

"I will need some sunscreen on my bottom," she said. "Do you think you could manage that without molesting me, baby?"

He discretely applied the sunscreen as instructed, and she turned over, placed sunscreen on her legs and thighs, and lay down on her back.

She put on her hat and scarf. Janine always wore her hat, and her scarf protected her top chest and neck from the sun. "Aren't you going to bake in the nude?" she teased Steve. "What's the matter, are you embarrassed?"

"Well, yes, I am!" he responded.

"Have you never sunbaked nude?" she enquired?

"Of course, I have, often, but this is different; I need to wait."

"Embarrassed to disrobe while the girls are on deck, are you? You have nothing to be ashamed about," she said.

"It's not that," he said.

"Then go on, take your pants off, you pussy!" she teased.

"OK,"he responded, "If you must insist."

He stood and dropped his bathers to reveal his erect cock that glistened in the sun.

"Oh my, God!" she exclaimed rather too loudly because the two girls on the deck turned to see what the problem was.

"I told you I needed to wait. Do you think I can rub your back and bottom and gaze upon your beautiful body without some reaction, do you? You are very, very sexy, and seeing you naked in the sun turns me on. I just needed a little time to settle."

Steve had sat down by now, and the girls had returned to their yachting duties but were laughing together about what had just happened. She was not bothered by their seeing him like that; in fact, she often felt it would be nice to tell someone just what a man she had and what a magnificent cock he had. Now all the girls on the yacht would know what she was getting every night; those that did not just see would no doubt hear the tale and, if not, would certainly hear them making love.

After a few hours of intermittent sun baking and periodic hosing down with cool water on the deck, Steve and Janine had a light salad lunch, served again by Angie, who could not take her eyes off her breasts as she served them. Janine was still topless and comfortable being naked in front of women, though she felt a little exposed by her intense gaze.

She wondered why this was different.

intercepted

Suddenly there was a distant sound of voices, and a large horn blew. They rose to see the captain take her post at the bridge and begin to lower the main sail. To the port, they saw a medium-sized naval frigate bearing down on them with a sailor up front shouting through a loud hailer for them to stop, drop sails, and prepare to be boarded.

Janine could see from the flag that it was an Israeli navy frigate.

Steve turned to Janine, saying, "We should go down below and dress. You will need your passport as well. Just be polite, and all will be fine."

They slowly made their way below and started dressing and retrieving their passports as the crew prepared to receive the inflatable speed boat now being sent from the Navy frigate with six armed Israeli sailors aboard.

They spoke English as they came alongside and requested that all crew and passengers present themselves on deck.

They asked for the captain of the vessel.

"They are searching all ships in their territorial waters," Steve explained. "To stop Hamas and Hezbollah from smuggling weapons. So we have nothing to fear from them," he added reassuringly. They made their way on deck as the Israeli sailors boarded.

When they arrived on deck, the senior officer was talking to Jessie and asked where they were headed, who was on board, and what cargo they carried. He advised Jessie that they must search the yacht entirely, which may take several hours. The other sailors were inspecting the passports of the crew.

The Senior Officer noticed Steve and Janine's arrival on deck and turned to them.

He asked for their passports, and Janine promptly handed hers to him, somewhat nervously.

Steve pulled out his passport. Janine noticed it was different from the one she had seen before. It was unlike any passport she had seen, with a large Star of David on the cover.

She had not discussed his nationality because he was Australian and knew he was born there, but this looked like an Israeli passport.

The Senior Officer took the passport from him, visibly relaxed, and opened it. He looked inside, looked up again at Steve, and immediately snapped to attention and saluted.

"I'm so sorry, sir," he said. "I did not recognize you. It is a pleasure to meet you and welcome back to Israel."

He turned and barked some orders at the sailors in Hebrew. They all immediately relaxed, placed the safety triggers on their rifles, and several came over, saluted, and shook Steve's hand.

Janine was stunned and looked at Steve with a very perplexed expression.

Steve lowered his voice to a whisper and said, "I told you I was a Nazi hunter. I did not say exactly for whom. I do not generally disclose this in detail, but I work for Israeli Intelligence as a consultant and have an honorary rank of Major General.

"I don't work in the mainstream intelligence section because my specialty is hunting down Nazis. Still, I have a reputation in the services and have been awarded several Presidential medals for my services to Israel. You understand that I cannot discuss openly.

"He has told his men not to bother searching the boat and advised them who I am. I'm sorry I could not tell you earlier."

The officer in charge advised Jessie that they were free to head on to Tel Aviv and they would escort them there as they were returning to their base. The sailors packed up, re-entered their tender boat, and returned to the frigate.

Jessie walked up to Steve and said, "I'm not sure what you did or who you are, but thank you. I don't like my yacht being searched. Not because we carry contraband but because the crew and I enjoy a little grass when off duty, not trafficable amounts, mind you, but small amounts for personal use. Sometimes the authorities can't or won't make that distinction. Mind you, no one has yet managed to find our stash," she added. "But I would not want to try my luck with the Israelis."

It took an hour after they raised their sails before they were lowered again to motor into the Marina at Tel Aviv. A suited driver met them, and Janine assumed it was the next chauffeur they had to take them on the hour-long drive from Tel Aviv to Jerusalem.

Steve was somewhat perplexed because he had not ordered a car to pick them up.

He had planned to show Janine a little of the Tel Aviv Marina area first and take coffee in a traditional Ethiopian coffee shop he frequented then when in Tel Aviv.

The driver introduced himself as one of the President's security detail and advised them that he was taking them to a helicopter five minutes away for the trip to Jerusalem. The President had been informed of his arrival and wanted to see him.

The depth of Steve's connection and obvious importance in this country fascinated Janine.

Ten minutes later, they flew in a helicopter across the coastal plain, headed for Jerusalem in the hills above these plains. The two-hour drive would now take up to fifteen minutes by air, and they would land directly in the Presidential compound.

The helicopter flew high at first, and Steve explained to Janine that this was to avoid hostile fire from the ground. He said this was rare when he noticed an expression of fear on her face. "It's safe, Sweet Pea. These pilots know precisely what they are doing and the areas to avoid. They will only get lower when over the President's residence, and the area around that is as secure as anywhere in the world."

Janine seemed to relax more and started to take in the scenery. From this height, she was struck by the narrowness of the country, the distance from Tel Aviv to Jerusalem. She was used to the vast distances in Australia. This seemed such a small country, particularly one to be fighting over.

Steve pointed out the city of Jerusalem, particularly the Old City. She could see the outline of the ancient wall encircling the Old City. "That part of Jerusalem was built around the time of King David," Steve explained. "Around 1000 years BC, he fortified the city because Israel and Judea, as it was known then, were under siege constantly."

"Underneath the old city are underground markets. People have walked the stone floors there for centuries, buying bread or spices. I will take you there," he added.

The helicopter started to descend, and the small building of the city grew more prominent. Seeing the ancient structures alongside modern buildings was a strange sight for her. Soon she could make out the outline of a large house and gardens.

Below them was a helipad, and their destination.

She could see several dark figures scurrying around the helipad like ants.

As they got closer and started to touch down, she realized these ants were agents, most likely the President's own Secret Service guard, and they were there to greet them, *well there to greet Steve*, at least, she thought.

As they disembarked the helicopter, Janine noticed several banks of heavy machinery on either side of the compound.

She looked at Steve again with a concerned look because they were definitely military. "Anti-aircraft and anti-missile rockets,"

Steve explained. "Don't worry, they have yet to be needed and are very accurate." Janine had not realized just how much this small country was still under siege.

The President's Private Secretary greeted them in the foyer.

He looked Janine up and down.

Turning to Steve, he said, "Welcome back, Major General. It's a pleasure to have you here, but we were not expecting to have company. This is a matter of utmost secrecy. Is this person to be trusted?" he asked with concern.

"I would trust her with my life," Steve said, his voice leaving no room for debate. "She's not just a friend. Janine is my partner—she knows who I am. What I do."

The man studied Janine's face for a moment longer before his posture softened.
"Then you are most welcome," he said with a slight bow. "Steve's trust carries weight with the State of Israel." He gestured toward the corridor. "Shall we?"

They were taken into a large room with a huge boardroom table. All around, computer screens and uniformed personnel were operating them. Several military officers sat at the table, and from the medals and glitz on their uniforms, Janine could see they were high-ranking.

Several suited men and about four women were also at the table, and at the head sat a grey-haired woman. She rose immediately and walked over to Steve. "Welcome, Steve," she said, "Welcome back to Israel. We have some exciting news."

"Thank you, Madame President," Steve said. "May I introduce you to my friend and partner, Janine?" He added as he turned to her.

Janine was still trying to take in the room. An *operations center*, she thought, *and the President was a woman*; she had been surprised for some reason.

"Welcome," the President said, "Welcome to my home; you are both most welcome to stay here. I have had the Presidential guest room prepared. My intelligence officers have informed me that only one bedroom is required. I hope we have not assumed too much," she added, looking at Janine.

Janine flushed red, somehow embarrassed that the President of Israel knew her intimate secrets, but quickly recovered as a warm smile broke out on the President's face.

She gave Janine a welcome kiss on the cheek but, as she did, whispered into her ear, "You are a fortunate woman, Janine; there are many women in Israel who would love to be in your place.

"Let's get to business," she suddenly commanded as she stepped back, her smile catching Janine one more time as she transitioned to her presidential face.

"Nathan, please proceed with the briefing," the President said as she looked across the table at a suited middle-aged man.

Nathan was built well and was likely to have been a former soldier, but he had a soft voice. As he spoke, he could hardly contain the excitement he was feeling.

"This is the big one," he said, looking at Steve. "We have tracked Herman Yultzer and have located him in Marrakech."

Steve jumped up immediately. "Yultzer," he said, "we have Yultzer?"

"Not quite have," said Nathan, "but we know where he is, his alias, his work address, and his movements. He has been there for seven years and is unaware that we have discovered him. We know you have been tracking him for ten years, but your last lead led to this discovery. So we thought you should bring him in."

Steve turned to Janine and back to Nathan.

He was torn.

He had been tracking this man for a long time and had almost believed he must have been dead. A year ago, he found a small clue that he passed on to Israeli Intelligence to follow up, but he did not expect this breakthrough.

He looked to Janine again. Would she understand? Would she forgive him for abandoning her to pursue this man?

The President was watching Steve's reaction and, after a moment, turned to Nathan and said, "We have agents watching his movements, don't we, so we do not need to spring the trap just yet, but it may be useful to have Steve slip into Marrakech undercover. He is well known in Nazi circles, so it may be useful for him to sail from here to Casablanca under cover of a couple's romantic sailing trip and spring the trap then."

Nathan agreed.

Janine was watching this exchange and thought that *only a woman could have detected the conflict in Steve.*

Janine had no idea who this *Yultzer* was. Still, she immediately felt that Steve wanted to get this man and was torn between that and continuing their holiday.

She also thought *the President very astute.*

"Then it's settled," said the President. "We will give these two lovebirds a little time in Jerusalem, and then they sail for Morocco."

"Steve," she added as she paused for emphasis and turned to him. "You must not involve Janine in the extraction operation; it's too dangerous and unnecessary."

"Of course, I won't," said Steve. "Janine is much too precious for me to risk any harm to her. For now, I only have two days and a city to show Janine."

Janine and Steve went straight from the residence to the old city. The trip was quick because they were escorted by two presidential guard vehicles and soon took steps into the Old City Markets. It was surreal; they were in the street, with stalls all along the labyrinth of alleys that crisscrossed in front of them, but there was no sky. They were underground, yet it felt like an outdoor market.

There were spices, clothes, carpets, old-looking pottery, religious artifacts, pots, and food stalls, all mixed with a weird assortment of stalls that sold mobile phones, snow cones of the Old City, and other modern items. She could have been walking down these worn pathways over 3,000 years ago, seeing the same items sold except for the addition of these modern wares.

They had lunch at a small café, and at the quiet corner table, Steve discretely explained that Yultzer was the lead Gestapo officer responsible for equipping the concentration camps with gas showers and crematoriums so that the Nazis could increase the pace of their plans to exterminate the Jews, homosexuals, and communists in the countries they had occupied in World War II. He was the youngest of Hitler's inner circle and the last to evade capture and trial.

He was now seventy-nine, but if such atrocities were to be prevented in the future, others had to know that no time limit would allow them to avoid responsibility for their crimes.

He would lead an operation to confront, sedate, and secrete him out of Morocco to face trial in Israel. He would be given a defense barrister and an opportunity to defend himself. Janine asked why they didn't just have him arrested and extradited to Israel. Steve explained that was why Yultzer had chosen Morocco to hide. As an Arab nation that did not recognize Israel, they would never extradite him there, no matter the crime.

They returned to the Presidential residence for an 'afternoon nap'. After all, they were unlikely to have the opportunity to tick 'Have sex in the home of the Israeli President' off their bucket list again.

They arrived at the Presidential Palace and were informed about dining with the President at seven. It was now four. They were escorted to the guest room.

While not large, it had a beautiful en-suite with marble walls and a large bathtub that rivaled most they had already had the pleasure of using. But if this was a guest room, they wondered what the President's room must be like.

Somehow, the very efficient secret service staff had transported their luggage from the yacht to the room. The aide that showed them through the room explained that this had been the same room many heads of state had occupied, including three US Presidents!

Another reason to add lovemaking here to their bucket list, she thought.

They ran a bath and soaked for a while, discussing the implications of their changed plans. Finally, Steve explained that they would need to sail directly to Morocco, so their trip to Egypt would have to wait. It would take about two or three days in Marrakech to complete his assignment, and he would ensure she was safe in a guarded hotel in Casablanca.

Once captured, Israeli Intelligence would complete the rendition to Israel. Steve would rejoin her in Casablanca before they continued sailing up the coast toward England and Scotland.

Janine was surprised to discover how thrilling this adventure had become. She felt like she was in a James Bond spy novel and was slightly aroused by the situation. Janine laughed to herself at that thought because she was constantly aroused with Steve regardless of any situation and decided then and there that she would do everything in her power to ensure a sense of excitement would always be part of their relationship.

Janine knew that that would take a conscious effort on both their parts, that they could never take each other for granted for them to keep what they had.

The first step in her plan to ensure this happened was to entice him back to bed, the bed of Presidents, and treat him like one. Once dried, she put on a very sexy dark green teddy she had been saving for such a moment. Her dark green matching panties were lined in black lace and were cut low but full.

Steve was shaving and brushing his teeth while she got ready, so he was pleasantly surprised when he entered the bedroom to find Janine seductively lying on the bed. Janine enticed him with chocolate from the basket on the dressing room table, and as he lay down, she kissed him deeply.

They embraced, and Steve ran his hands over her body, feeling her teddy's lace and satin material; he was fixated on how the teddy highlighted the cleavage in her breasts and kept placing little kisses on them as if to welcome them.

Their embrace soon turned to passionate kisses again, with Steve placing his hand over her mons and rubbing her firmly. Janine was wet, and she could feel it. She wanted him; she wanted his thick cock, which was waiting in the wings in full erection, somehow being held back to ensure his entrance was timed to perfection and for greatest impact.

She played the game.

Steve's continued rubbing the satin of her panties against her clitoris raised her excitement to an almost unbearable level. She wanted to cum, but she wanted to cum with him inside her.

She resisted its surfacing.

He stepped up the rubbing and placed two fingers inside her panties. Janine was very wet now, and he could feel it. He audibly groaned as he touched her wetness, and his cock responded by firming even more. It was hard against her side, and he was now pumping his hips against her.

She could feel it getting firmer, and she could feel his pre-cum oozing from its tip.

He could not stand it anymore, and he ripped off her panties in one sharp snap, and they gave way immediately as if surrendering to their passion.

He flung them across the room and had not even landed on the floor by the time he had mounted Janine, cock in hand, and was probing her wetness.

Janine was now in a frenzy of lust; she wanted him, this, she wanted to be taken, and his forcefulness excited her even more.

"Fuck me," she cried, "fuck me, baby, I want you, I want your cock deep inside me."

Janine had been on the edge of cuming for a while now.

As he entered her Flower, she came immediately, as she had never done before, fast, intense, and completely.

As she screamed in joy, he tipped over with excitement and filled her full of his semen. It was quick, and in any other situation, two lovers would have considered this too short, a premature end, but this was no normal sexual experience.

This act, this lustful extraction of each other's orgasm, was so total and intense that it was satisfying to both. And it was not the end of their pleasure that afternoon.

It had been a long day, and after the intensity of their frantic and passionate sex, Janine was exhausted. It was short, intense, and drained her energy.

They had a dinner engagement in several hours, and she needed to rest. He could see her tiredness but also that she was still highly excited. Her senses had been heightened, and sleep could be difficult.

He got up from the bed, went to his suitcase, and retrieved a small bottle. Janine was lying on her stomach as he returned to the bed, unscrewed the bottle, and poured the fluid into his hands.

He straddled Janine and started to apply the massage oil to her shoulders, kneading her tired muscles gently at first, then deeper.

Janine sighed as she relaxed into his strong hands on her skin. His massage was relaxing but sensual; he started with her shoulders, neck, and upper arms as she relaxed more and more.

He moved to her back; he used his arms to apply pressure to her spine and slowly moved toward her bottom.

After ten minutes of working on her back, he focused his massage on her thighs and bottom.

This part of the massage was different for Janine. The relaxation of her upper body provided calmness that relaxed her. The soft strokes of Steve's large hands on her thighs and bottom stirred her desire again. Janine was starting to become wet again, and she could feel her Button twinging with every sweep of his hands across her inner thighs. Her breathing became deeper and faster, and she gently moved her hips in unison with his hand movements.

She started to moan softly.

He continued this sensual massage but moved his straddled legs to have one knee between her legs and the other outside her left thigh.

Janine could feel his leg close to her Flower and subtly moved down the bed until his leg was hard against her Flower and Button.

Now her hip movements had a new sensation as she used the force of her movement against his leg to stimulate her Button. This was new, but its newness was just the thing to excite her. She moved her hips faster as he massaged her bottom.

Janine's breathing quickened as she felt a small orgasm rising in her. She was now almost mounted on Steve's leg, moving faster, pushing her Button harder and faster against his leg until she came. It was small and satisfying but not enough.

Janine unlocked her legs from him, turned over, and moved up the bed.

This placed him between her legs and halfway down the bed. She took her hands and parted the lips of her Flower, looking longingly at Steve. Her Button was now clearly visible and erect, large and throbbing. She looked at him with pleading eyes but did not need to ask.

He knew exactly what she wanted, and was already heading toward her Flower.

As his lips met the lips of her Flower, she sighed with pleasure as the sensation went down the internal nerves of her Button and spread inside her. "Yes, yes," she said, "more baby, use your tongue."

He took her Button into his mouth and circled it with his tongue. He started slowly at first, building the orgasm deep inside her as she moaned and, in an attempt to make him work faster, she pushed against him. He resisted. He knew that building the sensation would ensure a deeper orgasm and kept using his tongue to tease her, bring her close, and then let it subside just a little.

Janine liked this, she liked it because she knew where it was headed, but she was also impatient, wanted it, and wanted it soon. "Special!" she said finally, "I want the special," as she pushed down on Steve's mouth.

He finally engulfed her Flower, took her Button entirely into his mouth, and began to suck and bite her Button with his lips. He moved faster as she built inevitably and profoundly until she came and came quickly. Not one but three orgasms, each deeper than the one that preceded it. Janine almost fainted as these waves washed over her body, and she screamed in ecstasy.

"We better run a bath," said Steve after lying with her for five minutes; "we have to get ready for dinner."

They were finally dressed for dinner at around five to seven, just as the President's aide knocked on the door to escort them to the dining room.

They followed the aide along the long corridor silently.

They were still reflecting on their last lovemaking and had little smiles that broadened to a grin each time they glanced at each other.

The door to the dining room was on the left and was huge. As the aide opened the door, they prepared to be serious for the other guests awaiting the dinner party.

They were surprised to find just the President in the dining room. The table was set for three and at just one end.

Janine was seated on one side of the President, and Steve on the other.

"You will just have to be patient for a few hours while you entertain an old lady," said the President as she saw the two lovers glance at each other.

"I was in love before," she added as they both turned to her in surprise at her remark. "Yes, the spinster President of Israel was in love; it's not a state secret," she responded. "Do you think I'm so old I cannot spot true love when I see it?"

"If you can forgive a little advice. Advice from a woman and not the President, she said.

"Don't make the same mistake I made; I was in love once and let my perspective on life cloud my judgement. I was proud and had ambition. I had served the state for twenty years and was comfortable with my life when I met him. We both fell in love, but I could not give up the career I had built for a life with him. So now I serve the state as a lonely woman, full of regret for the love I missed, the lost passion, and the time I could have spent with the love of my life."

She looked visibly sad, and Janine felt sorry for the woman who sat before them, not as the President of a state but as another woman whose life had been touched by love and regret.

"Now I have to fill my life with a vicarious experience of love by inviting lovers like you to my table. So tell me, how did you meet?" The President asked.

Steve and Janine recounted their earlier relationship, the intervening years, Janine's search for Steve, and the *chance* meeting on the train orchestrated by Janine.

The President listened carefully, looking from Janine to Steve as they each took turns placing the respective details of their romance before her.

"That is an amazing story, but I hope you are both aware of the significance of the chance you have been given," she said. "I had one chance and lost my love; you now have a second chance. Please do not lose this opportunity, or you will wake up one day sad and full of regret like me. You must promise me this: take this chance and ensure you cherish each other and don't let this opportunity go just because it may change your comfortable life. Being comfortable is fine, but passion can help you live every moment fully."

They promised the President they would heed her warning, and they chatted about various things over dinner and dessert.

After dessert, the President rose and said, "And now I have taken enough of your time; you must be with each other, not a sad old lady; remember what I said and make the most of your time together; you will never get this moment back again. Use it to express your love in the way you know best."

She smiled as she said this, and Janine felt a little embarrassed and exposed as she was sure the President of Israel had just ordered them to bed!

They went straight to the bathroom and ran the bath. It was becoming their space, their place to debrief from the day, get to know each other more deeply, and express their feelings. Of course, they often ended up in some form of lovemaking, either in the bath or immediately after, but that made the experience even more precious to them both because their conversations were intimate and frequently left one another highly exposed and vulnerable. Such trust was comforting, made them feel safe, and was, at times, very erotic.

This time was no different.

Both were significantly affected by the President's pleas for them to cherish their love, and both were keen to reassure the other that this was their intent.

Both were clear that whatever their lives had been, they were committed to each other for the rest of their lives.

Their vows to each other led to intimate moments as Steve embraced Janine in their bath. He did not take long before he was visibly aroused and caressing her breasts with his mouth.

Janine was already aroused before he started, and she had felt her wetness long ago while sitting at the dinner table listening to Steve's voice as he talked with the President. Their conversation about commitment had aroused her even more, so when he started sucking and tugging on her erect nipples, it did not take long before she came.

It was the starter for their meal of passion together.

Now she wanted the main course.

They moved from the bath, dried, and climbed into the bed. It was a king-sized four-poster bed fit for a US President. With crisp white sheets, a thick down duvet, and the softest pillows they had ever used.

The room was large but intimate, with soft light that could be dimmed to any desired level.

He turned down the lights just enough to make it romantic but not so much that he could not take in the beauty of her body.

He put their favorite music on softly.

Janine had climbed in first and was dressed in a petite black nighty made of satin; it was sleek and sheer and highlighted her body in a way that entranced Steve.

He lay next to her, looking at her for a moment, hardly believing that this woman was the girl he had loved so long ago and was here. He wished he could time-travel back to those days and tell her he loved her. How different their lives would have been and how much he could have loved her over all those years. He moved closer and kissed her deeply.

Janine was aroused and wrapped a leg around him.

He sat up slightly and moved his head close to her stomach, just close enough to her Flower to inhale her scent. It aroused him.

Janine moved away a little and produced several scarves she had secreted under the pillows.

"Remember we talked about this a while ago," she said. "We could blindfold each other to heighten the senses and see where that went."

He smiled and just said, "Yes, baby."

Janine started first, blindfolding Steve so he could not see at all. She had him lie on his stomach while she used her hands to caress his body softly. It was slow, sensual, and deliberate. Janine explored his body thoroughly, seeking out the places that he loved her to touch in this way. She observed his reaction, breath, movement, and gentle sounds as she found those spots he liked.

His breath was deepened.

She started to kiss him where he had enjoyed her touch earlier, softly caressing his body with her lips. Occasionally, when he responded with a moan, she used her tongue.

His breath quickened.

Once she had finished with his back, she asked him to roll over onto his back.

Janine helped him roll over and was trying not to acknowledge his full, erect, and throbbing cock. She resisted her urges and managed to ignore it.

Janine had a role to play and would finish it. She started exploring his front side with her hands again, watching all the time for his response and then using her lips and tongue to increase the pleasure she was giving him.

Janine avoided the obvious parts and explored parts of his body she had hardly touched before. The inside of his arm, the side of his knees, and the top area of his stomach.

His engorged erection stood erect, like a monument, challenging her to resist.

He was very aroused now, and so was she.

Janine moved to an upright position and straddled him, leaning over him and using her hands to touch his neck to act as a decoy for what would come next.

Finally, she had had enough of resisting and lowered herself over his cock, and with one expert movement, dropped, so he penetrated her entirely in one go.

She gasped as he entered her.

Steve did not see or feel this coming and he gasped simultaneously.

She had never heard him gasp like this before and understood now how her gasp must sound to him. Erotic, primal, and lustful. But now he was deep inside her, very deep.

The sensation was intense and a little painful but complete and very sexual.

She moved upward, feeling the thickness of his cock move deep within her and then down again. Fullness, pain, pleasure, and satisfaction all together; she raised herself again, feeling his thickness slide deep within her and down, again and again. She did this as the rhythm of this movement built her orgasm deep inside her.

He started to move with her now as she controlled the movement and depth. She varied the pace as she carefully built her climax step by step. It was rising deep within her, and she knew this would be good.

Faster and deeper, they moved with Steve now breathing heavily, clearly building his climax as they fucked.

Janine was in control, but he was moving just as she needed him to.

He moaned louder and was close to his peak.

Janine was excited even more by this, and as she started to feel the signs of his orgasm, her excitement grew until it peaked.

She thrust herself onto his cock in a frenzy of passion, screaming, "I'm cuming, baby, cum with me; oh god, I'm cuming."

Then she did: writhing upon his thick cock, she exploded in ecstasy, moaning deeply as she succumbed to the bliss that was her orgasm.

Janine was so enveloped in her orgasm that she did not notice that he had stopped his. She only needed to believe that he was cuming to tip her over.

As she recovered, she became aware that the familiar feeling of his cum deep inside her was absent. She looked at him and said, "You did not cum with me, baby; why not?"

"It's your turn to be blindfolded, baby," Steve responded, "there is plenty of time for that, and we can only cum together once in a session; Soon, baby, soon."

As Steve wrapped the blindfold around her eyes and laid her on her stomach, he added, "First, let me take you where you just took me, and perhaps you will feel just how erotic that was for me."

Janine lay on her stomach, with Steve kneeling at her side. From this position, he could touch her anywhere without moving from where he knelt.

He started with a gentle stroke across her back as if he were about to massage her, gently lifting his touch and moving to her shoulders. Like Janine, he carefully observed her response to his every touch, noting the areas that responded with deep breaths or little moans. Next, he spread his sensual touching across her arms and back to her neck.

Slowly, Steve worked his way to her legs. The inside of her leg elicited the best response, with Janine deliberately opening her legs to afford him higher access.

He resisted going there. *Not yet*, he thought to himself.

He spent nearly half an hour moving from one spot to another, progressively introducing some kisses into his repertoire.

Janine was wet with anticipation by now and was visibly writhing where she lay.

She was getting even more aroused by the realization that soon he would turn her over and work on her front. She lay on her stomach, taking in the sensual stimulation of his hands and lips, thinking about how exposed she would be lying on her back with him sitting over her, studying every part of her, every very intimate place.

It turned her on just thinking about it.

Finally, he whispered to her, "Time to turn over, baby" as he guided her onto her back.

Janine could feel her obvious wetness and thought to herself, *Steve must be able to see and feel this.* She wanted him to know; she wanted him to desire her; she wanted him to understand just how much he excited her.

He started with her neck and shoulders, working his way down her arms and then across her stomach.

My breasts, thought Janine, don't forget the twins.

She wanted to say this but understood she had to remain quiet and mindful of the sensations he was creating.

He avoided the main intimate places as he worked down her hips and thighs to her feet but started moving up the inside of her legs.

Janine moved her legs open again, and he touched her so close to her Flower that she almost gasped in anticipation.

God, she was so wet, he thought.

He kissed gently on the upper part of her left breast, then the right, moving his fingers down to her nipples and encircling them.

He placed his hand on her stomach close to her Flower, and she could feel her Button twinge as he did. The anticipation was incredible and sexy and was building tension inside her. As he laid his hand on her stomach, she felt his lips touch her nipples. Softly at first, but then he started a gentle suction. Next, he moved his hand closer to her Flower, applying a slight pressure that stretched her skin and caused her Button to twinge again.

She could feel it was engorged. It was strange for her to take each stroke, each touch, each movement as it landed on her, not knowing where the next touch would be, but it was exciting. Her whole body anticipated the next move, and her Flower was the most expectant.

Now Steve moved his body, moved lower on her and placed himself between her wide-open legs.

She wanted him, she wanted his lips, wanted his special, his cock deep inside her, but she did not know what was next.

He placed his hand on the inside of her legs again and slowly worked his way up. When he reached her Flower, she pushed her hips toward him, seeking his cock or lips as a climax to this endless teasing.

She did not expect his fingers would start to probe first.

He touched her Flower, gently seeking the wet entrance to her womanhood and feeling the wetness of her lust. Then he moved inside her Flower, placed a hand on her tummy, and started searching for her G-Spot with his finger. It did not take long before she moaned with delight as he caressed her spot.

He picked up the pressure as she responded to his touch. Janine pushed back with him, writhed, moved into the sensation, and gradually began to feel the tension rise, the tension that sought release. It was just when she thought she would pee when it hit.

Janine had learnt to bear down at this point, and it paid off again, exploding into an intense orgasm, pulsating through her entire body, now heightened by the time being stimulated by Steve's touch.

She writhed and moaned as the sensation went through her.

Janine had no sooner begun to relax when she felt Steve move again. He was still between her legs but had now moved closer to her.

She felt '*HIM*' then. *HIM*, the thick cock she had come to love, and he was now probing the wetness of her Flower. He entered her roughly, with intense desire and lust.

He wants me, she thought; *he wants to take me; he wants to cum inside me.*

She took him in and gasped as he passed the point where his girth met her internal resistance. Then he filled her, again and again, as he thrust his cock into her and out, moaning with pleasure as he did.

Janine was excited by his lust and wanted him so much. She moved her hips with him, calling to him to push deeper, to fuck her, not to stop, to cum, babe, cum, and this time he did, and she did.

They both did as their passion culminated in explosive orgasms. Their passions merged at that moment in an orgasm that each could not have anticipated. It was bliss for both, satisfaction for the release of their sexual tension and the completion of their love.

Then, finally, they both collapsed in joy and exhaustion...

Neither Janine nor Steve knew the point at which they fell asleep. It was like that with them; comforted by their respective presence, they often drifted to sleep together.

Janine woke first as the daylight peeked through the window. She took a moment to comprehend where she was but did not have any doubt about who she was with.

It was like that from the moment they met. When she woke, she had an intuitive understanding that Steve was with her, as if she was conscious of him while sleeping.

He also had the same intuitive sense of her presence.

Janine rose and went to the small fridge in the room. She found some orange juice and poured them a glass each, and went to place his on the bedside table.

As she was about to put the glass down, Steve said, "Thank you, my love. Just what I need."

He sat up and drank deeply from the glass as if replenishing his energy. she climbed back into the bed, hoping he had.

"I had hoped to take you to the Holocaust Museum in Jerusalem today, but it seems from the text I got overnight from Nathan that I have to be flown to Casablanca today to finish this mission," he said. He believed our target may be heading off on a trip, so we have to spring the trap soon.

"You will come with me, and the girls will sail the yacht to meet us there in four days. They will chopper us to Tel Aviv airport at ten a.m. for our flight out. Business class direct to Morocco. I'm sorry you will miss the sail across the Mediterranean, but I promise we will do that on another trip."

"Then we have time for some morning delight," she said, scrambling under the sheets to investigate the current state of Steve's cock. She was not disappointed. He almost always woke this way, and usually, he subsided pretty quickly. Still, around Janine, he maintained this state for some time or until he had cum inside her.

She continued her exploration under the sheets and gently took his cock in her mouth. She loved the soft, silky feel of his cock.

He responded by hardening more and gave a muffled groan.

Janine also loved the way Steve regularly shaved his cock and his balls. Like her, he liked the soft feel of a hairless pubic area.

She loved his shaven cock, and it made oral sex with him so much better. She moved her tongue to the base of his cock and kissed his scrotum. He moaned again and opened his legs wider. She knew what he wanted as his cock grew even harder in anticipation.

Janine moved lower and started kissing him all over… gentle pecks with just a hint of her tongue providing tinny sensations of delight for Steve and building his desire even more. She knew what was about to happen because, at this point, he would nearly always say, " I want you, baby," turn her over, and fucked her till he came with her.

"I want you, baby," Steve said right on cue, and Janine looked up at him and smiled. She also understood that she was getting to know this man very well and he was getting to know her.

Janine moved up the bed; she was already wet from sucking his cock and needed no further preparation. She wanted him, and the thought of them cuming together was already starting to build her orgasm. She could feel her Flower twinge madly in anticipation.

He mounted her, his cock pulsating with desire as she raised her legs, opening her Flower to him.

He probed for her wetness, and she helped guide him, grabbing his cock and pulling him to her. He was always gentle and tentative because he did not want to hurt her, but sometimes she wanted him to just take her, and right now, she wanted him deep inside her.

She felt the thickness and caught her breath a little. Steve's morning cock was always a little easier, but as he thrust deep inside her, she gasped louder. His morning cock was never shorter, and his length penetrated her deeply. She loved this part, where her body accommodated him, where all the sensations of his presence inside her first echoed within her.

He thrust again, then again, as he built the rhythm of their fucking as she felt her orgasm building.

"Don't stop," she cried. "I'm building," she said. "God, I love your thick cock deep inside me," she continued. Janine knew just what to say, for him; for both of them. Her erotic talk and demands were always a feature of their lovemaking, and while she used this to heighten her pleasure, she also knew that this aroused Steve.

He was also building, but then he slowed. He pushed her legs onto the bed and urged her to close them together.

Janine knew this move and liked it.

She moved her legs as close as she could yet still allowed him to be between her legs. He was on top of her now, and his thrusts placed pressure on her Button.

Yes, she thought, *this is what I like*, as the stimulation on her clitoris pushed her closer to orgasm.

He picked up the pace and was now getting close.

Janine could feel it; she understood the signs, but as he built, Steve called out, "Yes, baby, yes, I'm there, baby."

That was all she needed. That was all she wanted, and they both tipped over into their orgasm.

They had a bath after their morning sex; chatted about the adventures they were about to embark on, her fear that Steve was on a dangerous mission, and sex.

They always talked about sex.

Their sex in particular: what they did; what they were going to do; their fantasies; their favorite things. They also talked about how comfortable they were talking about sex. Janine had never been used to talking this freely, but with Steve, it felt natural, normal, liberating, and very sexy…

indulgence

They had to rush in the end, as their conversation in the tub went way too long, and they had to pack in a hurry. They were taking their entire luggage with them as the yacht had already sailed early that morning to ensure it made the run through the straits of Gibraltar and down to Casablanca in time to meet them in four days.

The aide had sent a porter to collect their luggage, and soon they were in the helicopter for the trip to Tel Aviv Airport. The steep altitude climb as they first took off needed no explanation for Janine this time, and she felt as if she was almost comfortable in Steve's presence. She felt safe and that the steep ascent was the safest option given where she was.

Not so the descent into Tel Aviv.

There were thunderstorms on the coast, so the descent into the airport was very rough.

Steve was composed all the time, and she tried her best not to look scared, but at one point, He reached out and held her hand. He could see her discomfort and gave her a reassuring smile. It did not stop the unpleasant feeling of being thrown around in the sky, but it alleviated her fear.

Finally, they landed at the heliport next to the terminal. They were met by a small open-air jeep and taken to the airport. The person who drove them dealt with their bags. A military officer took them straight through security and to the El Al Airlines Business Class lounge.

They were greeted by name by the El Al staff member who informed them that their plane had been delayed due to the storms and that there may be a two-hour wait.

He took Janine to the bar and spoke to the barman in Hebrew. The barman disappeared out back and emerged with a bottle of Verve and two champagne glasses, poured them both, and handed the glasses and bottle to Steve.

They sat on an oversized couch in the corner of the lounge. It was a busy lounge with many people waiting for their flights. Four businessmen were sitting opposite, discussing their upcoming meeting and their strategy to get an agreement on their proposal.

Others were sitting around in conversation or on their phones.

Janine and Steve looked around and glanced at each other knowingly. Then, as was their tradition when drinking champagne, wine, and even orange juice at times, they each proposed a toast.

"May the world never distract us from our love," Steve said.

"And may our love become our world," she responded.

They curled up on the couch and cuddled, occasionally kissing passionately, oblivious to the envious stares from the businessmen and the middle-aged women in the lounge. They were like two young lovers who were so focused on each other that the world did not exist beyond them.

Janine was on her second glass of Verve and was starting to get aroused from all the attention Steve gave her. He had occasionally moved his hand discretely up her skirt and had come dangerously close to her Flower.

Sometimes his hand was not so discrete, and on one occasion, Janine had moved his hand inside her dress and under her bra. They both loved this game, but it was arousing her, and Steve's pants were starting to bulge a little too much to be a simple fold in the material.

Janine wanted him but excused herself to go to the bathroom. She returned in four minutes.

Because Steve did not comprehend that this was insufficient time for any woman to go to the bathroom, her ruse remained intact.

"Come with me," she said, grabbing Steve's hand. "I want to show you something."

He followed her dutifully until they reached the private shower rooms, and she opened one of the doors. She pulled him inside, locked the door, and said, "Now I have you to myself."

He looked around. The room was well appointed and had a large vanity with mirrors, towels, and a soft chair. He finally got the idea, turned to Janine, and said: "You are very resourceful, aren't you?"

He moved closer to her and kissed her. Janine responded with a passionate kiss that clearly showed she was very aroused.

He unzipped her dress, and it cascaded to the floor. She wore blue underwear, a deep blue bra, and deep blue panties.

Stepping back, Steve took in her beauty. Janine moved forward, undoing his shirt and pants. He slipped out of his pants and removed his underpants, his thick, erect cock bouncing as it was freed from its confines.

Janine trembled with delight as she saw it. Janine always did this, half from the sight of its size and half from the anticipation of having it deep inside her.

He beckoned Janine to the soft chair, but she nodded no. Instead, she grabbed a towel, placed it on the vanity, and sat back on it with her legs apart.

"Like this," she said, calling her lover to her.

He needed no prompting at the sight of her Flower glistening from her wetness and moved toward her. Then he understood. She had not been to the bathroom at all. Instead, she had been on a reconnaissance mission to find this place, this position, this aspect because as he approached her, he could see their reflection in the vanity mirror and the double reflection from the mirror behind them on the wall.

It was a perfect placement for them to see themselves from both front and back as they made love. He could see her in front of him, her side in the mirror she was leaning against, and both of them if he looked further into the vanity mirror at the mirror behind them.

Well played, he thought; *she was an excellent planner.*

His cock had been hard when they were undressing, but now it was rock hard; these three views of his lover were a real turn on, and by the look on her face as she gazed at the mirror behind him, she had the same reaction.

If there was any doubt about that, it was confirmed as he entered her. She was wet, very wet, and as he pushed his throbbing cock deep inside her, she felt her juices flow out of her Flower and down her perineum. Janine gasped. Steve's cock was easier to accommodate now, but still, he was thick and so firm.

As he started to build the rhythm of their fucking, Janine gazed at the mirror behind them; she could see him thrusting into her, his cute ass pushing in and out of her. Janine could also see the other reflection through the vanity mirror, showing Steve entering her, withdrawing, and entering again.

With each thrust, her orgasm built.

She also gazed around the room they were fucking in, the flight lounge bathroom— a public place— and was even more excited by their act's illicitness.

It was all a huge turn-on, but then as her lover started to moan and started to cum, she completely lost her control and started to scream, "Fuck me, baby, fuck me fast, I'm cuming."

Whether it was simply a total loss of control or her providing an added furtive aspect to this tryst by adding the risk that someone could hear them, she did not know, but it was all she needed. They both came together for the second time that morning, exploding in such pleasure that Steve was brought to tears by the experience, and she was moved to tears by his reaction.

It took them ten minutes to regain their composure, and then they dressed silently.

Carefully, they packed up and opened the door discretely. Janine went out first, and as she walked through the lounge with Steve behind her, she could not help getting the sensation that everyone in the room knew exactly what she had been doing. As she thought this, her Flower twinged in excitement and pride.

They sat back on the couch. They had not said a word since coming from the shower room. Janine knew Steve loved the experience but was so turned on that she feared he might think her strange.

Finally, he turned to her and said, "That was incredible; we must do that again. I was so turned on by the fact that we did that here. Let's see if we can find similar places and make love like that."

Yes, thought Janine. "Yes," she said to Steve, "I would like that very much."

Janine thought about their lovemaking in the airline lounge shower room as their plane took off. She was daydreaming about other places where they could have illicit sex when the hostess interrupted her thoughts with an offer of a glass of champagne.

It was a four-hour flight, so she gratefully accepted, fully intending to sleep for some of the flight so her Flower could recover.

Steve was already asleep. At least, she thought he was. He had headphones on, listening to music but had not spoken for the last fifteen minutes. He was also exhausted and had several days of intense work ahead.

She would let him sleep. She would sleep.

Steve woke to the sound of the announcement from the captain that they were on their approach to Casablanca and turned to Janine.

She was sound asleep, but he woke her reluctantly.

"We are arriving, baby," he said gently. "It looks like we both crashed, if you can excuse my using that term on an airplane," he added.

"I certainly did," responded Janine. "I have never slept like that on a plane before, but then I don't often get to fly in business class."

Janine gazed out the window, her thoughts drifting toward the danger that lay ahead for Steve as they descended.

The landscape was yellow, a desert. They were over North Africa now. Apart from some large rocky mountains and the occasional smaller outcrop, it was desert as far as the eye could see. She could make out a small town here and there and wondered how people could make a living in such a place.

As the plane banked to approach Casablanca, the Atlantic Ocean appeared on its left. It was an azure blue, contrasted by the yellows of the coast and the green of the coastal villages and towns. They were starting to see more housing, more buildings, and many ships.

Big ships. Ships laden with containers of freight or huge oil tankers, were dotted in the ocean, waiting to make port at Casablanca.

They landed and took some time to clear customs.

Janine noticed that Steve used a different passport here, his Australian passport.

He was patient and quiet. So well practiced, she thought. *So well practiced at slipping in and out of countries without attracting attention. It was a stark contrast to their arrival in Israel, where he was known and honored.*

Anonymity comes with a queue, she thought— *even in business class.*

They took a taxi to the hotel (*another way of not being noticed*, she thought): the Oum Palace Hotel and Spa. It was near the ports in downtown Casablanca.

It was early afternoon when they arrived. They had just under two weeks before the New Year, and Steve's plan had them reaching Scotland by then. It was not a five-star hotel, but he had booked a suite with a bath, which was very comfortable and had an ambience of old Morocco.

They were hungry and decided to go out for Moroccan food, so they took the desk clerk's recommendation and walked a block to a small, intimate café near the docks. They were not disappointed, as the place was full of locals, had exotic music, and had the ambience one would expect of Casablanca.

Everyone spoke French, which surprised Janine, who had forgotten that he was fluent. It made their ordering easier.

Janine was relieved as it meant he would fit in without being unduly noticed, making him safer during his mission.

They ran the bath back at the hotel, well-fed and a little drunk, and spent the next hour talking about the food, spices, and the movie Casablanca. she always thought that Steve would better fit in the 1930s, and they joked about him being in Rick's Café then, fighting the Nazi occupiers.

In their fantasy, Janine was a French singer who worked in the bar, and Steve owned the joint. They had a tumultuous relationship, but it was passionate and enduring. They drove around Casablanca in a 1930s black Humber sedan with running boards and chrome strips down the side. Steve would always carry a silver pistol under his white linen jacket.

They laughed about their fantasy, but she secretly wondered and worried about Steve's future danger in Marrakech and wondered if he would be carrying a gun under his jacket.

It was time for bed, so they dried off. Steve pat-dried her back, and she did the same for him.

He seemed to understand that she was worried and said, "I have done this many times; my target thinks he is safe and anonymous, so he will not be armed, and I won't be alone. I will be back in two days, safe and well, I promise."

They cuddled for a short while as Janine's fear for him had made her quiet, but his kisses soon aroused her spirits again, and the gentle kissing turned into a hungry melding of mouths, all heat and urgency, like they'd been waiting forever to touch each other this way.

He was quickly erect and firm, and her fear subsided as he deftly roused her passion with one of his specials. Janine loved the special, but that had just warmed her up, taken her to a place where she could recognize her desire again, and now she wanted that cock deep inside her.

He was attuned to her needs and guessed how she wanted him this time.

The bed had a vast bedhead, and he encouraged her to straddle him as he lay on his back.

As he probed her wetness, she observed his face. She saw the anticipation, the desire, and the unconditional love for her as he moved his cock to where she needed it. Janine lowered herself onto him, all the time watching his reaction. His obvious pleasure gave her pleasure, and she felt very desirable when he pushed back deep inside her and moaned with total joy.

She felt desirable, and she felt *Him*. Deep inside, his thick cock spread that familiar sensation throughout her body as he filled her. "Yes, yes, yes," she said, moving her hips with him as their rhythm built.

Janine was controlling the rhythm, but Steve was helping with the thrusting, pushing his cock deep inside her. Janine had now shifted back so that her legs were down the bed in the traditional missionary position, except that she was on top. She enjoyed the control and could look down at Steve's face.

This time, he was having trouble holding back his orgasm—she could tell. He had such remarkable restraint, but sometimes she wished he would lose it now and then, so now that he was struggling, she was pleased with herself.

I'm fucking him, she thought, really fucking him, and I can make him cum!

His thrusting also stimulated her Button, which added to her pleasure from this position; she was building and building fast. Half of her wanted to tip him over, but the other half wanted him to wait and cum with her.

Ultimately, it did not matter because as soon as Steve lost it, she came with the sheer pleasure of knowing she made him cum for her.

She felt very pleased with herself.

He loved this position also, and it gave him so much pleasure that he found it hard to wait for her to cum with him, but he focused, trying hard to wait for the signs of her impending orgasm.

In the end, he had lost it from the pure pleasure of watching her fuck him, but as he did, she tipped over and came with him anyway. It was hot, sexy, and so fulfilling to Steve, knowing that she had pushed him over the edge despite his best efforts.

So much more so, knowing that she had cum anyway.

He felt very pleased with himself.

They both collapsed following this short and passionate embrace; they were exhausted.

They were asleep in several minutes, with Steve cuddled beside Janine in a tender lovers' embrace.

arousal

Steve woke in the middle of the night, startled by his dream. He had been shot in the back with several bullets and was trying to regain his breath as he awoke. It took him a few seconds to comprehend where he was and that he was not shot, but the dream had disturbed him deeply. He felt the need for comfort from Janine, but she was deep asleep.

He cuddled up to her closer and began caressing her buttocks and thighs. Janine remained asleep, but she was physically responding to his touch and started to move her hips as if she were awake. She rolled over onto her back, so Steve moved his hand to her waist and slowly started to caress her upper thighs.

He was beginning to become aroused and desired her again. He carefully pushed onto his elbows and moved down the bed. It became a game to see how far he could go without waking her. As he slid down, he gently moved her legs so he could rest himself between them. Janine stirred but did not wake.

As Steve started to perform oral sex on his sleeping lover, she stirred but did not wake up into consciousness but started waking sexually. Unconsciously, her hips moved gently, and her pelvis tilted to meet his lips and tongue.

Her Button began to grow larger, slowly at first, but then it engorged as Steve commenced sucking it slowly.

Progressively, he picked up the stimulation with his tongue, flicking her Button to and fro to her now audible moans.

She was still asleep or pretending to be; Steve did not know, but it was hot for him to think he could arouse her while asleep. If Janine were asleep, she would not be for long, as he started to give her his special.

Janine went from sleeping (or pretending to) to full-on orgasm as she moaned in ecstasy.

"You woke me, baby, with such pleasure, and you woke the love deep inside me. I love you so much," she said when she finally caught up to the fact that it was not a dream.

It was very bright the next time they woke; they had four hours before Steve would be picked up in a four-wheel drive jeep for the five-hour drive to Marrakech and his assignment.

Despite his reassurance, she was still apprehensive. She clung close to him in bed as they ate a light breakfast delivered to their room. They chatted about other things, carefully avoiding the one subject that occupied their thoughts.

After breakfast, Steve cleared the trays and returned to bed. He was refreshed now, and their cuddles began to arouse his passion despite the unacknowledged fear he felt.

He was always fearful in these assignments; though outwardly, you would not know it, he feared failure, feared not getting his target, and most of all, he feared getting killed. The fear helped make him very cautious.

His love for Janine had quelled all his fear for now.

Janine was likewise preoccupied with her thoughts and was amazed at just how calm he could be in the face of all this danger. She was bothered by how composed he was and upset that she had to worry alone.

She was also surprised that on this of all mornings, his manhood was now presenting itself in all its glory.

Even as surprise was her first reaction, this soon turned to desire, and she felt that familiar wetness beginning to form deep inside her. She was amazed at how remarkable it was that he could even think of making love… and how amazing it was that she responded to this.

Then she had a dreadful thought. *This could be the last time they ever made love.*

It was a fearful thought that went to the core of her heart. Nonetheless, she strangely desired him more than ever and responded to his advances with such passion she could not believe was possible.

He kissed her and was surprised at the intense response; he was puzzled that she was so passionate so quickly.

He was also grateful and embraced her passion as they kissed and fondled each other.

Next, Steve turned his attention to Janine's breasts, her beautiful mounds with such erotic nipples. They always excited him, and he firmed as he started sucking on her right nipple.

Steve's desire drove her crazy this time as he sucked and tugged at her breast like it was his last meal. His pure lust turned she on so much as he sucked her breast that she almost came immediately.

Almost.

Now she wanted him, she wanted him deep, and she wanted him now.

He sensed her urgency and started to mount her, but she stopped him. "No, from behind, please; I want you deep in me, and I want you to take me from behind. Take me, baby, firm and fast, cum with me. I want to feel your desire for me and take your passion at the height of mine."

He was aroused before she said this; he was hard, but after that, he had such a desire for her he could not have imagined. He wanted this woman so much that it almost tore his heart apart. He wanted her sexually more than any woman he could imagine.

He rose to his knees and moved behind Janine, who had already positioned herself on two pillows, her hot ass presenting to Steve, who moved behind her with his cock throbbing with excitement.

He thought, *take this slow; HE's full and thick, and she will feel this.*

As Steve probed her wetness, seeking the familiar entry that would quench their passions, she called, "Please, I want you, don't go slow, I need you inside me now, fuck me, baby, I'm already close with anticipation."

He obeyed with one slow but deliberate thrust of his cock. Half in pain, half in ecstasy, she gasped and cried out, "Oh god, how you fill me, baby, now fuck me; I want your warm cum inside me, I want you to desire me, I want to drive you crazy."

He obeyed. He pushed deep and withdrew, deep again, deeper than he had ever fucked her before, and as he did, his passion for her exploded.

"Oh god, I'm cuming," he said, "cum with me, baby."

She needed no more than that to push her across the edge she had been on ever since he had made her cum earlier, sucking on her breast. Janine pushed back against him and fucked him passionately as they came together.

They rested for a while.

Steve ran their bath while Janine tried desperately to relax on the bed.

They only had two and a half hours before his companion would arrive to pick him up. Janine was reflecting on their time together, trying not to think about what her life would be like without him. Still, she was having trouble pushing those dreadful thoughts away.

She would miss his voice, his soothing reassurances, the way it made her wet. Yes, and there was that; she certainly would miss the sex; she found it difficult to comprehend that she could ever find another lover like him but did not even want to consider that possibility.

Finally, they moved to the bath, and she hoped that would end her torment.

It did not.

As they chatted about how hot their last passionate embrace was, she realized that she would also miss their baths and the conversations. So often they had talked in the bath, so often they had worked through issues, so often explored each other's previous lives in the tub together.

I would miss his companionship as well, she thought.

Janine tried again to bury these thoughts and re-engage in their small talk.

He was talking about the things she liked to wear, the tops that turned him on, and he had asked if she could wear the white top with the pale green silk skirt he loved so much. This did not help she as she immediately thought, *he wants his last image of me to be in his favorite clothes.*

She agreed just the same. *How could she resist a dying man, his last wish,* before she pushed that horrible thought away?

"Janine, I said, " I want you to book dinner for us on Saturday when I return," Steve commented, bringing Janine back to the moment. "Are you all right? You seem to have drifted off into thought," he added.

"I was just thinking about us," she said, not wanting him to realize how worried she was.

"I will be back, so we need to book the restaurant, Rick's Cafe. Remember seven p.m. on Saturday? I will meet you there as we will be returning that day, and I have a flight to get my captive on—it leaves at six, so I won't have time to go back to the hotel and change. But, of course, it's not the real Rick's Cafe; that is just a movie set, but I understand it is based on the movie and is quite a place."

"Of course, I will book it," said Janine. "And of course, you will be back," she added hopefully.

He dressed and packed a small overnight bag. They waited on the bed, chatting and talking about how they would not survive the next few days without sex. Of course, they both knew they would, but it was fun anyway.

In reality, Steve would be too busy to even think about sex, or so he thought.

There was a knock on the door, so Steve got up to answer it. He returned with two people behind him. The first was a large, well-tanned man dressed in clothes more suited to an African safari.

Steve introduced him as John, and she deduced from his accent that he was South African. Janine assumed that this was not his real name.

The less she knows, she thought, touched that Steve was protecting her.

The second was a surprise. A striking woman about ten years younger than herself, also well-tanned but dressed impeccably without a hint of someone on a dangerous mission.

"This is Rachael," said Steve. "She is going to stay with you. I have her booked in the next room, and there is an interconnecting door. Rachael is an agent like me, so do not be deceived by her refined looks; she is well-trained and capable of dispatching any man twice her size—and has."

Janine thought she saw Rachael exchange a look with Steve, making her wonder if they had been on assignments before and if there had been something between them.

She was also relieved Rachael was not going with him, as she was beautiful.

"We have to go," said John, "we are meeting our contact at three p.m., and we have a long drive ahead."

Steve turned to Janine and went to say goodbye. Janine assumed it would be a curt farewell in the company of others.

As if on cue, John and Rachael discretely retreated to the hallway to leave them alone.

They kissed deeply, and Steve hugged Janine tight. Janine wanted to say what she feared, but she held back. She had to show faith in him, or he might not have the edge he needed to survive this. They said goodbye one last time, and Steve walked to the door, turned and blew her one last kiss as he disappeared down the corridor with John.

Watching him leave, she felt a hollowness opening inside her chest. This separation wasn't just about missing his physical presence—it was the sudden, terrifying realization of how completely he had integrated into her sense of future. The possibility of losing him now wasn't merely disappointment, but a fundamental reordering of the world she'd just begun to imagine for herself.

Janine wondered if that would be her final image of him.

Rachael re-entered the room and closed the door. She approached Janine and said, "This is just a precaution; we have no intelligence to suggest that this mission is compromised or that you are in danger. Steve is very fond of you because he insisted I be here to keep you safe. As far as anyone else is concerned, I'm your friend from London, and we have caught up in Morocco.

"We will do the usual tourist things, go shopping, and dine together, but you will NEVER lock the connection doors to our rooms. Please do not open the main door to anyone; we will arrange to have the room serviced by staff we trust while we are out. Are you clear?"

Janine was a little shocked by her '*orders*,' but she delivered them with a voice that showed professionalism, genuine care, and commitment. She felt safer.

Rachael and Janine set out on a shopping trip fifteen minutes later. Steve had provided a generous expense float for their activities because Rachael insisted on paying for everything. They shopped for two hours before stopping for coffee. Rachael was most endearing, intelligent, and very fit. They chatted about all sorts of things, but their conversation avoided talking about Steve.

Janine was beginning to understand that Steve had organized this as much to keep her mind off him and the danger of his mission than her actual safety. Rachael was a perfect companion, and time passed quickly. *Keep busy,* she thought, that's the secret, but she could not help but picture Steve in the four-wheel drive heading toward some unknown fate that she dreaded.

After more shopping and a quick visit to a traditional art gallery, they returned to the hotel. Rachael had booked dinner in the hotel restaurant. "We won't go out at night," she said. "Two women alone in Morocco will attract unwanted attention from men looking for fun or Islamic extremists who think we should be inside with our husbands."

"Are you married?" Janine asked, realizing that she knew nothing about her.

"I was once, but my husband was killed in... "

She stopped mid-sentence, and Janine realized she had thought better of telling Janine this story. She guessed he was also an agent and was killed in action, perhaps in an operation like the one Steve was conducting.

"In 2004," Rachael continued, recovering from her momentary lapse in discretion.

"I have never found a man like him since," she continued. "I have had a few relationships, of course, but he was a once-in-a-lifetime love. I loved him so deeply in our few short years."

She had drifted into her own thoughts, just as Janine wondered about asking if Steve had been one of her lovers but was unsure she wanted to know the answer. She admired this woman and did not want jealousy to tarnish her friendship.

Janine showered, dressed for dinner, and met Rachael in the hall at five to seven as instructed. She sensed that she had to obey all Rachael's instructions and should not deviate from the plan. Rachael was dressed in a beautiful dress of teal. It was modest, befitting of an Islamic country, but its tightness highlighted her figure perfectly.

And what figure it was, Janine thought! *She was stunning, very well built, full in the breasts, had a slim waist, and, from the rear in her tight dress, had very well-toned buttocks.* She again imagined Steve must have slept with her.

Then she wondered *what it would be like to kiss her...*

heat

Steve was three hours into the four-hour drive to Marrakech and wondered why he was apprehensive. He was not feeling as confident this time, even though he had carried out operations like this many times before in far less stable countries. His thoughts turned to Janine, and then he realized that in the past, he had no one to return to, no one to mourn him, no one he wanted to be with so much that this time, it mattered that he survived.

He could not leave her alone, he could not let anything happen to him, or she might be devastated. It mattered now, and that is why he worried, not for himself but for the love of his life. He watched the desert pass endlessly as they drove the rest of the way to Marrakech, deep in thought about Janine, how he would approach his target and how he could avoid being killed. He swore then that this would be his last mission and never leave her side again.

If he survived?

Do avoid attention, they checked into a nondescript hotel, befitting a couple of quirky tourists. There were three other operatives in other rooms, but they had been there for three weeks since the target was identified. They had slowly tracked his every move, identified his movement patterns, his home, his work, where he ate, had a haircut—every minute detail.

Tomorrow, Steve would pour over these with maps and try to identify the best time, place, and escape routes to ensure all would go smoothly. He was in charge, and everything would only occur with his knowledge and approval. He had learnt to be patient, stalk carefully, and understand his target in detail; this would be no exception.

They ate dinner separately, John and Steve at one table in the hotel's dining room, and the others at theirs. They did not want to attract any attention. They had a jovial night, but Steve was always careful with his drinks. He needed to be alert. His thoughts drifted back to Janine, and he guessed Rachael would have taken her to dinner at the hotel. They had agreed that they should not go out in the evening.

Rachael was an excellent agent, and yes, they had had a fling for a short time in South America; after all, she was a beautiful and sensual woman. But, unfortunately, it had ended because Steve was incapable of a commitment then, and she wanted more.

Rachael was a professional, though, and would not let that get in the way of her protecting Janine. He had made it very clear to her just how much she meant to him and had noticed her brief, pained look when he told her that, but she had quickly composed herself and was clear on what she had to do.

At nine thirty p.m., they retired to their rooms, and Steve showered. The dust in this place was invasive, and he could not bear to go to bed with the desert dust on him.

He thought of Janine and their bath time. He stirred. He read some of the agent's notes about their target in bed, carefully committing every detail to memory before settling to sleep.

Sleep evaded him as he thought of Janine alone in her bed, and his thoughts started to turn to her body as images of her flooded his mind. His cock stirred and began to firm. It felt nice, so he focused his image on her. Steve was very visual, so it was not long before he had a picture of Janine lying on her bed, masturbating. He liked that and moved his hand to his cock and started to caress it, slowly rubbing his shaft and his balls. He firmed more.

He was getting very hard, so he changed his image to one of Janine on her knees; in his mind, they were in front of an open fire on a large, white, soft animal skin rug. Janine was in her green underwear and had her high-heel shoes on.

He stroked his cock up and down the shaft with his hand. His breathing intensified as he began to feel his passion rising and imagined slipping off her green panties and mounting Janine from behind. As he imagined probing her wetness, he firmed even more, and his strokes increased as his breathing deepened.

Finally, he imagined punching through deep into her Flower and heard her gasp as he did.

He almost came but slowed the strokes to delay his orgasm. He was enjoying this and wanted it to last. He imagined the feeling of her wetness and her calls for him to fuck her. He could almost feel her buttocks on him, but when he imagined her calling out to fuck her, he decided it was time.

He imagined her orgasm building and finally her screams that she was cuming. With this image in his mind, he started to stroke faster and faster. He grabbed between his legs with his other hand as his orgasm exploded in a pulse across his body, and his cum spurted from his cock onto his belly. He continued the strokes milking his cum completely as he settled, satisfied for the moment.

He imagined them lying on the rug, the fire crackling as they cuddled and drifted off to sleep...

As he drifted off to sleep...

fantasy

Janine and Rachael talked all evening about their lives, the men in their past, and their families, but both women steered away from any conversation about Steve. If Janine had suspicions that Rachael had a history with Steve, they were confirmed by her total avoidance of discussing Janine and Steve as a couple.

Rachael did not ask about her relationship with Steve at all. This would have been a typical question given the situation and their other discussions, but she did not go there. Janine conspired with her on this by also not discussing him with her. At one point, she almost decided to ask her outright if she had slept with him but held herself back as she had developed a close friendship with Rachael and did not want to place her in an awkward situation.

Janine was not confident she would answer truthfully anyway.

One thing for sure was that she had unfinished feelings for him, and all she could think was that she could not blame her.

They finished dinner around nine p.m., and as they stood to retire to their rooms, Janine realized that she had consumed too much champagne. She steadied herself and smiled at Rachael, "I think I'm a little drunk," she said. "I need to go to bed."

They went upstairs, and Rachael checked her room before saying goodnight. "Remember, I'm just in the next room; if there is anything you need, any noise that worries you, call out. I sleep lightly and will hear you."

Janine thanked her, and Rachael went through the interconnecting door to her room. Janine almost called her back to ask her to stay for company, but she did not. Instead, she dressed for bed, cleaned her teeth, removed her makeup, and settled into bed with a book. Her thoughts once again turned to Steve.

The wait was tough for Janine as Steve could not use his mobile to call her. The possibility that their phones were being monitored was too high to risk using them, so Janine would only know if Steve was safe once he met her at the café in a few days.

It was difficult for her not to imagine the worst.

Janine returned to the book and began reading to take her mind off his danger. It was a romantic novel from the 19th century and had now turned to describe a particularly erotic scene. The head of the manor was having a steamy love affair with his children's nanny, and at this point, they were making love in the stables. Janine's Flower stirred, and her thoughts turned to Steve.

She began to imagine him as the master and that she was the nanny, in the stables with his head under her large skirt, her bloomers down to her ankles, and his tongue working magic on her Button. Her hands were touching her Flower before she even realized it.

As she felt her Flower, she noted that she was already quite wet and used her wetness to help slide her fingers over her Button. Now and then, she placed her fingers deep inside her Flower, imagining Steve's large cock entering her.

Then she remembered.

Pinkie. Her vibrator.

She called it Pinkie because it was a pink penis-shaped vibrator, not as large or thick as Steve's cock but pleasant nonetheless. It had held her in good stead in the past.

She slipped out of bed and retrieved it from her suitcase. She pressed the start button, and it hummed. *'Perfect'*, she thought; it was charged, and Janine slipped back into bed and resumed her touch.

As she retrieved the image in the stables, she became more aroused by her touch and turned on the vibrator. She started with a light touch on the upper part of her Button using the tip of her vibrating penis. She wanted to build this slowly.

The image of Master Steve under her skirt was arousing her, and she lubricated her Button with her wetness to emulate the sensation of his tongue on her. She moved the tip so it was fuller on her Button and felt the vibration bring her closer to her climax.

She shifted her image so she was on a hay bale, her shirt over her front, and the Master standing before her with his huge cock waiting for her. She moved the vibrating penis to her Flower and probed her wetness.

Master Steve moved closer, placing his engorged cock on her Flower. He thrust it in as she inserted Pinkie into herself; she drew a quick breath.

Not from the size of Pinkie but from the memory of Steve's thick cock entering her.

She moved her other hand to her Button as she changed the setting on Pinkie to a pulsing throb and pushed it deep inside her, withdrawing and pushing in an attempt to emulate Master Steve fucking her.

Her hand provided the rest.

As Janine fucked herself with her Master's penis, she rubbed her Button faster as she built her climax. She was close but needed more. Finally, she imagined the master groaning, saying he was cuming and pushing deeper inside her. Again, she rubbed her Button harder and faster.

As she imagined her master cuming, she tipped over into a very satisfying orgasm. It expanded throughout her body and slowly settled as she continued to rub her Button in an attempt to prolong the sensation.

Janine held her Flower as she slowly drifted to sleep, with images of her in the stables, lying on the hay in the arms of her lover and master...

rendition

Steve woke late.

He was not used to waking late anymore because now he usually had his lover next to him and always woke aroused and early. This morning, he was aroused despite her absence and recalled his masturbation of the previous night. He almost revisited the fantasy of the open fire but was late, so he had to dismiss this urge.

He ate a fast breakfast that he ordered into the room, showered, almost revisited the fantasy in the shower, and then met his colleagues in John's room at nine a.m. as planned.

They spread the maps and notes on the dining table in John's suite and started considering each route and stop their target would use the following day.

Steve always called their quarry 'the target' because it helped him not focus on the fact that the target was a human being with a family. He believed their crimes had lost them that right, but he still needed to depersonalize them so he could carry out their mission without being influenced by his compassion.

They painstakingly cross-checked every detail before he was even called in to capture them specifically to ensure they had the right person; they would face a trial and be able to defend themselves. The judgement and decision on punishment were the concern of others. Israel did not have the death penalty, a kindness not afforded by his target to the millions of his Holocaust victims.

It took eight hours, including a short break for lunch, for Steve to finally decide on the optimal place and time to take the target into their custody. He had progressively taken a list of ten prospective places and times; one by one, the team pulled them apart for faults, risks, and weaknesses.

Steve made the final decision but always tried to ensure consensus among the team. He could only risk their lives or liberty if they were committed and convinced the plan was the best.

The plan, however well executed, could always be better, so the team planned to spend three hours after dinner rerunning scenarios, carefully rehearsing options should unexpected events occur as they executed their plan.

They had options for rain, a child crossing the street at the time, the target not turning up as planned, a mechanical breakdown in the car, intervention by third parties, the police—everything conceivable. But, at the end of the evening, they were all satisfied they had it all planned and knew each step where they could exit the operation if something went wrong.

Throughout the day, Steve's attention drifted to Janine. He had to force himself to push these thoughts from his mind. Instead, he had to focus on the mission.

He had never experienced such thoughts before. Never had he constantly thought of someone; she was never far from his mind, and it pained him that he was not with her. He loved her passionately and wanted to be with her.

It pained him even more that he was on such a dangerous mission and could not even call her on the phone.

He went to sleep that night with a deep sadness in his heart and could not find the desire to be sexual in any way.

The grab was to be at around two p.m., so Steve slept in, ate breakfast, and rejoined his colleagues once more to rehearse the plan.

They would leave Marrakech almost immediately after the robbery. With a four-hour drive back to Casablanca and a detour to a small airport outside the city, he would barely make it to Rick's café to meet Janine on time.

The target would be having his usual lunch at a corner café in the lower part of the city. He had his regular table, but they would wait until he left at around one forty-five p.m. to walk back to his home. It was four small blocks, but at the third, he had to cross over to a small laneway, where they would grab him.

They planned a ten-minute leeway on either side. They had special radios connected to small earpieces that were not traceable so that one of their team would signal as he left the restaurant.

Steve and John would be at the four-wheel drive parked just in the laneway with another of their team on watch across the road pretending to repair a puncture on his bicycle. If there were any sign of police or people who could witness the grab, he would signal, and they would revert to their second option.

That would mean another day in Marrakech, and Steve did not want to delay his return to his love.

This had to work.

By one thirty p.m., all the teams were in place. Steve and John had driven their four-wheel drive into the laneway from the other end, so when they stopped, they were just at the edge of the intersection where the target would cross.

They got out of the vehicle, opened the front bonnet, and made it look like they were having mechanical trouble. Then, through his discrete earpiece, Steve checked that the others were in place, checked his sidearm for the last time, took it off the safety, and waited.

It was one forty-eight p.m. when he got the signal from the agent outside the restaurant that the target had just paid for his meal and was now leaving. Ten minutes, they estimated from previous observations of his walk. They had to be prepared for random stops to talk to someone, but he always went home and took this route.

He rechecked his sidearm, and John did likewise.

They waited, staring over the open bonnet, looking at the engine, and occasionally tapping or pointing at specific parts.

He thought of Janine right at that moment. He thought of her lying on the yacht's deck, naked in the sun, and his cock twinged again.

Focus, he said to himself as the agent with the bicycle whispered in his earpiece that he could now see the target a block away and walking in their direction.

All was ready.

The agent whispered every fifteen seconds, "400 meters, 350 meters, 300 meters," until finally, the target was fifty meters away and still alone.

The street was also empty, with no police, traffic, or other pedestrians.

They had chosen the spot well, off the main roads and when most people avoided the midday heat.

"Ten meters…" It was his cue.

"Es ist dein Auto, weißt du nicht, wie du es reparieren kannst?" Steve yelled at John in his best German accent (it's your car, don't you know how to fix it?), hoping his German would attract the target's attention. They knew the target was a keen amateur mechanic, and they were sure combining two 'Germans' with a mechanical problem would attract his attention.

"Ich nehme es immer zum Service-Center, ich habe keine Ahnung, was falsch," John responded. (I always take it to the service center, I have no idea what's wrong).

The target immediately walked toward them and said in English, "Can I help? I know a bit about engines."

He was well-practiced at hiding his German background, only spoke Moroccan or English, and never broke character.

"Do you speak English?" he added.

"Yes, we do," said John drawing on the Germanic tones of his South African-Germanic accent, "and we certainly could use some expertise right now. I have a toolbox in the back. You could show me which tool is best to tighten the fan belt. I know enough to realize it might be loose and not charging the battery enough, and the red light came on."

"Of course," said the target, unable to resist an opportunity to tinker with an engine. He followed them to the back of the four-wheel drive and further into the laneway.

John opened the back door while Steve stepped back and waited. There was a toolbox on the boot floor, and John opened it for the unsuspecting target. As he leaned over to inspect the contents for a shifting spanner, Steve stepped forward and placed a large rag soaked in ether over his mouth and nose as he and John held his struggling body down against the boot floor until he was nicely asleep.

Steve and John bundled him into the back of the car, bound his hands and feet with cable ties, and threw a rug over him. It was all over in thirty seconds, and with the bonnet closed, they were off in another thirty.

The other agents melted into the background, returning to the hotel to check out and disappear in different directions and across the border.

John drove while Steve sat in the back seat so he could keep an eye on their target. He would be asleep for around thirty minutes, but by then, they would be on the dirt highway back to Casablanca.

The target roused on cue thirty minutes later, so Steve asked John to pull over. The road was deserted, and they both opened the back door and removed the blanket as the old man demanded in English to untie him, but he was groggy still and slurred his words.

They sat him up and gave him a drink of water.

They did not want him to die before facing trial.

As the target began to wake, he said, "I have money, contact my solicitor, and he will arrange to pay your ransom."

Steve laughed and said, "We have not kidnapped you for ransom, you fool."

Steve stood upright and said very formally, "Herr Herman Yultzer, on behalf of the State of Israel, I am arresting you to face trial for crimes against humanity, for your role in the murder of 568,000 innocent Jews in the Bergen-Belsen Concentration Camp, 720,000 in the Auschwitz Concentration Camp, and 420,760 in the Dachau Concentration Camp."

Yultzer's face went ashen.

He started to protest that he was not Yultzer, but Steve cut him off.

"You are to be taken from this place to the State of Israel, where you will be provided with legal counsel so you can defend yourself. You will be given the same legal rights as an Israeli citizen and will have your day in court. Unlike your victims, you will be treated humanely, but you will face a jury for your crimes."

Steve drew his sidearm, and he and John moved him from the boot to the back seat. John restarted the car while Steve got into the other rear seat next to Yultzer and buckled him in.

Finally, Steve said, "If we are stopped, and you attempt to call out, I will shoot you on the spot. You can cooperate and live out your life in jail or die in the desert today. It's your choice."

Yultzer was silent, scared, and had stopped protesting.

He knew his life in hiding had ended.

They drove off down the highway.

Three hours later, they pulled into a side road and, after ten minutes, arrived at an old, disused French Air Force aerodrome.

John drove up to a large and rusty airplane hanger, and as they got closer, they could see a gleaming small private jet hidden inside. As they entered, the pilot acknowledged them from the cockpit and started the engines.

Two men exited the plane as three others appeared from an office at the back of the hanger.

They warmly greeted Steve and John, speaking in Hebrew, and removed Yultzer from the car. They cut the cable ties from his feet and walked him to the jet.

Yultzer initially tried to resist but then appeared to resign to his fate.

The men treated him with dignity, did not manhandle him, and carefully guided him up the stairs to the jet. All the other men entered the plane except John, Steve, and one man who lingered.

He walked up to Steve, saluted, and said, "Thank you, Major."

He entered the plane, and in two minutes, the jet was taxiing down the disused runway. It took off within three minutes, making a steep climb to avoid the Moroccan radar systems. Within two hours, it would land in an Israeli Air Force base, and Herman Yultzer would face the families of those he had killed.

Watching the plane take off, Steve felt the familiar post-mission clarity—that heightened awareness that came with danger successfully navigated. But this time, something was different. The thought of returning to Janine wasn't just pleasant anticipation but urgent necessity. Each mission before had been self-contained, but now his life had expanded to include her. Success meant nothing if he couldn't share it with the woman waiting for him in Casablanca.

John and Steve did not linger; they had another mission to complete.

lust

Janine woke the following day with Steve on her mind. She had been dreaming about him.

In her dream, she was in a large city and was wandering around. Now and then, she could glimpse Steve in the crowd, but he would disappear every time she tried to get to him.

She sensed that he was also trying to get to her, but whenever they got close, suddenly, they were further apart. He was there but always just out of reach. Her dream disturbed her, and she felt alone. More than anytime since she had known him, she missed him, even more than when she had first loved him. she wanted to see him but knew she could not.

She hoped and prayed that he would be safe.

She had planned to meet Rachael for breakfast at eight a.m., so she automatically went to the bathroom and turned on the bath. She stopped and thought. *No*, she decided; *it would not be the same without him. It would only cause her heart to ache and remind her of his absence.*

Janine had a shower instead and dressed in modest clothing. They planned to visit the markets and needed to ensure they were sensitive to the local sensibilities. She was in the dining room at eight a.m. as instructed, and

Rachael was waiting. They enjoyed a light breakfast and chatted about nothing in particular before heading to the markets about two kilometers away.

Janine enjoyed walking, so they did not take a cab. They would see local sites on the way, and she would get her exercise. She particularly liked that walking helped keep her legs and buttocks toned. At first, because she wanted to look good for herself, but now she also wanted to look good for Steve.

Janine and Rachael chatted as they walked through the streets of Casablanca, looking at the various stores and the Moorish buildings as they did. Hues of red, ochre, and blue dominated the road, and typified this style. Now and then, they would stop at a store to look at ceramic pieces, scarves, and the occasional carpet.

They arrived at the markets around ten a.m., having taken an hour to walk what would have been a twenty-five-minute stroll.

The market was busy with many locals and a smattering of tourists. It was colorful, vibrant, and full of bustle. Janine and Rachel joked about the carpets. "There are so many carpet vendors," Rachael said. "I'm surprised the whole of Morocco is not carpeted."

Janine purchased a beautiful dark green pashmina; she had tried to look disinterested as she examined the shawl, but her excitement at finding it must have been evident as the stall owner called her bluff in their negotiations on price.

She thought *this would be very cosy to wear in the colder climates of Scotland.*

Janine wondered why such items were so common in hot countries and could not understand the need for women here to wear so much clothing. She loved to dress light when it was hot and found their desire for modesty frustrating.

They had lunch in a small café in the rear of the market area, and Janine was left alone while Rachel went to find a bathroom.

Janine checked her mobile.

She knew Steve could not call her, but still, she checked her phone often to see if he might have emailed her or texted her.

No messages.

She had expected this and did not want him to do anything that would put him at risk, but she was saddened just the same.

She opened her photo album. She had taken photos of Steve, and occasionally, they took a selfie. He looked so happy in these photos, and she did as well. She only had about thirty pictures of him and about fifteen of them together and thought *this would be all she would have to remember if something happened to him in Marrakech.*

She wondered if he was thinking of her and what he would be doing now.

Rachael sat down next to her again and gave her a knowing look, and she realized that Rachel would have seen the photo of her and Steve she was looking at as she passed by her chair to sit on hers. Janine flushed.

"He broke my heart, you know," Rachael said, breaking the mutual conspiracy of silence about Steve.

"I'm over it now, so don't worry, but I understand how you would fall in love with him. We had a cozy relationship, and he loved me in a way, but I always knew I was not the one for him. Frankly, I never thought he would ever find his one true love, but when we met in the hotel, I knew instantly that you were special. I have seen other women come and go, but I sense that you are different. I hope you don't mind me talking about this. I enjoy your company, but I could tell you knew that Steve and I had a past, and the tension of that has gotten in the way of us being friends."

Janine was surprised at her candor but relieved that she had finally broached the subject. "I have never known a man like him," Janine said. "So completely sensual and caring. He understands me as if we had been together all our lives. In a way, we have. Did you know we met each other thirty-three years ago? We lived together for a short time before he moved on for his work. He did not know I loved him then; he did not know I never stopped loving him. Somehow, I found him again, and now I'm afraid I will lose him."

Janine could not stop herself; she broke down and cried. The patrons in the café looked at them as Rachael moved to comfort her.

"He is very experienced," Rachael whispered. "And has done this many times. He will be fine, I have no doubt."

She put her arm around Janine to comfort her, and Janine and Rachel became real friends at that moment.

The next day, Janine and Rachel were inseparable; the night before, they had stayed up late talking about Steve and trading stories about him. Still, Janine kept her stories discrete, not because she was embarrassed but out of concern for hurting Rachael's feelings.

Janine would have loved to tell her how fantastic the sex was but knew in her heart and from how Rachael talked about him that she was not over her love for him. Yet, she took some pride in that Rachael sometimes expressed her envy that she had managed to overcome Steve's fear of love and have him fall for her.

She thought of Steve often and missed him badly, but Rachael's presence had lightened her heart and made the time pass faster.

She was grateful for her friendship.

The following day, Rachael came into her room before breakfast. They planned to get ready together, and

Rachael had brought her make-up and several outfits. She was asking Janine's opinion on what she should wear.

Janine thought that was cute.

Rachael still had her nightie on, and Janine could see the outline of her nipples through the sheer material. She was attractive and extraordinarily fit, which showed in her body. Janine had always been comfortable acknowledging the sexuality of another woman.

Rachael asked Janine which dress she should wear, so Janine suggested the blue one she had over her arm. Rachael immediately pulled off her nightie and started to climb into her dress.

She was naked, had no panties on, and was completely waxed.

Her breasts were larger than Janine's but were firm, and Janine felt her Flower stir.

She dismissed the feeling and asked Rachel which dress she should wear. They went to her wardrobe, and Rachael picked a green dress.

Janine now wondered how to go from here. She would not normally undress so brazenly in front of another woman, but Rachael's actions required some form of reciprocation.

Janine did not want Rachael to think of her as a prude.

She took a deep breath, dropped her lightweight dressing gown, and started pulling the dress over her head.

"I can see why Steve is so attracted to you," said Rachael, staring at Janine.

Janine caught her head up in the dress and was having trouble getting the dress on.

The sleeve was entangled.

"Here, let me help you," said Rachael, stepping forward to help adjust the dress. As she did, her arm brushed against Janine's nipple, sending a shiver down her body. Her Flower twinged for the second time.

Rachael was now right next to her, so when Janine turned to thank her, they were face-to-face and very close.

They paused and looked into each other's eyes for signs of what was next when Rachael moved closer and kissed Janine.

She kissed her softly at first, awaiting her response but did not have to wait long as Janine surrendered to her desire and kissed her back.

Soon they were embracing, Rachel's hand caressing her back and sides and Janine's across Rachael's firm buttocks.

They kissed passionately before collapsing onto the bed in a tangle of lust.

Pure lust drove them from there as they embraced and stroked each other, and as Janine felt Rachael's wetness for her.

She massaged Rachael's clit, rousing her even more before Rachael did likewise; it was quick; Janine's orgasm was fast in building as Rachel stimulated her Button adeptly. Rachael had a firm touch and knew how to apply the pressure Janine needed to cum.

The excitement of this illicit encounter and the few days she had not been with Steve ensured her orgasm was full and satisfying.

Janine turned her attention to Rachael.

First, she kissed Rachael's breasts, gently sucking on her nipples as Rachael's breathing deepened. Then, she slowly moved her kisses across her stomach until she was at her soft, hairless Flower.

Janine moved between her legs, using her tongue to stimulate Rachael's clit.

She smelled good and understood Steve's desire to breathe in her own scent.

Janine could feel Rachael building.

She clasped Rachel's clit between her lips and started to flick her tongue and suck; she enclosed the whole area and sucked and flicked forcefully. Rachael went from a slow build to an explosive orgasm in seconds, writhing on the bed with Janine firmly between her legs.

Janine moved next to her as she recovered.

"Wow!" said Rachael, "Nobody has ever done it like that to me before; that was incredible. I'm not sure what you did, but only a woman would know what to do to make me feel that."

Good, Janine thought; *Steve's special was hers alone as he had not used it on her*.

They showered and dressed quietly, only occasionally chatting about make-up.

They had both silently decided that this was just a bit of fun, and since they may never see each other again, it would likely not happen again.

They shopped again, had lunch, and did not mention their encounter.

As Janine wandered around the shops that afternoon, the memory of Rachael's touch mingled confusingly with thoughts of Steve. The experience had been pleasurable, undeniably so, yet there was a hollowness afterward that surprised her. Physical connection without the emotional foundation she'd built with Steve felt incomplete now, like a language missing key words.

She wondered if this revelation was simply part of growing older, or something specific to what she and Steve had created between them.

They returned to the hotel, got ready for dinner together, dressing, putting on make-up, and chatting inconsequentially as if trying to erase their earlier passion from their minds.

Tonight was Rick's Cafe, and Steve would be returning.

pursued

Steve and John sped down the highway from the old airfield; they had forty-five minutes to make it into Casablanca and Steve's date with Janine. Steve had hoped to get to the hotel before and shower, but the timing would have prevented that.

As it was, he would be there about 15 minutes late.

They had caught and dispatched Yultzer, and all had gone well. He was proud of himself, but he was most pleased that he would never do this again, never leave her in this situation, and risk never seeing his love again.

"I am retiring, John," he said out loud. "That was my last mission."

"I'm sorry to hear that," John said, "but you may have to wait a little longer; there has been a black SUV behind us for the last twenty kilometers. It is now about 300 meters behind. I have tried to slow down to let it pass us or speed up to break away, but every time I do, it slows or speeds up to match our speed, so I think we have a tail."

"I'm surprised you did not notice my speed changes," he added.

"Sorry, John, I have been deep in thought, and I must admit I had relaxed my guard since we got the target away," Steve replied.

Steve thought for a while, then said, "OK, here's the plan."

echo

Janine and Rachael arrived at Rick's Cafe around six forty-five p.m., and as Janine entered, she cast her eyes around the room for Steve.

Unfortunately, he was not there yet.

The place was amazing. It looked just like a scene out of Casablanca, the movie, and there was a piano player in the corner playing 1930-style music.

They were taken to a table for two in the corner. Despite Rachael's pleading, Janine asked the waiter to set another place. She thought that Rachael had been such a friend that she could not make her dine alone.

They sat down and ordered champagne. Janine was very pleased that they had Verve on the wine list. The waiter provided menus and advised them that around eight p.m., there would be a singer to accompany the piano player.

Janine and Rachael chatted for a while as the time ticked past seven, then seven-fifteen. Janine kept glancing at the stairway near the entrance. That would be where Steve would enter. Rachael appeared detached for a while and finally said what she was thinking.

She asked Janine if she would mention their little encounter to Steve.

Janine was surprised by this and had not even thought that it would be inappropriate to do so. She knew Steve had fantasies about seeing Janine with another woman, and she thought it would please him to know.

"I am honest with Steve," she said, "Don't you want me to tell him?"

"I'm not sure," Rachael replied, "I'm worried that it might hurt your relationship, and I also don't want personal issues spoiling my professional relationship with Steve. It was awkward after we broke up, and I missed out on critical and interesting missions. I don't want my future missions limited because Steve is uncomfortable working with me."

It was now seven-forty-five, and Janine was getting very worried. Finally, she pushed her concerns aside and told Rachael that she would test the water with Steve and tell him at an appropriate moment, even though she was sure he would not mind.

"I'm sure if you were a man, it would be very different," she explained. "But then if you were, it would not have happened. But I believe he trusts me and will understand I would only do this if it were purely sexual."

"You are a great friend, and I feel very close to you. We had a bit of fun, and Steve will understand and, I'm sure, even find it sexy!" She added to reassure Rachael.

Rachael sighed visibly and thanked Janine for her understanding. She told Janine that they might never cross paths again, but if we were to, I would be glad to have a little more fun with you.

Janine smiled for the first time since they entered the café.

A spotlight appeared across the room and focused on the stool next to the piano; the show was about to begin. Janine looked at the clock. It was eight. The pianist started a short intro tune, and a man in a white suit walked up to the stool, sat down, looked at the pianist, and nodded to start.

The music was familiar to her.

"You must remember this, a kiss is just a kiss," he sang as the audience broke out in applause.

Janine clapped as she distractedly glanced over to the stairs.

There he was!

Her Steve was standing there!

The relief that washed through Janine at seeing him stand in the doorway of Rick's Café was physical—her knees actually weakening, breath catching. She hadn't allowed herself to fully acknowledge the fear that had been her constant companion during his absence. It wasn't just about losing a lover, but losing possibility—the future they'd only begun to sketch together, all the conversations yet to have, discoveries to make. His safe return felt like a gift she hadn't earned but desperately needed.

Steve waited for the applause to die before he started crossing the room to her.

Her next thought was that *it was typical that he would time his entrance so perfectly, so romantically*, as she rose to her feet and started walking over to greet him.

They met halfway, embraced, and kissed as if no one else was in the room.

"It's still the same old story, a fight for love and glory, a case of do or die. The world will always welcome lovers; as time goes by," the singer sang as a second spotlight moved across the room and highlighted two lovers passionately kissing in the middle of the café.

The crowd clapped and cheered, oblivious that this was not part of the café's show.

Janine and Steve suddenly became aware of the attention they were attracting and broke from their embrace, slowly walking back toward the table.

As they did, Janine looked at Steve and said, "I hope you don't mind; I asked Rachael to join us for dinner; she has been such a great friend."

"When does she arrive?" asked Steve.

Janine turned to look at their table. Rachael was gone.

She thought about how she had just greeted Steve, then realized that she had been insensitive. Rachael still loved him, and her display of affection must have hurt.

They enjoyed their meal, danced, and chatted.

Steve apologized for being late and quietly explained that the mission had gone well and that they would have made it close to on time but had to deal with a car following them.

They finally managed to do this when the road passed through a wadi, a desert oasis that was lined with trees, and several curves in the road as it went across the creek. They stopped and positioned their car blocking the road, and Steve got out and hid behind the trees so that when the SUV finally turned the corner, it had to stop.

Steve had moved swiftly, gun drawn, and confronted the startled driver before he knew he was there.

They forced him out of the vehicle at gunpoint and started to interrogate him.

It turned out he was an older man whose eyesight had been so bad lately that he had to keep his distance from cars ahead of him because the dust trail they generated on the dirt road made it impossible for him to see the road.

After some apologies and cash compensation for his troubles, the old man agreed not to mention the incident to anyone. After being given more than his annual salary in cash, he had decided it was an honest mistake.

Janine and Steve walked back to their hotel.

It was a full moon, and the streetscape was very romantic. They held hands as if they never wanted to be apart again.

Janine did not say just how scared she had been but showed him with her affection that she was very happy to have him back. Safe.

The hotel lobby was crowded when they returned from dinner.

Janine noticed her first—a striking woman with olive skin and piercing eyes that missed nothing. Those eyes locked on Steve with unmistakable recognition.

"Darling," the woman said, approaching Steve with casual confidence. "What a delightful surprise." Steve's body tensed beside her.

"Leila." His voice was carefully neutral. "It's been a long time."

"Not so long." She smiled, her piercing gaze sliding to Janine with a cool assessment. "Aren't you going to introduce me to your... friend?"

"Janine, this is Leila Navari. We worked together in Cairo." The slight emphasis on 'worked' told Janine everything she needed to know. "Leila, my partner, Janine."

"Partner? How serious." Leila's smile didn't waver. "I need to speak with you. Privately. Old business."

"Anything you need to say can be said in front of Janine." Leila's expression hardened.

"I don't think so. Unless you want her involved in what happened in Damascus?" She responded pointedly.

Janine felt Steve's hand tighten around hers. His jaw clenched. Whatever 'Damascus' meant, it clearly wasn't good.

Steve was clearly conflicted but finally agreed to talk to Leila in the bar next to the lobby. He told Janine he would only be ten minutes and suggested that she ran their bath and he would join her shortly.

It was the longest 10 minutes of her life. The bath was running, and she was getting worried. It was now fifteen minutes, and she was just about to return to the lobby when Steve entered their suite alone.

"She's gone," Steve said, his jaw tight, his eyes uncharacteristically guarded.

"Going to tell me what that was about?" Janine kept her voice steady despite the unease settling in her stomach.

"Damascus was a covert operation. We called it 'Operation Mirage,' and it's still classified, even though it was six years ago. It did not go well." He ran a hand through his hair. "Three agents died."

"And Leila blames you."

"No." He met her eyes. "She and I were the only survivors, but it was complicated, and I am afraid I cannot say anything more without putting you at risk." Steve added, wanting to close the conversation down. They ran the bath, climbed in, and relaxed despite the unfinished discussion they needed to complete but for the secrecy it demanded.

In the familiar routine of their bath, Steve felt the last tension of his mission dissolve, and he buried the issue with Leila as fast as it was raised. That was then, and this was now.

With Janine, he could be all of himself—not just the determined hunter or passionate lover, but the man who existed between those roles, the person he was still discovering himself to be. Her acceptance wasn't just of his body or even his past, but of his potential—who he might become with her influence shaping him.

For Janine, the unfinished secret would have to wait; she needed to trust Steve's judgement about what she should know about his work. She decided to put it aside for the moment despite suspecting that this was more than a work-related issue.

Besides, she had her own secret to spill.

They were in their discussion and truth place now, so she told Steve about her little encounter with Rachael. She did not tell him that Rachael had mentioned their love affair. She wanted to see how he responded first.

"It is another thing we have in common," he said. "I did not tell you before as we did not have time, but I was once in a relationship with Rachael. I ended it a while ago."

"I know," said Janine, smiling, "I know, baby, and I hope you don't mind that we had a little thing. It was just the moment, and I felt lonely; we played around for a while."

Janine could see Steve did not mind as his cock had grown since she confessed, and it now grew bigger every time he asked what she did, and she told him.

Recounting the encounter with him also turned her on.

They went to bed and embraced. Janine was so glad to have his body next to hers again, and their bath-time conversation had made her very hot, wet, and horny. But, most of all, she wanted her special, particularly now that she knew it was only hers and hers alone.

Janine was not usually demanding in bed, but this time she pushed Steve's head toward her Flower, saying, "I want you to suck my Button, baby. I want you to make me cum. I want you to do your special, our special, god how I need that now."

He was a little surprised by her insistence but, at the same time, turned on by it. He complied, and as he applied his lips to her Flower, the image of Janine doing the same to Rachael came to his mind.

If Steve had appeared to enjoy this before, he was positively excited this time, and he sucked, nibbled, and flicked her Button ravenously.

Janine could feel his desire and lust; she loved that he wanted her so much, and her orgasm came quickly and intensely. Janine screamed as she came, partly because she was ecstatic and partly because she knew this had turned him on.

It certainly did.

He was lustful, and it was his turn to be demanding. "I want you on top, baby. Sit on me. Let me fill you with my cock."

Janine complied without hesitation, straddling him and raising herself so that he could probe for her wetness.

And wetness there was.

Janine was so wet that her juices dripped onto Steve as she mounted him. He found her entry and allowed Janine to lower herself onto him.

She held her head high, closed her eyes, and paused at the point where his thickness met resistance. She waited, anticipating the sensation, then dropped and gasped as his thick cock punched through.

He gasped as well as he felt her Flower open and then close around his cock to engulf him.

Janine cried out as his cock filled her. "Oh baby," she cried, "I have missed you, missed your tender touch, and god, I have missed how you make me feel when you meld with me in this way."

She raised herself again, slowly; this time, she moved back to the point where his cock resisted her.

She wanted to feel him break through again. She paused again, then lowered herself, gasping as she did. This time she dropped totally as Steve's cock filled her and pushed beyond, stretching her internally and stretching the flesh around her Button.

"Deep," she cried. "I want it deep, god, how you fill me."

She moved up again, then dropped and again, and each drop was total, and he sensed she wanted this now.

It excited him, and his now hard cock grew even firmer.

As she built the speed, Steve responded with his forward movement, plunging his cock even deeper than she thought possible.

"Fuck," she cried, "oh god, fuck me, baby. I'm going to cum," she screamed, "For god's sake, I want you with me, baby."

Janine pushed down on him and, as she did, pumped his cock with her Flower.

He pushed back but withdrew further on each stroke by pulling his hips back into the bed. This action made each stroke longer and more pleasurable for him.

"Yes, baby, I'm going to cum," he cried, as he felt the building sensation shift to the point where he knew his orgasm was inevitable.

"Cum, baby, cum," he cried, "cum with me!"

And she did.

Janine exploded into orgasm as Steve's orgasm began, his semen spurting forth in successive pulses deep into her waiting Flower.

Finally, they collapsed with Janine on top of Steve, his cock still inside her. "I could not imagine life without you now," said Janine.

"Nor could I," responded Steve. "Nor could I."

Later, watching Steve sleep, she gently traced the lines around his eyes—marks of experience, of a life fully lived. She'd known other men, shared pleasure and even affection, but never this sense of recognition, of finding someone who seemed to understand her without explanation.

The thought of building a life with him no longer frightened her. Instead, it felt like the most natural progression imaginable—not jumping into the unknown, but finally finding solid ground.

They spent the next few hours exploring each other's bodies. Steve loved to take her beauty with his eyes, and Janine found this very sexy and hot.

He would spend some time just looking at her pert breasts and nipples, touching them softly, teasing Janine before he moved closer and began to suck her nipples slowly and gently.

As he did, he would take her nipple between his lips and tug them till she could not take it anymore.

"Suck them, baby, please," she pleaded, and Steve would take her breast entirely into his mouth and suck another orgasm out of her. Then, they would bathe again, talk, and return to their bed.

There he would turn his attention to her Flower.

Janine would open herself to him; her recently waxed Flower was soft and naked. He loved the feeling of her Flower against his face. He would breathe in her essence, take the beauty of her Flower in with his eyes.

Janine, in turn, could feel the desire in Steve's looking at her so intently and loved that he adored her womanhood.

He would then kiss her Flower and move his tongue across her soft and naked places, slowly stimulating the skin around Flower.

Janine would open herself up completely, allowing Steve to touch her everywhere with his tongue. This slow stimulation built her desire for him, made her so wet, and ensured that when he moved to her Button, he took her over the edge to her climax wholly and quickly.

This time was no different because as Steve moved his tongue to her Button, she pleaded for her special.

He would delay, but not too long, and then he would take her in his mouth and suck and flick her Button until she exploded again.

Janine would then be impatient with him, impatient to have him fill her with his thick cock. She would move to him, down to his manhood, and feel his softness.

Janine would also use her tongue, and Steve would open up to her, allowing her to explore him entirely. His cock would stir and rise to this, but before it grew too large, she would take him into her mouth completely and use her tongue to pleasure him until he was hard once again.

He would fuck her from behind, on the side, or sometimes with Janine controlling the pace on top, but often they would fuck with Steve on top and Janine underneath, his weight on her and her legs together.

It was this way they finished this night as Steve's hard cock penetrated Janine deeply and as the pressure from this position stimulated her Button until she was close.

"Oh baby, I'm going to cum, fuck me, want me, give it to me, baby," she cried as Steve stepped up the pace and depth of his motion.

"Yes, baby, yes, I'm with you, baby, now," he cried as he tipped over just as she tipped, and they both cried out together as their climax merged into one expression of their passion and love.

nine

They woke late the next day, made love in the glow of the morning sun in their room, and spent an hour in the bath talking about the last few days, how she worried and how Steve was retiring from his dangerous work. Janine was very pleased as she could not contemplate her life without him.

They returned to the bed as they often did for a quick '*Special*.' Janine lay on the edge of the bed as Steve knelt on the floor before her, praying to his goddess and kissing her Flower slowly. As he applied his Special, she built quickly and came intensely. This time she wanted more. He had her turn over and kneel on the bed as he stood on the floor and entered her from behind.

Janine sighed with pleasure as he entered her, and his thickness passed that point. Janine was now getting used to his thick penis, not its girth, as that always made her gasp, but she was better able to take him without any pain. The intensity his size gave increased her pleasure immeasurably, and now she wanted to experience that thickness even more.

Janine asked Steve to withdraw back past the point where he entered and push past again. She asked him to repeat this, and gradually he started fucking her in this way. He thrust into her, making her feel his thickness, and each time he did, her pleasure grew as she built her orgasm to an intensity she had not experienced before. His cock slid across the tightness of her Flower repeatedly until she exploded.

The sensation was great for Steve because he came with her quickly this way. He could feel her Flower tight against his cock, like it was sucking the orgasm out of him.

They dressed. Janine showered her Flower with the hand shower in the bath, tempted to use it to cum again, but she decided she wanted to save it for a time with Steve.

He skipped the shower as he wanted the smell of Janine to stay with him. He loved that he could smell her as he went through his day.

Her scent excited him; occasionally, he would go to the bathroom to wee and when he opened his trousers, her natural perfume would fill the cubicle, exciting him so much that he would masturbate then and there. It was his secret, and she did not know how much her scent drove him wild.

They finished getting ready and packed their bags. Today, they were to meet the yacht in the marina. The girls had sailed her through the Mediterranean and down the coast and were due at two p.m. Steve and Janine would buy some provisions and stay on the yacht that night before setting sail at first light.

They took a taxi to the markets near the marina armed with an email list of supplies for the next leg of the QT's long journey to Scotland. They purchased fresh fruit and vegetables from the market stalls, meat from the butchers, and groceries from the large indoor supermarket.

He had hired two men who followed them through the markets with a large trolley, and now they were taking these supplies to the QT.

They went for coffee as Steve said it would take the girls a few hours to load the supplies and put them away. So they chatted in the café and planned their last evening in Casablanca. Janine found a nice-looking Asian restaurant on the internet that sounded good, and as it was attached to a major hotel, she thought *it was bound to be good.*

"Yes," said Steve, "I have heard that it is good, the Fat Noodle; it's attached to the hotel with the casino. It might be busy, but we can book it when we get to the QT, have our bath, play around a little, and then get ready."

They soon headed to the berth at the marina where the girls had moored the yacht, secretly excited by the prospect of 'playing around a little.'

They both pretended to be keen to rejoin the boat but were more excited to spend time in their private bedroom and bath on the yacht. Had it not been for Steve's assignment, they would have spent four days luxuriating on the yacht, sunning on the deck, retreating to their bath, and making love most of the day.

Now they had time to make up.

When they arrived at the QT, Jessie greeted them.

The Captain had been preparing the QT for the next leg of the journey and had sent two of the crew to get some marine supplies. In the galley, Angie and Evelyn were unpacking the stores they had purchased from the markets and walked past them as they went below to their cabin.

Angie smiled at Janine in a way that made Janine think about her little fling with Rachael and wonder what it might be like with Angie.

Steve asked Evelyn to book the restaurant as Jessie stood to the side. She wore her white uniform, and her shorts showed that her legs were strong but feminine.

By the time she got to the cabin, she was already wet with desire, and as she closed and locked the door, she turned to Steve and said, "Bath later, baby, I want you now; I can't wait."

He was a little surprised but did not take long to recover and soon had Janine on the bed, kissing her passionately as he progressively removed her light clothing.

He moved his hand to her Flower and realized she was already very wet. He moved toward her Flower, took her in with his eyes, and breathed her scent deeply. The sound of him inhaling her increased her excitement, and she pushed her hips toward him in a plea for attention to her Flower.

He took her Button in his mouth and began working magic on her.

Janine was writhing by now and had intermittent images of Steve between her legs, between Rachael's legs, and Angie's redhead being between hers. Now and then, she imagined Angie also being there with her and Steve. This fantasy was enough to bring her to orgasm quickly and left Janine wanting more.

Janine asked Steve to fuck her now, telling him that she wanted him on top and to cum inside her.

He mounted her, probing her wetness as she lifted her hips to help accommodate his thickness as he entered.

She gasped as he pushed through, lowered her legs, and placed them as close together as she could with Steve inside her.

He was excited by this position and began to fuck her fast and deep, carefully ensuring he placed most pressure on her Button to maximize her pleasure.

They both reached a climax fast, and as they approached their orgasm, she called him to cum with her.

He could not resist this and increased the pace of his thrusts until he was on the edge of his orgasm but waiting for the signs of hers.

It was soon after her breathing became erratic, and she began to cry out. "Yes, baby, yes, yes, yes."

He let go and came as she did, increasing their pleasure with the knowledge that the other was also cuming.

He was moved by her passion and love for him and held her close to him for a long time. His cock stayed inside her, his semen pooled in her Flower, and his love for her filled the room.

Finally, after about twenty minutes, she said, "Now it's time for our bath, baby."

It was the afternoon, and they were in port, so Steve closed the electronic blinds that closed the view of the bath from passing boats and people on the jetty.

Janine lit some romantic tea candles.

They poured a Verve each and waited for the bath to fill. Steve toasted to their future, and she retorted, "May it be everything we wish it to be."

Finally, the bath filled, and they both settled into the hot water, sighing.

It had been a busy week.

They chatted about the voyage ahead and what they might do at the destinations they were planning to stop. But most of all, they talked of Scotland.

He was uncharacteristically quiet, so she finally asked, "What's wrong, baby?"

"I've been thinking," Steve said, tracing patterns on her skin. "About our future. What you said earlier about it being everything we wish." He hesitated. "But we haven't really talked about what that looks like, have we? What we both want?"

Janine looked away. "I'm not sure what to say." Her voice softened. "This is something we need to decide together. What if you don't want what I want?" She turned back to him, her eyes searching his. "All I know is I see my future with you. After waiting so long to find you again... I can't imagine my life without you in it."

"That much is clear to me," said Steve. "I feel the same way. I ask where from here because I would like us to live together, and as I have retired, I will need to find a base for us to be. We should find a place together rather than live in either of our current homes. Where would you like to live?"

"Are you asking me to live together, or are you asking me to marry you?" she asked.

"Well, it's not very romantic, but if you have me in your life, I would love nothing more than to marry you. I know it is still early, but we have known each other for a long time; I feel we have been together all that time. We could wait for a little, and I could get a ring and propose romantically," Steve replied before adding. "But I was asking where you want to live."

Janine thought for a while and then said, "I guess if you were ever to propose, it would be appropriate to do so in our bath. The ring can wait, but I would like nothing more than to spend the rest of my life with you. You really get me, and we have such a great time together as friends and sexually.

"On where, I'm attracted to living in a cottage somewhere in the south of France, preferably on the Mediterranean coast. But if we could afford it, I would like to keep a small place in Perth so we could go back each year and visit family and friends." she added.

"Sounds perfect to me," Steve said. "We could get a cottage with some extra rooms so we can also have family and friends visit us in France. We could spend most of the Australian winter there and return to Australia in their summer. I want a cottage with black walls and a roof, and we should have a large bath and a huge bed. A four-poster, I think, with lots of erotic photos in our bedroom," he added.

"We can plan this together, and I would have to retire from my work," she said, "buy and create our dream home together. I like the sound of that. It must be near a large town with markets and lots of cafés, a small village with cafés and an artistic community."

Janine was excited about planning their home, and Steve found this endearing.

"We need to get ready for dinner," Steve said reluctantly, not wanting to dampen her enthusiasm. "It's getting late."

They dried off, and Steve took Janine into his arms once more. They were both naked and kissed passionately. He laid Janine back on the bed, taking her Flower into his mouth. It was a passionate moment, and as she came intensely, she cried out to Steve, saying she loved him.

Dinner was full of exciting discussions about the décor of their French home; Steve appeared to agree with her choices of rustic furniture, iron, and old wood, using old items in new ways for furniture. It was a mix of cottage and modern but seemed to please Steve.

The Fat Noodle was an excellent choice; the food was spicy, and they had a romantic and secluded table on the balcony.

He could not be happier, and Janine seemed on a high. Unfortunately, they drank too much, so she suggested they pop into the casino for a look as they left the restaurant.

They purchased $100 in chips and went to the roulette table.

"Just one bet," said Janine, "then we go back to the yacht," she suggested.

"OK," said Steve, "you choose; I'm not a gambler," he added.

Janine chose her birthday and her lucky number and placed the $100 on number nine. The croupier closed the bets as the wheel spun and the little ball circled around the wheel. It seemed to take forever, but eventually, the ball fell into the slots and jumped around before finally settling on number nine.

Janine was excited. "My number won!" she cried. "How much do I win?" she asked.

Steve did not know, but the croupier placed a pile of chips on the table next to her $100 worth of chips. It was a large pile and a different color from hers.

"That's $3,500 plus your original bet, Madame. Would you like to place it on another number this time?" he added.

"Oh my god!" she said, "I had no idea it would be that much. No, thank you," she responded to the croupier, "I will finish on that high," she added as she turned to Steve with a beaming smile.

They cashed in their chips, left the hotel, hailed a cab, and returned to the QT.

They were both laughing and excited about her luck. "I'm sure this is an omen," Steve said. "You and I have been fortunate to find each other again, and we will be good luck to each other. We are going to have a great life together," he added.

"I know," said Janine. "I have known since we first met all those years ago. I'm just so happy you have finally realized it too…"

Walking back to the yacht, their winnings tucked safely away, Janine leaned into Steve's embrace. The unexpected luck felt symbolic somehow—a universe conspiring to bless their union. She'd never considered herself superstitious, yet she couldn't help seeing signs and portents everywhere now, little assurances that they were moving in the right direction. Perhaps that was what love did—made meaning out of coincidence, patterns out of chance.

They arrived back at the QT around ten thirty p.m. to the sound of the crew singing.

One or two had been drinking and were slightly off-key, but they were all enjoying themselves. Steve wondered about their life, crewing such a ship, and whether they had partners or occasionally took lovers while in port. He was clear that they did not take men on board, at least not when he was on board; there was never any sign of that.

Janine wondered the same thing at the same time, but she was considering if they took men or women on board and even wondered if some of the girls were in relationships with each other.

They did not discuss these thoughts with each other. Even though it was late, Janine ran another bath, and they finished an open bottle of Verve they had earlier.

They laughed about her luck at the casino and discussed how she might spend it.

Janine wanted to put it toward the ring, but Steve was adamant that he would manage that.

Finally, they agreed they would save it and put it toward decorating their new home once they found it. Janine was excited and suggested buying one thing from each place they visited. She already had a pashmina from Casablanca, and even though it was clothing, it could decorate their home.

Janine was very happy, and when she was happy, she always became very aroused with Steve.

Her body responded to his lovemaking, but it also responded to her mood, his looks, and his voice. Talking in the bath had become foreplay for her, and she knew that, bath water aside, she was very wet internally and now sitting there looking at her lover.

She wanted his cock inside her. "Let's go to bed, baby; I want you, I want you inside me; let's make love."

He needed no further encouragement; her forthright plea excited him, and as he stood, it was clear it did.

"Looks like I'm not the only one that is eager. Come here, big boy," she said, as she sat up and took his cock into her mouth.

He was not yet fully erect, so she took him into her mouth, running her tongue around it as she did. It was not long before she could no longer hold his entire cock in her mouth as Steve became very hard, thick, and long.

She could not wait.

Janine turned around, presenting her rear to Steve and said, "I want you now, baby, right here in the bath; take me, baby, take me like I know you like it."

She leaned over the bath; their music was playing on the *iPhone* through their portable speaker. A Thousand Years had just started, and this always made Steve feel close to her.

He knelt to meet her, placed his hands around her hips, and his cock probed her wetness without any guidance.

He found her quickly as his cock was firm, erect, and standing tall.

Janine gasped as he entered her. It was easier now, but she still felt his thickness as he entered. It always thrilled her, always made her feel full of him.

"More, baby," she cried, "deeper, baby, god, I love your thick cock inside me."

He pushed deeper inside her and fucked her rhythmically.

Janine was beginning to show signs of her rising orgasm. He loved it when she came with him inside her. It excited him, and now he was also building. He fucked her even firmer and was now committed to giving her an orgasm and cuming inside her. So as he fucked her deeper, he had to ignore the tsunami of water from the bath that was now spilling over the bath wall.

Janine was so in the moment that she also did not notice or did not care.

As she reached the point where she started to cum, Steve's excitement peaked, and he began to cum as well.

Their cries were loud and most likely heard across the Marina, but they were unaware of the world outside their intimate moment.

The bath was still hot, so they sat back and basked in the glow of their love.

He washed her back and massaged her neck and shoulders. Janine was now very relaxed and decided that it was time for bed.

They dried each other, poured their usual orange overnight juice, and climbed into the crisp sheets on their bed.

He cuddled up to Janine and kissed her goodnight.

It was a soft goodnight kiss at first, but soon became passionate, and despite her tiredness, she began wrapping her legs around Steve and pushing her Flower against his hips. Next, he moved his kisses to her breasts and was soon sucking hard and fast on her nipples, taking her entire breast into his mouth.

It was sexy and quick, and she cried out again as she tipped over with a satisfying orgasm.

He now knew the difference between her full orgasms and those that were less intense, so not wanting her to sleep without another full orgasm, he moved his kisses down her stomach until he had positioned himself to give her his special.

This time he started slow, teasing her with his tongue, asking Janine to hold back the hood of her Button so he could touch it directly.

Janine closed her legs this time and found that this helped intensify the sensation as Steve's tongue moved fast across her now engorged and exposed Button.

Again, she built quickly, but this was a different sensation from his usual technique, and she loved it very much.

He was now on his knees at her side so that he could reach her Button with his mouth quickly, and he was so excited by her response that his cock had risen again, and he was pulling it with gusto while he flicked her Button with his tongue.

Janine loved seeing Steve pull his cock, so her orgasm built deeper, and she deliberately exaggerated her moans and cried out. Finally, she was cuming so that Steve's excitement rose.

This trick worked because as she exploded into an intense orgasm, Steve came also. As he came, he sat upright, and his cum spurted over her stomach and Flower.

Janine spread his cum over her stomach and rubbed it in her Flower as her orgasm settled. They cuddled again, but this time they were satisfied and soon fell asleep together, both thinking about their love, the life ahead, and the voyage they would start at first light the following day.

merged

They awoke to the swaying of the yacht. It was early in the morning, and from the porthole, they could see the sun rising across the silhouetted buildings of Casablanca as they sailed parallel to the shoreline.

They were now about 300 meters off the coast and were heading north along the coast of Africa. It was a magnificent sunrise, reddened by the desert dust and seemed to foreshadow a new dawn in their lives.

Steve had emailed his boss and was now retired. Janine also emailed the school where she worked that she had now retired, and they were on a yacht heading north to Scotland.

They had decided to find a new home and live together.

He thought about the time they lived together in the past, how young they were, and how he had not appreciated that the young girl he knew then would become such a beautiful woman and a strong force in his life.

While he understood from the moment they met on the train in the US that this was what he wanted, in the quiet of this morning, he knew at that moment that this was their destiny.

He was very content.

Janine lay there on the bed, watching the expression on Steve's face as he was deep in thought. He was not even aware she was watching him.

She knew he was deep in thought and wondered what he was thinking. Janine did not doubt that he loved her, that much she could tell; it was written across his face every time he looked at her.

She was worried about how he was now feeling about the discussion they had just had about making a life together.

Janine was in no doubt about how she felt; she loved him deeply and had wanted this all her life.

Certainly, she had gone on with her life, even loved others, but he was always there, like a missing part of her, so whenever she felt something was missing, her familiar feeling for him kept bubbling to the surface. It was true love, but it was a curse without him.

Now she was on the verge of a new life with him, complete and with a fantastic sex life.

She was content.

Janine was only worried about him, what he felt. She even wondered if he was the same man she had known so long ago. He looked like him and had his memories and family, but he was very different. This Steve was attentive, committed, generous, and most of all, he loved her.

Yet, the Steve she knew in the past was not committed and certainly not generous with his love; he had hurt her and fooled around with other girls while living with her.

Yes, they were not in a 'relationship' as such, but he must have known that she loved him and that it hurt her to see him with others.

Janine could not imagine this Steve ever hurting her.

Had she gotten this wrong? Was he still really the same but deceiving her with his charm?

Steve's words about dedication echoed in her mind as she watched the coastline drift by. She'd spent so long searching for him, yet now that she had him, a part of her still held back—still feared that opening completely would leave her defenseless. Old habits of self-protection warred with the undeniable truth that she had never felt more at home than in his arms. Was she brave enough to believe this could last beyond their journey?

Doubt started to creep into her mind. Could she trust him with her heart? She had to know and discuss this, or it would poison her love for him.

They were having their morning bath when she raised it.

Steve had been a little surprised when she jumped up from the bed and put the bath on. They usually fooled around a bit first; she loved her morning special, and so did he. He had dismissed this as her enthusiasm to greet such a beautiful day.

"OK," she said, "I have to ask you some questions before we go any further with this."

"All right, my love," Steve said nervously, "ask away."

"When we were together in the past when we lived together, you never really seemed to be that much into me; what's changed now that you are so much in love with me? You do realize you broke my heart, don't you," she added, not planning to add that to the discussion, so she wondered if she had really forgiven him for hurting her.

"I do now," Steve replied. "I don't know what to say, baby, other than I'm truly sorry, sorrier than you could ever know. I was very young when I first married, and she broke my heart.

"I now realize that that love was not real love, but at the time, it hurt deeply, and the only way I could cope was to deny love existed, to deny my feelings—I did that through sex and by not getting close to anyone. You were the only one I liked at the time, you were a real friend to me, and that's why I asked you to share a house with me, but because I was still hiding from love, I pushed you away. I'm sorry, baby, for you and me. That was the biggest mistake of my life. I did not even know you loved me; you never said, baby."

"How could I, you were Mr. Cool, and I was only seventeen; I never dreamed you would love me back, so what was the point," she said.

He considered this carefully for a while and said, "Baby, I never understood then, but you must believe I now love you more than I ever believed possible. You have healed my heart and opened me to love once again. You have given me the greatest gift I could ever want or deserve. If you could find it in your heart to trust me again, I promise. I will never hurt you again. I'm what you see today because of you, and I will dedicate myself to your happiness."

Steve's sincerity moved Janine, and although she never consciously thought she had never needed to, it was then that Janine finally forgave the boy she had fallen in love with and accepted that here was the man she loved.

Yes, he was different. She was right about that, but it was because he was no longer the boy who had broken her heart; he had become the man that had healed it again. *So now,* she thought, *I can fully trust him again and surrender my heart to him once again, safe in the knowledge he will care for me, my love, our love until the end of time.*

Their lovemaking after the bath was particularly passionate as she opened up to Steve totally; they spent a little time making up for the missed early morning special with two glorious orgasms brought on by Steve's tongue flicking against her Button as his lips held it firmly in place.

Janine was so wet when he entered her that she did not need any play lube. They were so fixed on each other that their build-up to orgasm was almost identical, and they came together without even thinking about it.

It was about fifteen minutes later, as they lay in the bed enjoying the afterglow of their orgasm, when there was a knock on the door, and a voice called out. "If you two have finished in there, breakfast is ready."

It was Nellie, as she was on galley duty, and it was clear they could all hear their vocal session.

They ate breakfast and drank two glasses of orange juice each to ensure they rehydrated themselves. It was still summer here, and despite the sea breeze, it was hot, and they had expended quite a bit of energy during their lovemaking.

The morning went quickly; the QT sailed swiftly up the coast with a full spinnaker. The sea was calm, and they made good time. Janine was very pleased, as she was uncomfortable with open sea sailing.

She watched the crew handle the yacht as she sunned herself on the deck with Steve. Now and then, Steve would get up and assist in resetting the spinnaker as they tacked up the coast. She could see the coastline of Morocco as they sailed parallel to it, which was also reassuring for Janine. She was not looking forward to being in the open sea with no land in sight.

He seemed to understand her thoughts because as she sat there watching the coastline, Steve said, "This crew is one of the most experienced yachting crews in the world;

they have sailed every ocean, around the Cape of Good Hope, and have come second in the Sydney to Hobart Yacht race three times.

"So we are in very safe hands," he added.

"Is it that obvious?" she asked.

Steve responded, "It's not uncommon for people to feel insecure on a yacht. The large sail gives you the feeling that the yacht could tip over, and that is scary, but this yacht has a sizable winged keel underneath. It would take a hurricane to tip her, and none are forecast. Furthermore, we have a large engine, and as we will always be no more than a hundred kilometers from the coast, we could motor to land if we lost our sails."

Janine seemed to relax after this explanation and started moving around the deck a bit more. She was slowly getting her sailing legs.

Lunch on the deck was a light Moroccan salad with chickpeas and spices. "They are not only good sailors," she remarked to Steve, "they are pretty good cooks as well."

"Yes," said Steve, "it's not easy cooking on a yacht. It takes much skill to choose the right foods, store them well, and then throw them together in a galley that keeps moving, but they have mastered the art of yacht cooking."

They were inseparable all day, sunning on the deck. He put sun cream on her back, and she did likewise. They chatted continually, talking about house décor, what he liked, what she liked, and how they wanted a big black bath in their house. The bedroom would be a focal point in their home, and the kitchen would be well-appointed. They both loved food and enjoyed cooking.

"I wonder if we could cook a meal together on the yacht," Steve asked her rhetorically. "It might be fun," he added. "I will ask Jessie."

Janine looked forward to spending time in the kitchen with Steve in their new home and even fantasized about how many ways they might make love in their large kitchen. She imagined cooking in her apron with nothing else on, and Steve helping her, not knowing she was naked under the apron.

In this fantasy, Steve would be talking to her when she would reveal her bare ass as she turned around and reached up for the salt in the top cupboard. Then, Steve would approach her, dropping his trousers and taking her then and there as she leaned across the countertop.

Her fantasies were getting her wet and very horny, so finally, she said, "I'm getting hot (she was not lying), so I'm going to have a cool bath. Do you want to join me?"

They had bathed together since they met, so Steve was not about to stop now.

They moved to their cabin, and Steve poured a glass of Verve while she ran the bath. They toasted to their new life together. Janine was very thirsty, so the glass of champagne went down quickly, and Steve poured another.

They bathed and talked more, and another glass of champagne disappeared. Steve was on his second, and as usual, when he had his naked lover in front of him in the bath, he was visibly aroused.

Janine was admiring his erection and getting quite impatient to get to bed, so she stepped out of the bath and dried off quickly. She slipped into an emerald-green lacy bra, matching panties, and a pair of high heels.

Then she seductively posed herself in the comfy chair in the corner of their cabin—legs draped up along the side wall, a glass of Veuve in hand.

When Steve finally walked in, she purred, "Come here, big boy. I want you—and I want you now."

He was firm as he walked across the room to the vixen before him. Here was his lover, the sultry Janine, who was into role-play and spicing up their sex with little surprises like this. It was very hot, and by the time he reached her across the room, he was rock hard and standing to attention, ready to do his lover's bidding.

"Well, lover boy, Mr. Sex on Legs, do you like what you see? Do you think you can handle it?" she said in her sexiest voice.

"Does he look as if he can handle you?" He responded, brandishing his huge, thick, and very firm cock in his hand and waving it at her. "I eat vixens like you for breakfast," he added.

"Well, go right ahead," she demanded, "eat me."

He looked at the vixen in front of him; his eyes cast across her entire body, taking her in with looks that showed his pure desire for her body. He held back, staring at her half-naked body, then focused his stare on her Flower, her womanhood, that opened up to him as she sat with one leg on the wall and the other on the arm of the chair, wide open and inviting.

She was glistening in the light, highlighting just how wet she was, and Steve noticed that drops of her nectar had escaped and were flowing down the space between her vagina and her anus, her Ani, as they called her.

He knew that taking her womanhood fully with his eyes turned her on, but if he needed any confirmation, it came from the additional flow of her nectar that was now trickling down past Ani.

He hardened even more and knelt before her, his body between her thighs and leaned forward and breathed in her essence.

Janine visibly heaved from the excitement; she was trying to play it cool, appear indifferent, and hard to get despite having her Flower open to him, but she could not hide her arousal when Steve breathed her in.

He loved her smell, her womanhood, as it filled his nose, and her pheromones rushed in to play havoc with his senses.

He firmed even more.

Now Steve moved closer and slowly used his lips to kiss and tease his lover. He held back his tongue while he used his lips to grasp her Button and tug it gently.

Janine moved her hips and pushed toward him. She was not going to beg this time.

He now took his tongue and teased her more, using it at the entrance of her Flower, tasting her nectar slowly and deliberately. He savored her juices as his tongue rolled around the edges of her Flower's opening.

His cock thickened even more.

Finally, he moved up and engulfed her Button with his mouth and started to flick her now engorged Button with his tongue before taking it entirely in his mouth and sucking her orgasm from her very being.

It did not take long as she was almost there before he even touched her, but then the suction and the flicking took her over the edge as she came explosively, writhing and screaming as she did.

He lay his head on her tummy as she slowly bathed in the glow and recovered from its intensity. It was not long before she was ready again. "I want that cock, baby, fuck me and fuck me firmly," she pleaded. With her legs wide open, Steve moved onto his knees and quickly found the wet and welcoming entrance to her Flower.

He was firm and thick now, so he took her slowly, easing his manhood into her and pausing at the point he knew Flower would resist.

"Now," she cried, "fill me, baby, fill me with your thick cock."

She gasped as he filled her, plunging deep after he punched past his thickness.

"Oh god, you feel good," Steve cried as he did, resisting all temptation to fuck her fast and cum immediately.

It was like that at those first moments.

The foreplay they engaged in was often so intense that Steve could enter her and explode in orgasm, but she needed him; she needed his thickness and length to fill her and bring her to her climax.

Then he did, as he plunged deep inside her and fucked her fast.

She built quickly, begging Steve to cum with her; he was close and crying out and knew he was ready, but he also knew that she would want more of him, so he let her believe he was about to cum and held back.

She did not hold back as she cried, "I'm cuming baby, oh god, I'm cuming, fill me, fill me with your cock."

Janine tipped over into another explosive orgasm.

She was horny and hot tonight, a little drunk and very relaxed, so her orgasms came strong and fast.

Janine realized that Steve had not cum with her, and while a little disappointed, this soon changed to gratitude, as she understood she could have him inside her again.

He had withdrawn and was now touching her Flower with his fingers.

Janine, as she often felt after orgasm, intertwined their fingers, their tips wet from her juices. They had the play lube handy, but they hadn't needed it so far. Her juices were abundant; she was wet all over her Flower and oozing down over her Ani.

He started to touch Janine around her perineum; she liked this and showed it with a gentle moan and movement in her hips. As he got closer to her Ani, she writhed a little, and Steve took the cue that she was up for a little finger play.

He circled her Ani with his finger, teasing her with gentle pushes but no penetration. He did this several times before he knew she could stand it no more, then gently slipped his finger in deep and stimulated her inside.

Janine moaned and started to rub her Button. He was still on his knees, and his cock was hard; he began to probe her Flower while stimulating her with his finger deep inside her. Janine could see his cock standing firm waiting to penetrate her when she said, "No, baby, I want you inside me."

He was puzzled and said, "I'm almost in, baby; what do you mean no?"

"No," she said, "not your finger. I want him inside me, to fill Ani, but please go slow, you are big, and I'm not sure I can take you."

He was surprised and asked her if she was sure. "I know I want it, that's for sure; I'm just not sure I can accommodate him," she replied. "Use plenty of lube, baby." she added.

He used lots of lube on himself and his fingers and filled her with the lube using one finger and then two. Janine was surprisingly relaxed, so then he started to probe her entrance with his erect cock.

He pushed in slowly.

Janine quivered as he entered her but signaled, "More baby, keep going."

It was then that he fully penetrated her, for as he passed his thickness, his cock slid in effortlessly.

Janine moaned softly as he did and cried out, "Oh god, that feels amazing, so sexy baby, so hot; I feel so open to you, my love."

He was tentative at first, but the sensation of her Ani grasping the shaft of his cock was too much; he started to move in and out as her tight butt caressed his cock with the motion.

Janine was building.

She was surprised by this and cried out for Steve to move faster and deeper and then cried out for him to "fuck her hard, to fuck her up the butt."

She was getting off on the sensation but also the dirty talk, and so was Steve.

"Oh god," cried Steve. "I'm going to cum, baby," he yelled.

"Yes, fuck me, baby, fill my butt, baby," she cried with him. "I'm cuming, baby; fill me with your semen."

This time they came together, both writhing with the pleasure of their orgasms and with the erotic and intimate nature of their pleasure.

He stayed in her as they settled, his thickness reducing as he rested, still glowing from his release. Then, finally, she looked at Steve and said, "I thought that would be impossible, but it was so sexy, baby, I loved it, and I have never had anyone cum in me like that."

"No, thank you, baby," said Steve. "I would never have asked you to do that, but you need to know that this was also the first time I have ever had sex like that."

Janine was amazed; Steve had been so sexually active that it never occurred to her that he would be an anal virgin.

She told Steve that she was honored to be his first and pleased that she could introduce him to a new experience.

He finally said, "Baby, I'm the one who should feel honored," he said, his voice low. "That you would trust me like that... " He shook his head, at a loss for words. "And to be my first—" He pulled her closer. "It means everything. What we just shared—it's a gift. To both of us."

Soaking in their bath later, she smiled at the memory of their mutual surprise. There was something profound about discovering new pleasures together, about being equally inexperienced in certain territories. It balanced the occasional intimidation she felt at Steve's worldliness in other areas. They were writing their own story together, creating experiences that belonged solely to them.

inquisitive

They tracked further up the African coast that day, making their way to Bordeaux in France, and it would take about three days in total, two and a half if the winds were favorable.

Between passionate sex, baths, and meals, they spent their time during the day sunning themselves on the deck, playing cards, and occasionally engaging in a little game they played from time to time.

It was a confronting game at times because it required absolute truth, and each took turns being an Inquisitor.

It went like this:

The Inquisitor would ask a question, and the other had to answer with a simple YES or NO.

It seemed easy for the person asking the questions, but if the other could not truthfully answer yes or no, they could say NEITHER.

Phrasing the question was critical.

The person responding could also have a hard time because sometimes the answer required a qualification, but they were not allowed to do so.

It also required absolute honesty. They were entitled to only ten questions each and no more, and they could only play once a week.

Steve started as the Inquisitor, and the first question was simple.

"Do you love me?" Steve asked.

"YES," was Janine's reply.

And from there, it continued…

"Have you always loved me?"

"NO," she responded.

Not the reply he expected, but Steve realized that 'always' predated even their first meeting.

"Did you love me from the very first time we met?"

"NO."

"Did you love me when we lived together all those years ago?"

"YES."

Now he was getting the hang of this.

"Did you continue to love me while we were apart all those years?"

"YES."

"Do you believe you will always love me?"

"YES."

Steve smiled.

"Do you believe I love you?"

"YES."

"Do you want to live with me?"

"YES."

"Do you believe I want to live with you?"

"YES."

And finally, just to be absolutely sure, Steve asked.

"Is my cock the largest you have ever had?"

Janine laughed and played with him, looking like she had to think and even used her hands to 'estimate' the sizes of imaginary past cocks in her mind's eye.

Why are men so obsessed with size? Of all her lovers, very few were too small, she thought, *but many failed to satisfy her because of their poor anatomical knowledge, technique, or indifference to her needs. Size was never the issue, but when they had all three—WOW.*

He was looking a bit deflated at her long pause, so she finally said "YES."

Now he grinned.

It was her turn now, and she thought hard.

She felt Steve's questions were good, but he was not as careful as he should have been, for he had asked her questions from which she could deduce information. He should have waited and let her ask if he wanted to live with her, if he loved her. He had wasted some of his turns!

She thought she would start with some basics.

"Have you ever made love to two women at the same time?"

"NO." Steve grimaced, color rising to his cheeks.

Interesting, she thought, enjoying his discomfort. *There's a story there.*

"What about with another man and a woman?" she pressed.

"NO." His shoulders relaxed slightly—he wasn't nearly as bothered by that question.

Telling, she thought. *Very telling.*

"Have you ever fucked anyone up the butt before?"

"NO."

OK, she thought, *he was honest about his anal virginity.*

"Have you ever had sex in a plane?"

"NO."

That answer surprised her; she was sure that with his track record and travels, he must have managed that sometime. *Well, that's one more I can give him as a first,* she thought. She then worried he might ask her the same question and was not sure how he would cope with her answer.

"Before we did, had you ever made love on a train before?"

"YES."

Well, she thought, *he was playing the game honestly*, not really loving his answer.

"Did you consider me as a girlfriend when we were first together?"

"YES."

This was not the reply she expected, and she thought carefully about how to pump him for more information.

"As a boyfriend/girlfriend?"

"YES."

"As lovers?" she asked quickly.

"YES."

Damn, she thought, *that's obvious; they were friends and lovers. But, of course, I knew that already, so that did not help. Now I have wasted a few questions. I will have to explore that further in our bath conversation.*

She decided on a different tack.

"Do you want to live with me?"

"YES."

Good, she thought.

"Do you think that we will be together forever?"

"NEITHER," Steve responded without hesitation.

Janine was shocked. *He seemed so sure of their relationship. So why was he not able to answer yes?* She pondered.

"Are you not sure about us, baby?" she asked.

"That's the eleventh question," Steve replied.

Janine was now worried; she had a week to wait and wanted answers.

They had dinner early that night, and Janine was quiet; Steve seemed content to let this lie, and she started to get cross and very concerned. Then, finally, she bit her tongue and said nothing but was not about to let this go on.

They ran a bath after dinner, and after some general banter about what they would do in Bordeaux, she finally burst out—"What do you mean you don't know if we will be together forever? I thought you loved me; our song is a 1,000 years!"

He looked shocked; it had not occurred to him that she would take his answer this way or be so upset.

"Sweetheart," he began with conviction, "you asked me if I think we will be together forever; I could not answer NO because I believe that I want to be with you forever, but I could not answer YES because I cannot speak for you. It will take both of us to last forever, and if you decide you don't want this, then it cannot. So I had no choice but to answer NEITHER because it is not all up to me. If it were, it would be a resounding YES."

Janine's expression changed instantly. "Oh baby," she said, "of course, I believe it will; you are the love of my life. I have always wanted this, and I don't intend to let you go."

Janine smiled; she smiled a beaming smile that lit up her eyes and her face.

"There is my Janine," Steve said. "That's the happy girl I have come to love."

As he said this, his eyes welled up with tears. "You are so beautiful when you smile, my love; it brings joy to my heart."

"Oh my baby," she said, clasping Steve's head in her hands. "Nobody has ever cried tears of joy for me; that is so sweet," and all her anger and concern melted away as she loved him more than ever.

It was late afternoon on the second day, and they were below deck again. They just had a bath and were relaxing after making out in bed. Janine had just experienced her first orgasm for the afternoon when they heard the loud crack from above. Steve jumped up from instinct and told Janine to stay there while he checked what had happened.

He was in protective mode.

Pirates were rare on this side of the African continent, but he was taking no chances. He did not tell Janine this; he would not have wanted her worried.

He headed up on deck to find all the crew above around the central mast.

"We have broken the main boom," said Captain Jessie. "Fortunately, the main mast is intact, and we have not damaged the sails, but we cannot sail her until it's fixed. I will have to radio our company headquarters, and they can suggest the nearest port where we can get the boom replaced or repaired," she added.

When Steve returned to Janine, they had turned the diesel motors on, so she knew something was wrong. He explained the situation and reassured her that it was just a temporary setback, that Jessie was in contact with her company, and that they would fix it as soon as possible.

Jessie knocked on their door after about thirty minutes and informed them that they could schedule repairs in Lisbon, Portugal. It was approximately 100 kilometers away. With their dual motor and front sail, they should be able to reach Lisbon overnight and arrive at the marine repair shop when it opens. With their assistance and the crew's help, they should be able to leave the following day around lunchtime.

There was not much else to do, so they did what they knew best, resumed their lovemaking, and retired early for some much-needed rest and sleep.

They woke early and, after their usual morning delight and a bath, took breakfast on the deck as the sun rose across the landmass that was now getting closer.

Jessie was spot on. They were now only twenty kilometers from docking in Lisbon, and she had already lined up the repair shop to meet them at the marina to dismantle the boom, take it to the repair shop, and fit the rigging to the new bare boom that would replace the broken one.

The repairs would take most of the day as they refitted the boom and tested the yacht.

As they watched the crew work on preparation for the repairs, Steve's arm settled around her shoulders—a casual claiming that felt both protective and possessive.

She leaned into him, realizing how quickly they'd established their own silent language of touch and presence. This unexpected delay didn't feel like an interruption to their journey, but simply another opportunity to discover each other in a new context. With him, even setbacks became adventures.

Jessie suggested that Steve and Janine spend the day on shore and return late that afternoon.

Lisbon was not a city they would have chosen to visit, but as the opportunity presented itself, they decided to explore the shopping area and some of the older buildings.

They decided to have lunch in the city to savor traditional Portuguese cuisine. Janine had heard that Lisbon was renowned for its linen, gloves, and handmade luggage, and that the prices were remarkably low compared to European standards. Consequently, some shopping was also on their agenda.

They took a taxi from the marina.

It was different from the standard of the cars they usually took lately, but it was fun as it was an old French Citroën.

The driver was pleasant, adept at weaving through the chaotic traffic, and proud of his city. He pointed out every interesting building on the way, told them where to have lunch, and gave them a potted history of Lisbon from the 1700s to today.

He was fluent in English and talked very fast.

Steve arranged for him to pick them up from the café, where he suggested they have lunch and take them to a few historic buildings and churches.

He was effusive in his thanks when Steve tipped him twice the fare for their twenty-minute ride.

He had dropped them at the traditional craft shops in Baixa and the old area of Lisbon with ornate façades. The same families had owned some of the shops for over 300 years.

There were haberdasheries, fabric stores, and a few leather stores that had handmade luggage their families had produced for many generations. Janine was not keen on the embroidered linen but purchased a small number of linen table napkins as a gift for an older woman at her now former workplace.

The handmade luggage attracted her the most, and she bought a beautiful, small overnight suitcase with stunning brass fittings.

She thought it would make a perfect home for her favorite printed photos and letters. They were currently home in a cardboard box, and she was constantly worried about potential damage. Most important were her letters from Steve when he first left her and moved to Melbourne. She had kept them all this time as they were some of her favorite possessions. In the meantime, she could use it as an overnight case as they took short trips from the yacht.

They lunched at the café and enjoyed a traditional Portuguese stew, but both were not impressed by its stodginess, even though the chili gave it a fiery flavor. The driver arrived on time and greeted them like a long-lost relative.

They spent the afternoon with their private tour guide and driver, providing a fascinating and sometimes amusing narrative about each building they stopped to explore. It was almost as if he had lived in every building for the last 300 years. Their driver knew every character that had ever inhabited the building and every secret intrigue in which they were involved.

Janine sometimes wondered if he just made it up but did not even care if he did. It made for great entertainment as they 'toured' the city.

It was five p.m. when they finally returned to the marina, and after saying almost tearful farewells to their driver Jaspeh, they left him waving to them on the dock with more than a month's usual takings in this pocket.

Jessie was cleaning up when they arrived at the QT; the crew had fixed and tested the boom, and all was in order. The crew had been working all day non-stop, and Jessie explained that she and the crew would take the night off to relax in town. She explained that the girls generally hit the city hard and would leave in the afternoon the next day as they likely would not return until late the next morning.

Angie had drawn the short straw and would stay on the boat, provide the security, prepare and serve their dinner, and tend to their needs as required.

Janine cheekily wondered what *needs* they would *desire* from Angie before going down below to run a much-needed bath.

three

It was getting colder as they traveled north, and winter was well underway in England and Scotland. They would be in Bath in England by Christmas if they stayed on schedule. It would be her first white Christmas, and she was looking forward to the atmosphere, if not the cold.

The bath was hot, and they sat soaking in the bath, laughing about their driver's stories that afternoon. They agreed that he had been the one redeeming feature of an otherwise average city.

They dried off and spent a little time in bed relaxing and fooling around, mimicking their driver by telling weird stories about the boat and the secret events in their cabin over the years.

Most of their stories involved some sexual component, ranging from secret meetings between illicit lovers to full-blown orgies involving multiple partners. Each story got more erotic, and soon Steve was nestled between her thighs, bringing her to a stunning orgasm with one of his specials. He was hard and thick by then, and he wanted Janine, and she, in turn, wanted his cock inside her.

As they were about to satisfy that desire, there was a call from the lounge room.

"Dinner is served, you two; it's hot, so don't let it get cold," it called.

Angie was serving their dinner, and her call was so adamant that they both felt they should postpone their desire to have dinner while it was hot.

"It would be rude to ruin the food she has made for us," Janine said, somewhat torn between good manners and her lust for her lover. Reluctantly, they put on their dressing gowns and moved to the lounge dining area, where Angie had left their food before returning to the galley.

The food was good, and they realized they were both quite hungry.

It was easy to forget about their other daily desires when they were so into each other. So even though their lovemaking had been interrupted, they were pleased to have taken this break, as it would restock their energy.

Angie had chosen the wine and had left a lovely bottle of Pinot Noir, and by the time they had finished their meal, they both had two glasses each.

They had moved to the sizable modular couch opposite the dining table with their wine. They were starting to get flirty, and Steve had his hand inside Janine's dressing gown, caressing her nipples.

Janine was beginning to rouse again and was getting wet. She soon explored his dressing gown, looking to see if Steve was responding to her flirtations. He was. He responded with his hand probing her wetness under her gown.

Suddenly Angie appeared at the door to ask them if they would like dessert. They jumped apart and were a little embarrassed, but Angie took it in her stride. Angie made no attempt to hide the fact she had seen what they were doing and smiled and said wryly that she suspected they might still be a little hungry.

She had prepared a caramel soufflé and served them in small dishes with hearts.

"They say that soufflé is the dessert for lovers," Angie said, casting a knowing smile in Janine's direction.

"Perhaps you should join us then," said Janine, "Do you have more of this Pinot? You could get another bottle, a glass, and a bowl for some soufflé."

"Sure I can," she replied, "I will be back in a few minutes."

Steve noticed Janine smiling and admiring Angie as she left. Then, he smiled and said, "Are you flirting with the crew?"

"I might be," she responded, "At any rate, she is on her own tonight, and it would be cruel for her to be sitting alone listening to the sound of us fucking all evening; inviting her to join us seemed the right thing to do," she added.

"Oh, I don't mind," said Steve, "If you would like to have her company this evening, I would be pleased as well."

Angie was back at the door before Janine could respond. She had a bottle of wine, a glass, and a bowl for her dessert.

Angie poured them all, another glass, and sat on the couch next to Janine.

Although Steve did not even notice, Janine noted that she had brushed her hair and changed her top. It was sheerer, and through the material, Janine could see her firm nipples. She was not wearing her bra now and had also applied some lipstick.

Mmmmm, thought Janine, *this could get very interesting tonight.*

Janine was not sure how she felt about what was to emerge that evening; she certainly felt that Angie was hot and attractive and would possibly enjoy a bit of fun with her. Still, she was unsure about being in a threesome with her lover sharing in the action.

Janine was a little drunk, so she let the evening roll where it would.

Angie had never shown any interest in Steve, so she figured her focus would likely be on her. Finally, Janine thought, *I could get thoroughly spoilt tonight,* and settled in to enjoy the evening.

Janine asked Angie how she got into sailing, and Angie explained how her father sailed regularly. She had been on sailing boats since she was six, and when her father died when she was 23, she inherited his yacht and some money. It was a thirty-five-footer, and she renovated the yacht with the money she inherited and started entering races.

Angie had worked as a marine biologist after finishing university, which had always kept her close to the sea. Her skills with boats and qualifications had earned her the front-running on research expeditions around the world, so she had also been able to travel. So when Jessie decided to start an all-female yacht charter, she was among the first chosen for the crew.

They talked about Steve and Janine's earlier relationship and how they had reunited after all those years, and Angie commented that it was so romantic. She also said that from what the girls could hear on the yacht day and night, it certainly was a passionate relationship, then admitted it had made her somewhat envious, given she had been celibate for four months.

"There's not much opportunity when you work on the QT," she said. "The others seem to manage to find one-night stands when in port, but I'm not keen on meeting total strangers in random ports for sexual liaisons like that. I prefer to choose my partners carefully, even if it is not for a committed relationship.

"There are always opportunities for a bit of fun, but I prefer *quality* to quantity any day, and I know quality when I see it," she added and smiled very deliberately at Janine as she emphasized the word *quality*.

Janine's Flower twinged, and she looked at Steve to see if he had picked up Angie's clear signal. He was close to Janine, and as she looked at him, he placed his hand on her leg, discretely moving her dressing gown aside to reveal more of her legs.

He's showing me off to Angie, Janine thought; *he certainly had gotten the cues, and he was enjoying this.*

They had finished the second bottle of Pinot, so Angie offered to get another.

Steve jumped up, insisted that he could get the wine this time, and headed down to the galley.

Very clever Steve, thought Janine. *It was now or never.*

Janine turned to Angie, who was now quite close to her on the couch, and warned her, "If I have any more wine, I won't be responsible for what happens."

Angie looked straight at her, placed her hand on Janine's bare leg, and replied, "What happens will happen, no complications, let's just have a bit of fun."

Angie then leaned in and kissed Janine softly on her lips while moving her hand slowly up the inside of Janine's thigh.

Janine's Flower twinged again, and she felt her wetness rising.

Steve returned with the wine, having taken too long for what should have been a quick trip to the galley, making it evident to both girls that he was giving them time to get 'acquainted.'

They certainly did because when he returned, they were embracing on the couch, still dressed but enjoying each other's presence.

"Hope I'm not interrupting," Steve said, keen to ensure that Angie expected that he would be with them for her intimate moments with his lover.

"Just warming up," said Angie, eager to get her intentions out in the open. "What took you so long? We have missed you," she said, quite pointedly.

All was clear now, and the fun was beginning.

As Steve sat down and poured the wine, Angie began to kiss Janine more passionately, and Steve felt his cock rising rapidly.

He had seen this in movies, even the occasional porn flick, and had discretely observed a lesbian couple kissing passionately in the park one day, but he had never been in a threesome.

Even though he was currently a passive participant, he found the idea quite exciting. The anticipation enhanced his arousal.

He placed his hands on Janine's other thigh, carefully ensuring his focus was on her as Angie started to open the top of Janine's dressing gown to reveal her pert breasts and now erect nipples.

Game on, thought Janine.

Angie reached over to caress Janine's breasts, and Janine sighed at her touch.

Despite her hard work sailing, Angie had managed to keep her hands soft.

Janine's nipples stiffened as Angie touched them, and she glanced over at Steve to see his reaction.

"Oh, he's enjoying this, don't worry about that," Angie said, smiling at Steve.

"We'll put on a good show for your lover."

With that, Angie moved from the couch to the floor in front of Janine and, in one swift movement, removed her top, revealing her tanned body and firm breasts.

They were larger than Janine's, and her nipples were wider but nowhere near as long as Janine's.

She cradled herself between Janine's legs, still focused on her breasts, and leaned forward to suck Janine's nipples.

Janine, in turn, placed her arm around Angie's back and shoulders and caressed her gently.

Janine was now getting very wet with the attention her breasts were receiving, but she was also getting hot at watching Steve next to her.

The two of them caressing each other transfixed Steve, as Angie moved up to Janine and took her firm breasts into her mouth. He started to writhe in his seat next to them. Janine knew this meant he was also hot and sporting a firm, thick erection under his dressing gown.

Janine's gown had now disappeared from her shoulders and arms, and she was naked on the couch. They were taking turns sucking each other's nipples, kissing occasionally, and caressing each other's arms, shoulders, and backs.

Then, finally, Angie stood up and slowly, seductively dropped her pants, revealing a pair of dark blue lace panties. She stepped out of her trousers and slowly lowered her panties, revealing the bare pubis.

Janine smiled and said, "Snap, we have the same style down there."

"Can't stand hair there," Angie replied, "now where were we?"

Janine thought it was time to initiate some action and asked Angie to sit on the couch as she moved to the floor and between her legs.

She started at Angie's breasts first and then kissed her slowly. Janine made a point of rubbing her breasts against Angie's breasts. Angie clearly liked it as she began to moan and writhe her hips. Next, Janine slowly worked her kisses from Angie's lips down her neck, lingered on her left breast before moving down her stomach and paused to feel her soft bare Brazilian mound.

By this stage, Angie was practically crawling up the couch, trying to move her hips to position Janine exactly where she desperately wanted her.

He watched on, curious to watch how his lover would pleasure Angie. He still had images of her pleasuring Rachael, but these were only in his imagination. Here it was live and happening now. His cock was bursting from the excitement, and it took all his strength not to intervene and join them right now.

He understood he should wait.

They would get to him in good time.

Janine began by caressing Angie's labial lips with kisses. Gradually, Janine moved on to tasting her with her tongue. Then, she enveloped Angie in her mouth and used her tongue to stimulate the opening of her vagina. Strategically, Janine held back on her clitoris, teasing

Angie while simultaneously enjoying the obvious wetness of her womanhood.

Angie was getting frustrated and started to rub her clitoris with her fingers, so Janine moved Angie's hand back and circled her clit with her tongue.

Angie writhed and moaned very loudly.

Next, Janine started to flick her tongue across Angie's clit faster, and this increased Angie's breathing rate as she built her orgasm.

He almost wanted to coach Janine and tell her to use the special now, but he resisted the temptation. Janine was a capable woman and he now knew she had experience with another woman.

As Angie built, Janine engulfed her clit, started to suck, and firmly flicked Angie's clit with her tongue. That was just enough as Angie heaved, screamed out, and moaned audibly as she came with a shudder that lasted twenty seconds.

Janine tried to continue, but Angie could not take the sensation so soon after cuming.

Angie needed to subside.

Steve had almost forgotten that most women could not stand touch on their clit just after an orgasm. He had gotten used to Janine's ability to cum immediately, one after the other, and the fact that she often wanted stimulation immediately after she came. It was another thing he loved about their lovemaking.

Finally, Angie settled as Janine stoked her gently across the breast.

As Angie recovered, Janine moved closer to Steve and kissed him.He could taste and smell Angie's womanhood on Janine, and this aroused him even more.

Janine had her hand under his dressing gown and stroked his erect cock. She seemed not to want to bring him into their action yet and keep him all to herself.

Steve was building the sexual tension inside him and could have cum with little effort. Janine seemed to understand this and stopped teasing him. She had no intention of taking him there.

Yet!

Janine decided it was now time for her to get some attention and to get it from both of them. She moved to the couch and lay down lengthwise as Angie moved to the other end where she could lie between her legs. Janine placed one leg on the edge of the couch and the other over the back, so she was open for Angie.

Steve had now moved to the floor beside Janine and kissed her. He was kissing her passionately when she jumped just as Angie settled her tongue on her Button. She had been surprised by the sudden sensation from her Button when her lover was kissing her.

It was an unexpected but lovely surprise.

Steve understood she needed to breathe deeper with all this stimulation on her Flower and Button, so he stopped kissing her on the lips and moved to her breasts.

Steve could see what Angie was doing from this vantage point, and the image aroused him. He still had his dressing gown on, and he could feel his erect cock pushing on the material, trying to break free to join the party.

Later, Steve told himself in his thoughts, *not yet; bide your* time. He started to suck on Janine's nipples slowly at first.

Janine loved his breast plays, but a breast play and oral sex at the same time? This *was going to be good*, she thought.

It was.

Steve sucked her pert breasts and flicked her hard and erect nipples with his tongue, and as he did, he paced his technique, mindful of Angie's progress with Janine's Button.

Angie was now licking Janine's wet Flower fast, capturing her Button in the furious up strokes, bringing Janine closer and closer to her climax.

Janine thought, *this is different; Angie was skillful but not as ravenous as Steve.*

The feeling was different but very satisfying, and as Janine built her orgasm, she could feel the sensations of Steve sucking her nipples, reaching out to merge with the rising ecstasy from her Flower and Button.

Steve then took her whole breast into his mouth, creating a full suction that drew the electric sensations in Janine's body to the surface. Somehow, he also used his tongue to flick her nipples.

Janine could not work out how he did this.

Now, the rising orgasm from her breast play and the orgasm from her Flower began to merge, and when they did, she exploded in a deep orgasm.

Steve and Angie had collaborated to achieve a double orgasm simultaneously. It felt like one orgasm at the same time. Each experienced as a breast orgasm *and* a clitoral orgasm, but the total pleasure they provided was greater than the sum of each individual orgasm.

They settled with Angie's head on Janine's stomach, and Janine's head on Steve's chest.

Janine could hear both their heartbeats, both fast from sexual arousal, both warm and full of life.

They rested for a short while before Janine turned over, grabbed the cord of Steve's dressing gown, and started to undo it, saying, "Now, where is he?"

"Where are you, big boy? I need you, and I suspect I won't be the only one."

Steve moved to the couch, sitting up as Janine removed his dressing gown, revealing his naked body and a huge erection.

Angie stared at it for a few seconds, then looked at Janine.

As if communicating in telepathy, Angie's expression was *Oh my god,* and Janine's telepathic reply was, *I know, really thick, isn't* it?

It took Angie a minute to compose herself, and when she did, all she could say was, "Now I know why you two are at it all the time."

Janine was now kissing Steve, and Angie was working out how she would approach this. Finally, Angie decided to continue her attention toward Janine as Janine focused on Steve.

Janine was now kissing and sucking Steve's nipples, and he was enjoying this. He had found it unusual, to begin with, but every time she did this now, he started to feel his nipples wake.

Angie stood behind Janine and caressed her back and buttocks. She chose right because Janine moved her hips in anticipation as Angie got closer to her Flower.

She was beckoning for more.

Finally, Angie moved right under her as Janine leaned over Steve and took his cock in her mouth.

Janine moaned as Angie probed her wetness with her fingers and stimulated her Ani with the other hand. Fortunately, she had enough passion juices in her for the Ani stimulation to be smooth, and Janine was pushing back for more.

Steve was moaning as Janine sucked him deeper and as he watched his Janine being aroused by whatever Angie was doing behind her. It was enough just for him to see that Janine was getting off on whatever she was doing.

Janine was getting wetter and hotter, and she decided she needed more. So she straddled Steve on the couch as Angie reached between her legs and took Steve's cock in her hand, and helped probe Janine's Flower for its entrance. Janine moaned and lowered herself just a little, leant forward, placed her head on Steve's shoulder, and then lowered herself past his thickness, giving an audible gasp.

"I'm not surprised at that gasp," said Angie, "I can see from here as it went in, very erotic and oh so big; you must be full," she added.

"Certainly am," said Janine, "full and deep."

Angie was now sitting on the floor between Steve's legs and had a full view from the rear as Janine and Steve started to fuck. Slowly at first but getting increasingly faster.

"This is so hot," Angie said again, "you should see this, Janine," hinting at what she might like to be doing soon.

Angie reached between her legs and wet her fingers with her juices, then returned to Janine's Ani; she circled her at first, then punched through to stimulate her internally. Janine gasped as she did; Janine liked this even more with Steve's thick cock inside her.

"I can feel your cock filling her," Angie said, and she finger-fucked Janine up the butt in time with their vaginal fucking, "god, this is so hot," she added. Angie took her other hand and started to masturbate, wetting her fingers with her thick juices and rubbing faster as Steve and Janine fucked each other harder.

They were getting close, and Janine started screaming, "Fuck me, baby, fuck me harder, BOTH of you, fuck my cunt, fuck my Ani, god this is good, deeper, deeper, god I'm going to cum, cum to, baby, cum with me," and with that, she exploded into her orgasm and so did Angie, screaming and writhing as she did, "oh god this is hot, fuck I'm cuming too."

Janine and Angie came together, filling the room with moans, screams, and religious profanities.

Despite the intensity of having two girls cuming in front of him, somehow Steve did not. He had more work to do and more fun to have.

They all rested a little, recovered, washed, drank, and moved to the bedroom. There they had access to play lube, a large mirror, and a comfortable bed.

They were all completely naked now and comfortable with this; Steve was still partially erect when they hit the bed. Janine lay down first, lengthways on the bed, head on the pillow, and beckoned Angie to treat her pussy to some more oral sex.

Steve was unsure of what to do, but when Angie climbed on the bed between Janine's legs on all fours and started to kiss her Flower, Janine said, "I'm sure Angie could use some attention from that impressive cock, my lover; it's fine, I'm good with that."

"And I certainly am," said Angie, wiggling her raised firm arse a bit as she enticed him to mount her.

Before Steve could even get on the bed, Janine was moaning to Angie's adept tongue, and as Steve watched the sight of his lover and Angie, his cock grew hard and thick. Pre-cum oozed from the tip.

He climbed the bed, but wary that he may need to prepare Angie, he started using his tongue on her from behind. As Angie had raised her butt high and her legs spread, access was not an issue.

She moaned as he touched her with his tongue, and he could feel immediately that she was very wet.

He had forgotten that Angie and Janine had been attending to each other, and this alone would make her hot, wet, and ready for him

Angie appeared to enjoy what he was doing, so he lingered for a while, carefully teasing her with his tongue to the sounds of his lover Janine saying "yes, like that, more and firmer, faster," to Angie as she taught her what turned her on the most.

It was very erotic, and he soon grew hungry for Angie's cunt. He moved, grasped Angie by the hips, and, with his left hand, guided his cock as he probed her wetness for her opening.

As Steve pushed gently forward, he felt the difference; it was hard to explain, but every woman was different. He pushed forward; she was tight and had said she had not had sex for three months. Steve felt her resistance, felt her tighten from the anticipation of what was to come next, then punched through her. She moaned loudly; she did not gasp but cried out, "God, that's good," as he filled her.

Janine was looking at Angie as she lifted her head to breathe and smiled at her and said, "I never get used to it and never tire of it either; he has the best cock ever."

Angie smiled back before she returned to pleasure Janine.

It was hard for Angie to focus on pleasuring Janine's Flower, but Steve fucked her in a way that he did not move Angie too much so she could still pleasure Janine.

He started slow, with deep, deliberate thrusts that Angie seemed to like. He had moved as far forward as he could, so the angle put most of the pressure from his cock on her G-spot.

He waited as Janine built her orgasm. Janine was now trying to teach Steve's special technique to Angie as she sucked and flicked her Button. As Angie went faster with her sucking and Janine got closer, Steve timed himself to give Angie her orgasm as Janine came.

He could tell Janine was close, so just as she tipped, he thrust deeper into Angie's cunt. Now freed of her task with Janine, Angie moaned louder as Steve plunged deeper than he had before. Angie tipped and screamed, and pushed back against him hard again and again as if she was seeking more to heighten her climax. Steve held back.

Somehow, he had managed not to cum, despite the intense and sexy pleasure this threesome was giving him, but he was on the verge of exploding.

It was time to change positions and mix it up a little. They positioned the large mirror now so they could all get a good view of their passionate sex. They had been so excited earlier that they had forgotten all about it. It was now in the corner of the room, high up and tilted so they could see the entire activity on the bed.

This time, Angie took the prime position, lying on the bed on her back with her head on the pillow. Janine had suggested that Steve teach Angie the special so that she could, in turn, provide it to her. So Angie lay back, knees in the air, anticipating something, even as she had no idea what the 'special' was.

Steve was crouched on his knees, head in Angie's cunt, and was starting to taste her as lay on her back. Janine now had her head between Steve's legs and was caressing his balls with her tongue from underneath him, moving it across his perineum and his Ani as she did.

Steve had trouble concentrating with this stimulation but managed to focus enough to ensure Angie's pleasure.

Now and then, Janine would grab his thick, erect cock and run her tongue down its shaft before taking it completely in her mouth. In this position, she could accommodate him completely, and occasionally, Steve nearly came.

He tried to focus on his lesson for Angie and now had her engorged clit in his mouth and was sucking it. Angie was impressed and said, "So this is the special, it's wonderful, thank you for sharing this, Janine."

Janine called from under Steve, "Not yet, wait for it, you'll know when it is special."

With that, Steve started to take her clit between his lips and flick it hard and fast. It did not take long for him to take her from pleasure to ecstasy; and as he did, she cried out, "Oh mother of Jesus, Christmas has cum early, my god, I'm cuming already, fuck, fuck, oh my god," and she screamed her orgasm out of her.

Janine was now very aroused at hearing Angie's pleasure and sucking Steve's pulsing cock, so Steve and she moved into one of their favorite positions. As Steve mounted Janine from the rear from the side of the bed standing, with Janine across the bed on her knees, Angie lay across the bed masturbating herself. Steve used a little play lube to ease into Janine and began a slow and deep movement that filled her.

Janine still gasped as he entered, savoring the full sensation of his cock filling her. Steve started to pick up the pace, as he could tell that Janine was building fast. With the sight of Angie getting off on their fucking (she could not take her eyes off them) and the image of them fucking from behind from the mirror, it did not take long for all three to build close to orgasm.

They were not sure who tipped first, but regardless of whoever did, it was only seconds later that they all followed as Steve fucked Janine hard and deep to the sounds of Janine's call for him to fuck her faster and Angie's moans as she rubbed her engorged clit fast.

They all came together in a chorus of groans, moans, and "oh god, I'm cuming."

Steve came this time, moaning as he spurted his warm semen deep into Janine as she pushed back, squeezing her Flower to get every last drop of him.

Finally, they collapsed on the bed, exhausted from their lust.

Steve ran a bath after he recovered. The girls lay on the bed, gently touching themselves, Janine on her Button and Angie using her fingers inside her vagina as she was too sensitive to touch her clit.

It was a glowing thing, a wind-down to recover slowly.

When the bath was ready, they all got in, soaked for a while, and talked about sex, their lives, and the yacht. Steve confessed to Angie that this was his first time with two women.

Angie was surprised and commented that he appeared to manage it quite well.

He had maintained his focus on his lover, waited for them to give the OK for what happened, and most importantly, saved his semen for Janine only.

They laughed because Janine was not of childbearing age now anyway, but Janine soon confessed that this part of their lovemaking was special to her, and it may have hurt if Steve had cum in Angie *first*.

They took turns washing each other's backs slowly and gave each other a short back and neck massage. Steve washed Janine's front, lingering on her breasts for a while, massaging her nipples, and Janine squirmed in the water, getting wet deep inside her.

Next, Janine started to wash Angie's front, and as she did, Angie's nipples firmed and grew. Angie's nipples were very sensitive, and it was evident from her response that she enjoyed having them touched. Janine wondered.

She looked at Steve, and he understood straight away.

They both moved toward Angie and started to kiss and suck one of her nipples each. Angie enjoyed the attention and liked the sensation. It was always one of her favorite foreplay moves, and she started getting aroused again. She was about to start masturbating in the water, but as she placed her hand on her clit, Janine moved it away.

"Patience," she said, "just go with the sensation for a while."

Steve and Janine now stepped it up a bit. Janine had felt this many times before, so she knew what to do.

He started to flick her left nipple with his tongue and suck deeper, and Janine followed on her right breast. Then he took as much of Angie's breast in his mouth as he could; this was most, but not all, as she was fuller than Janine.

Janine did likewise. She could not get as much in as Steve, but it was enough because, as they both started sucking deep and flicking her large, firm nipples with their tongues, Angie responded as planned.

"Oh, that's good," she said at first, then, "oh my god, what are you doing that goes right to my... Fuck, I'm cuming, oh god," Angie cried loudly and moaned her orgasm moan and heaved in the water with a climax.

Angie almost went underwater as she arched her back and would have if Steve and Janine had not been firmly clasped to her breasts.

"How the fuck did you do that?" Angie said as she regained her composure. "I did not think that was possible," she added.

"Welcome to the breast play club," said Janine. "I only recently joined thanks to Steve, and I never knew it was possible either. Great, isn't it?"

Angie agreed with a smile and a nod of her head.

They slowly dried each other, and Angie got dressed.

They kissed goodnight, Steve on her cheek and Janine on her lips, and Angie returned to her cabin. Steve and Janine climbed back into bed and kissed passionately.

"Thank you," Steve said as he cuddled up to Janine's back. "That was very generous."

"The pleasure was mine too," she replied. "But I thank you also for the sensitive way you approached it. At least we can tick off having a threesome at the QT with a cute redhead off our bucket list."

They woke late the following day; it was around three a.m. when Angie had left, and she did not wake them for breakfast.

Not surprisingly, they were hungry by lunchtime, and the crew had returned from their overnight exploits. Janine mused about them, thinking they had fun and poor Angie had to stay on duty.

Little did they know that she likely had one of the best nights she had ever had.

The crew readied the yacht for the trip to France, and by four p.m. they departed.

The yacht moved quickly; the repairers had included a full service, so the QT was in peak condition. They were headed to Bordeaux and would be there late afternoon the next day, given the favorable winds blowing across the Atlantic Ocean.

Janine was relieved that they would continue to track the coast and land would not be that far away.

They retired to their cabin after dinner and ran their bath. They usually took the opportunity for a little oral while the bath was filling. The large bath gave them time for him to warm Janine up and build her slowly before giving her a special.

Steve loved oral before the bath because it ensured he had her when her womanhood was strong, and he could taste and breathe her in. It always turned him on and made his manhood respond accordingly. He went to the bath with a full erection that she always liked to see.

She loved that he was hot for her, and it always made her wetter. After a little oral for Steve in the bath, they settled down for their bath conversation and the inevitable discussion about what happened with Angie.

Steve said he was excited about it, but most of his excitement came from watching them together. He had to confess that fucking Angie was also enjoyable, but even then, fucking her with his lover present had made it quite an experience.

Janine reassured Steve that she was OK and had enjoyed the excitement of the threesome. It was, for her, a bit of fun, sexual, and titillating, but she did not have any longing or sexual desire for Angie or even frequent threesomes. If it happened again, she might, but she was not looking to construct situations so they could do this regularly.

He agreed that he was also not after regular threesomes.

They decided that Angie was a one-off and that they would not try to engineer another get-together with her. They dried off, climbed into bed, and kissed passionately.

Steve told Janine that he valued the way they could talk through any issue and come to an understanding. He said, most of all, he appreciated her honesty.

He kissed Janine again, then moved to her breasts.

His cock was already firm, and as she stroked it, she admired its thickness and anticipated it filling her. As he sucked on her breasts and flicked her nipples, he used his other hand to stimulate her Flower and Button. He first placed his fingers on the outside of her Flower and felt her wetness before inserting his fingers. Janine moaned. He used her juices to stimulate her Button while increasing the suction on her nipple.

Janine's passion was rising. Again…

She was roused and wanted him inside her, so Steve mounted her on top. Janine lifted her knees so she could feel him deep, and as he probed her Flower for her entrance, she almost came. She caught her breath as he pushed through and felt his thick cock fill her.

She was very aroused now, and he was deep inside her.

They fucked like this for a while, savoring the sensation of building toward orgasm, and then Steve started to suck her breast again while slowly fucking her deeply. Janine was now building her breast orgasm as well. He knew just how to tip Janine when breast-playing her and knew the signs of her impending climax.

As she was getting closer, he asked her to close her legs flat on the bed while still inside her. Janine knew what was coming. He started to build his rhythm inside her. This position was good for both of them. She had pressure on her Button, and he felt her tight.

They both built fast, and she knew then that Steve would cum with her.

That excited her more so that as Steve sucked her breast harder, flicked her erect nipples, and fucked her faster and deeper, she tipped over both ways. Her breast orgasm joined the orgasm from her vagina and melded with Steve's as they both moaned their climax moan and called out to each other that they were cuming.

It was intense, hot, and a surprise for Janine.

They spent the next half hour caressing each other, basking in the glow of their passion before Steve gave Janine a goodnight special, and they fell asleep locked in a warm embrace.

primal

They arrived in Bordeaux the following afternoon, excited to be in France again and keen to get off the yacht. They had had little contact with Angie since their encounter, and she was on deck and on duty the day they arrived.

Angie called out to say have a good day as they left the yacht, and they turned to see that Angie was smiling and walking over to them. As she did, she said, "It's OK, you know, it was a bit of fun for me too; you don't have to avoid me; I was not expecting more."

They smiled back at Angie and said that was a relief because they had felt a little uncomfortable and embarrassed.

They bid her farewell and headed to the center of town.

As they passed a French deli, they noticed it had ready-made picnic hampers and decided to check it out. They thought a picnic lunch the following day might be an excellent idea.

The deli was much more than they expected. They sold the whole picnic experience. A blanket, basket, plates, glasses, cutlery, and even small chairs could all be rented and stocked with the deli's delicious picnic foods. They could include wine or champagne and hire a small Renault with a map of the most romantic and secluded private picnic spots. They even could include a gas heater for those who found the chill of the southern French winter a little too much.

They ordered the full deluxe experience.

As they explored the local shops, Steve purchased a small bracelet that Janine liked. It was antique and had green tourmaline stones. He said the green highlighted her beautiful eyes.

They went back to the yacht, bathed, and had passionate sex before going to sleep early. Angie had served their dinner that night, and they were relieved that things were no longer awkward between them.

They were very excited when they woke, as yesterday they had studied the picnic map and found what seemed to be a beautiful spot by a running creek in the middle of an ancient cedar forest carpeted in green grass. They had called and booked this with the deli.

They had their usual morning delight (a special followed by passionate sex), bathed, and ate a light breakfast to regain strength.

Then, they departed around ten a.m. in their rented Renault car, packed with their picnic supplies, for a two-hour drive to their picnic spot. They drove out of town and up the river valley, passing by the hundreds of small wineries.

It was the most beautiful farming country they had seen, with the patterns of the vines across the low hills creating a patchwork of greens, ambers, and reds across the countryside. As they climbed up the valley into the higher country, the farms became less frequent, and the ancient cedar forests of France became dominant.

They had chosen their picnic spot carefully, privately run, and off the tourist routes.

Better still, the deli arranged an exclusive booking to ensure their total privacy. They drove into the small farm driveway that straddled the forest. This driveway was the only way into this section of the forest, and the local farmer had boosted his income by hiring access and the privacy it provided to exclusive high-income customers of the deli.

They paid the farmer the required fee, and he let them through the locked gate that led through the forest to the river and the small secluded picnic spot.

They parked the car near the river and unpacked their picnic, blanket, and food. The river was beautiful, slow-running, and a small river beach looped around their picnic spot.

They lunched on French bread, cheese, and antipasto washed down with a lovely local Pinot noir.

It was surprisingly warm and sunny as the picnic spot was open to the sun at this time of the day.

A wall of cedar trees circled the area, creating a windbreak and insulation. Janine was getting hot and took off her blouse, so she only wore a bra. She had on a long skirt and had rolled this up to sun her legs.

Steve took off his shirt. He had a deep tan from his work, and although not muscular, Janine loved his physique. Janine was pleased that he was not hairy and that Steve shaved his nipples so that when she sucked his nipples, it was not uncomfortable for her.

They lay down on the blanket and kissed.

Soon their kisses became passionate.

The idea of being in pure nature emboldened Janine. She stripped down to her dark green panties, then helped him undress until he was completely naked. His thick manhood never failed to surprise her, and she breathed deeply with anticipation.

They cuddled as Steve sucked on her breasts. Her initial reservations about being outdoors quickly vanished when his attention moved lower. The sun warming her skin, the gentle rustle of the breeze, and the erotic thrill of being naked in the forest combined with his skilled touch to send her spiraling.

She responded quickly to his ministrations, occasionally thrusting her hips when he paused to admire her body. "More," she pleaded, "give me a special, baby, please."

When Steve finally took her engorged Button between his lips, sucking and flicking with increasing intensity, she cried out in ecstasy. "Yes, that's it, more, firmer!" Her orgasm hit with such force that for a moment, she forgot to breathe.

It only took thirty seconds before she was on her knees, "I want you," she said, "I need you, serve me, baby, take me here in the forest like an animal. Fuck my cunt, baby, fuck it deep."

She was now like an animal herself, circling Steve on all fours, goading him with her sexuality, presenting her butt to him, lustfully eyeing off his thick cock as He rose to his knees and also went on all fours.

They abandoned the blanket.

The grass was soft and natural; they were animals full of pure lust; they wanted to feel nature as they moved around each other.

He moved to her side, trying to get to her, but she played with him and moved away.

His cock was aching, bulging, and thick, and he was getting impatient.

He moved behind her and sniffed her from behind to breathe in her wild scent.

It drew him further toward her.

Then, finally, he caught her and rose behind her, grasping her hips to lock her in his grip.

She could not escape now that he had her, and she was his. He did not need his hands as his erect cock moved between her legs; he had her pinned now, and although she feigned struggle, she could not move; his cock probed her; she was wet and ready for his semen.

He pushed forward but met resistance, so he went firmer until he punched through.

As he did, she gasped louder than she had ever before, but not in pain.

It was primal, an ecstatic gasp as if she had finally found her mate and was reveling in her seduction of him.

Then he filled her completely with his cock, deep and total, soaked in her juices as it slid deep within her. "Oh god, that's good," she cried, "fuck me, fuck me, fuck me like an animal."

He did not need coaching; he was pumping Janine like it was his last fuck, deep, faster and faster, as she screamed, "Yes, yes fuck me, baby."

They were on the grass, naked in the forest, alone and fucking like two primal animals.

Janine was lustful, taking her mate completely, and her orgasm was building fast.

He was getting close but held his orgasm back; he wanted this to last; he wanted to cum with his lover, and he knew she loved that.

He was groaning, and she could tell he was on the verge; she tipped over, screaming through the forest's silence.

"I'm cuming baby, god fuck me fuck me," she cried.

He fucked her, pushing himself through without control, tipping with her as his building orgasm exploded deep within him. He could feel his semen rise from deep inside him, travel up his cock, and fill her, filling her deep as his climax continued pulsing throughout his body.

"Fuck," he cried, "oh baby, I'm with you, I love your cunt, baby, I love your Flower," He added, groaning and screaming so that his cries melded with hers in a passionate song that echoed throughout the forest.

Janine tightened her Flower and squeezed his cock as they both came, holding him deep inside her, pumping his semen from him, savoring his girth, his firmness as her orgasm continued to pulse through her body until satisfied, she relaxed and lay down; feeling very pleased with herself for her seduction of her mate.

They sat for a while, taking in the sounds of the forest, the river, and the birds and talked. Then, they slowly re-emerged from the glow of the lovemaking, and Steve caressed Janine tenderly.

She was aroused again and started sucking Steve's now-soft cock, coated with the taste of her and his cum.

He stiffened at her touch, but it was too soon, so he moved his attention to her Flower.

He straddled her sideways this time, and with one hand, he placed his finger inside her and the other pressure on her pubis. Janine felt the soft grass on her back as she lay there, her legs raised and open to him. She felt the familiar sensation his G-Spot stimulation caused, a rising orgasm with a strange sensation that if she did, she might pee.

It was incredible, and she silently signaled him with her eyes when he was in the right spot for her, and her orgasm built as he did. It was not long before she was at the point where she needed to bear down, to let go even though her brain said pee, but trusted Steve's assurance that even if she did, it would be OK.

Finally, she pushed through, and suddenly came a deep orgasm that shuddered throughout her body.

Her G-Spot orgasms were nice but not as intense, so she was always left wanting more. They were getting more intense as she learnt how to let go, and she understood that it would take time to learn how to do this just as she learnt how to feel her clitoral orgasms.

He was patient, did not push her, and reassured her.

He always followed with a special, and this was no exception.

He suggested she stand with her arms against a nearby tree, so she did. Her legs were open, allowing Steve to sit underneath her, back supported by the tree and giving him access to her Flower and Button in a way they had not tried before.

As he started to taste the juices of her Flower, she stood naked, looking around the forest and the river.

It was very natural and erotic and was making her very hot.

She was standing there but with a sensation between her legs that was so familiar.

As she could only see Steve's head if she looked down, it was very erotic to look around the forest while he pleasured her, imagining the stimulation was just there, that no lover was under her. She imagined this feeling was magically happening as she stood alone naked in the forest.

It was hot.

The sensation was now moving to her Button. It had slowly crept up her Flower and was now sliding across the hood of her Button. Now and then, it would slip under the hood and connect directly with her Button.

It sent a tingle through her.

She moaned. She could feel the familiar building of the tension between her legs as something clasped around her Button; it was like two soft lips holding her Button firmly.

And then suction.

Oh, the suction; it was drawing her orgasm out, sucking her orgasm to the surface, ready to be liberated.

She savored this sensation between her legs and squeezed her nipple with one hand, and then it happened.

As if from nowhere, a firm touch on her Button, direct and firm, mingling with the suction. Then again, it happened; it sent electric sensations to her core.

Faster this time, yes, yes, faster, she thought. It was all happening, suction and flicking, bringing her closer.

"Yes, yes," she cried to whatever was causing this, "faster, deeper," she screamed, "oh, suck it."

Janine could feel her Button had become enormous, and the sensation of this sucking and flicking finally tipped her over as she came like no other orgasm before it.

It had the intensity of having oral from her lover and the control of her masturbation; Janine almost had forgotten Steve was there, but she was delighted he was.

They chatted periodically in the afternoon that day, went for a bracing nude swim in the river, fucked again like animals as Steve took Janine on her back on the banks of the river, and he gave her three more specials before they finally packed up and left late in the afternoon.

Walking back to the car, leaves and pine needles clinging to their clothes, she felt a curious mixture of satisfaction and wonder. Their connection had transcended the civilized boundaries they typically observed, revealing something primal and honest.

Yet even at their most animalistic, there had been tenderness between them—a fundamental recognition that survived when all other pretenses fell away. She wondered what other discoveries awaited them in the months and years ahead.

They stopped at one of the wineries for an early dinner. It was busy, and they chatted about their naked forest romp and swim. They always liked to talk about their lovemaking.

It was almost as erotic as the actual act for them.

Almost.

They were deep in conversation when a loud gunshot rang out.

Steve's instinct kicked in as he jumped up to protect Janine from whomever it was before they both realized from the laughter that the bang was from a balloon that had burst and echoed through the stone walls of the winery restaurant.

A man was making balloon animals for a party group at the other end of the restaurant and had overfilled a balloon with his gas bottle.

He relaxed from his heightened alert status, but she began to worry if there was a connection between his 'Damascus issue' and his jumpiness. She asked him if this was why he was so jumpy and if it was an accident that Leila had bumped into him in Casablanca.

"Her timing isn't coincidental," Steve said. "Leila doesn't do coincidences."

"You think she's tracking you? Why?"

"I don't know. But there's a file—from Damascus. It was supposed to be destroyed."

"But it wasn't," she guessed.

"If the wrong people get their hands on it... " He didn't finish the sentence.

"I thought that chapter of my life was closed."

Janine watched him, this man she'd only just reclaimed...

"Is anything ever really closed in your line of work?" She added rhetorically to break the long silence that ensued.

The question hung between them, heavier than she'd intended.

They returned later that evening, bathed, and talked about their day, lovemaking, and even the 'shooting' incident, but carefully avoided mentioning Leila before retiring to make love one more time.

Again, it was a passionate session, lustful sex, with Steve on top and deep inside her as they both came together, embracing and wrapped in the love that had grown between them.

It was not erotic like the forest or with Angie but deep, meaningful, sexy, and loving so they both felt deeply loved.

With this warm feeling of complete connection, they drifted off to sleep that night and dreamed of each other.

The next day they spent a little more time in town looking at shops, art galleries, and a veterans museum built by the French in honor of the Allies in World War Two.

Then, of course, they had their bath, and Janine her special. He pumped his cock for Janine until he came over her breasts, partly because she really liked this and partly because she was sore deep inside her Flower from their animalistic fucking in the forest. She was not so sore last night, even when they fucked, but when she woke the next day, she ached deep inside.

He said he had to go to a covert office that the Israeli secret service had in town; he had to finish some of his retirement paperwork to access his retirement superannuation, and that it would take about an hour.

Janine suspected that this had more to do with the Damascus incident and Leila but joined his conspiracy to avoid the topic.

She spent this time at the shops, hoping to find time alone and get Steve a little Christmas present so his 'work matter' was also timely and convenient for her.

It was in a small antique shop that she found something. The owner was Jewish, and she had found this small, narrow silver case with what looked like Hebrew letters on it and had asked what it was.

He explained it was a Mezuzah, containing a special prayer and placed at the front door of a Jewish home. It was traditional for all Jews to have one on their front door frame.

Janine thought it might be nice for Steve to have one for their new home when they purchased one, so she bought it.

They met again at the art gallery entrance as planned in an hour.

Their day went fast, and they had lunch at a cute café before returning late in the afternoon.

Steve insisted that all the crew enjoy an evening off the yacht and said that he and Janine would cook their own dinner that night. Jessie agreed, not to rest the crew but to allow Steve and Janine some private time.

Jessie had been the mistress of discretion and had ensured the crew kept out of their way when below and at the other end of the yacht when they were bedding! As a result, the crew spent a lot of time cramped together at the other end of the yacht.

She was pleased to give her crew some space the night off.

Once out of the bath and alone, Steve handed Janine an apron for their cooking session but suggested that was all he wanted her to wear.

He had an apron for himself and put it on without anything underneath.

They headed for the galley where Angie had placed all the ingredients that Steve had asked for so he could cook his favorite meal.

They joked and laughed as they prepared a beautiful rack of lamb with rosemary and a mint jus and prepared a salad of mixed lettuce, capsicum, avocado, vine tomatoes, feta cheese, and fresh green chili.

Steve made a simple dressing of lime juice, sea salt, and vinegar. As they cooked, he occasionally cupped his hand on her bottom, feeling her 'curvy' bit as he did.

He loved the feel of that curved bit that marked the border between the lower part of her cheek and her thigh next to her Flower.

It turned him on to look at and it drove him wild to touch it. Janine, in turn, cheekily felt his bottom and occasionally gave him a little smack so that he knew she was still there.

They had fun cooking together, even though they had different ways of preparing the lamb dish they were cooking.

He placed the lamb in the oven and turned to see Janine at the galley sink finishing the last of the dishes.

The vision of her butt, the gap between the top of her legs and the definition view of her Flower from behind made his cock stir, and before he even realized it, it was firm and holding up his apron.

He approached her from behind, his thick cock seeking the gap between her legs and womanhood. He was aware of her need to be wet, so he placed his hand under the cheeks of her butt and felt for her Flower.

She jumped a little to feign surprise, but she was not. She had been waiting for this, anticipating the lust, fantasizing as she cooked that he would take her here.

She was already very wet, as he found when he probed her with his fingers.

"OMG!" said Steve, "You are dripping. I never knew cooking made you so aroused," he added.

Janine laughed, "Not sure I have been so aroused while cooking before, my love; it's the sight of you naked in the apron, knowing that that impressive cock is there waiting and anticipating your lust for me, that does it. I'm surprised it took you so long."

He responded that they would not eat that evening if he had not shown such restraint, but for now, they had forty-five minutes before the lamb was ready.

He was still behind her and kissed her back. Janine stepped back and leant forward over the sink as he guided his cock to her Flower and probed for her entrance.

God, she is wet, he thought as he found her quickly and pushed her to make Janine gasp. He filled her and went deep as she enjoyed it, and as he started to fuck her, she became more vocal, asking for more, deeper, faster, as she built her climax.

The dishes started to fly as she grabbed anything to steady herself while he pushed his cock deep in her, pushing deliberately upwards to stimulate her G-spot.

"Take it, baby, take it all," Steve cried, "take my thick cock, baby, god this is good, let me fuck your wet cunt, god, take it, baby," He screamed as Janine, in turn, responded.

"Yes, baby, I am. Fill me, baby, faster, fuck me, baby. I want you. I want your cum, fuck, I'm going to cum, baby. Please cum, baby. I need you to cum. Oh god, yes, yes, yes, ooohhh," as she tipped over with Steve groaning as he came with her orgasm pulsating his cum deep inside her as he did.

He had no intention of cuming then. He had wanted to take her face to face on the galley table, but her plea was so desperate, so erotic, he could not hold back.

He had let go, and she loved it.

Indeed, she wanted him again and again, but she had learnt he was capable of a quick recovery, and he had so many other ways to please her and make her cum.

Janine yearned for him to lose control, wanted to feel that he desired her so much he could not stop himself. Not all the time, of course, but it pleased her that she could make him lose control this time.

It was hot and erotic.

She was very pleased with herself and her lover.

They had a lovely evening, enjoying their rack of lamb and salad, had an excellent red Bordeaux wine they purchased from the winery with the balloon man, an intimate conversation in their bath, and by then, as he had recovered, were able to fuck on their now-favorite chair in their lounge.

emerald

The crew returned latish but were up early and had set sail for England before Steve and Janine even woke.

Their next port of call was Bristol on the west coast, and from there, they would visit Bath, where Steve's late mother was born and grew up.

It would take two days.

The two days flew by as they took turns napping, engaging in passionate sex, playing board games with various crew members, and indulging in long baths and deep conversations. Additionally, Steve and Jessie were teaching Janine the art of sailing.

They were very content, and she slowly put Damascus to the back of her mind.

They arrived in Bristol just before lunch, nearly Christmas Eve.

They had made good time, and they were keen to explore Bath.

They had a car waiting for the hour's drive to their hotel in Bath. The hotel was built around old Roman baths and was in the city's center. The original owners built the hotel with a sensitivity toward the historical Roman baths, and they complemented them with several private baths for their wealthy guests to enjoy. They were replicas, of course, with the traditional opulence of the Roman baths and all the modern conveniences of today's plumbing.

They indulged in a delightful high tea in the hotel's grand dining room, savoring tiny cakes and Darjeeling tea. Steve, a coffee connoisseur who rarely ventured beyond his preferred brews, made an exception. He insisted on having tea here in honor of his mother, a tea enthusiast who cherished her tea.

Their room was a stateroom with two bedrooms, a lounge, and a dining area. It had a beautiful bathroom and a lovely double-clawed bathtub, but Steve had reserved one of the private Roman baths for several hours that afternoon. They undressed and slipped on the traditional Roman togas that the hotel provided with the Roman bath experience and headed down to the area where the baths were.

They were greeted at the bath reception by a valet who escorted them to the private area they had booked. He provided them with a key and explained that they wouldn't be disturbed for the three hours and that there was antipasti, cheese, and fruit, orange juice, and, of course, champagne on ice.

They had provided Verve as Steve had requested.

He then discretely left them to their privacy.

They entered the baths and locked the door behind them.

It was vast and looked just as you would expect a Roman bath to look. The room was about the size of their entire suite and had high ceilings. A large square bath was set at the backside of the wall, three meters square, with steps on one side.

The water was hot as it was steaming in the slightly colder air of the room. There were two sizable waterproof sun chairs with towels, food, and drinks on the table.

The hotel had installed a phone in case they needed anything else.

They did not.

Steve had ensured he brought the play lube in his dressing gown. He made some joke about having a bath in Bath, and as usual, she was not always amused by his dad joke humor but smiled just the same as it reminded her of her father's corny jokes!

They disrobed and stepped slowly into the hot bath.

He was always in awe of her body, and she noticed how he looked at her as she dropped her robe.

She smiled inside and felt a little wetness rising in her from the knowledge that this man, her lover, thought she was sexy, beautiful, and very desirable.

Steve, in turn, stiffened at the idea of their time together in this Roman bath.

They had champagne in glasses and toasted their time together.

Janine's toast to Steve's mother touched him.

Then, they chatted about their time with Angie and the sex in the forest. They liked reliving these experiences and discovering what each other particularly enjoyed about their lovemaking.

It also aroused them.

It was not long before he was breast-fucking Janine, bringing her to a small but enjoyable orgasm to warm her up.

They were very relaxed in the bath and had plenty of time, so she sucked his cock as he sat on the side of the bath. Steve lay back on a towel with Janine still in the bath, his legs wide open as she teased him with her tongue on the shaft of his cock, his balls, and his Ani.

Janine used a little lube around his Ani, causing him to move his hips, seeking more. She used more lube and slowly slipped her finger in.

He gasped at this, but it was a good gasp.

With her other hand, she held his cock as she sucked it deeply and stimulated him inside with her finger. She could tell he was building and she was getting wetter from this erotic foreplay. Janine did not want to take him over the edge; she wanted that cock inside her, and now it was time.

She washed her hands in the little side basin at the edge of the bath and rinsed herself with the hand shower connected to the tap.

It had good pressure, so she had to try it.

She sat on the top step of the bath next to the basin and hand shower so her Flower was just out of the water and invited him to watch her cum with the water pressure.

He found this erotic as he loved watching his love pleasure herself.

Janine started using the hand shower the usual way and enjoyed the pleasure it gave her until Steve suggested an alternative position.

He suggested that she turn over and get on her knees and use the hand shower upwards against her Button. He was always turned on by this view of Janine, and his cock hardened at the prospect.

He found the play lube and started to stimulate Janine's Ani, and Janine, just like he had done, pushed her butt back against Steve's hand, wanting more.

He slowly slipped his finger into Ani and started to finger-fuck her, placing pressure downwards onto her vaginal wall.

Janine was building fast with the water pressure, and the added stimulation of Ani was bringing her rapidly to climax. "More," she cried. "More, deeper, more, baby, yes, that's good," she called, but when he inserted a second finger, she immediately tipped over, crying out; "Yes, yes, oh baby, I'm cuming, fuck me, fuck my butt, oh god, this is erotic, ooohhh," and she heaved as she came with a deep orgasm.

He was rock hard by this stage, excited by Janine's reaction to his finger-fucking her Ani, and when she saw him standing firm and thick, she wanted him more than ever.

She sat back at the bath's edge, where the bath's bottom was the right height for him to enter her while he was standing in the water. Janine placed her legs up and was wide open as he approached her, his throbbing cock in his hand, heading straight for her waiting Flower.

He probed her, and she groaned, "Fuck me, baby, I want you deep; please, fuck me, firm, baby," she said before he entered her.

She gasped as he did and moaned loudly as his cock filled her and went deep inside her.

"Yes, baby, that's it, that's my big boy, that's my sex on legs, fuck me deep, yes, firmer, yes, faster, babe, oh god, this is good, I'm going to cum," she cried.

"Yes, baby, me too," he replied as he fucked her deeply.

"Not yet, baby," she called. "Not yet, please, hold back," she added as Janine tipped over into her orgasm, heaving as she did and squeezing her vagina as if to pump his semen from him.

There was none to pump as, somehow, he had held back despite his highly aroused state and desire to fill her with his semen.

Janine lay back, glowing from her climax, recovering fast, and then leant over, grabbed the play lube, poured a generous amount on her hands, and grabbed Steve's still-erect cock and smeared play lube all over it.

He liked the sensation and said, "Do you want me to pump my cock and cum over you?"

Janine smiled and explained, "No, baby, I want you to fuck Ani, and I want you to cum inside her."

He looked down; she was still in the same position, and he could see her Flower, but as she lifted her legs a little higher, her Ani came into view. She took her hand and smeared the rest of the play lube all over her Ani area.

He moved closer and used his finger first to get her used to the sensation.

It was not long before she said, "No, baby, your cock, I want your cock in me. Now!"

He gently probed the entrance of her Ani; he could feel and see where it was.

He pushed, and as he looked down, he could see his cock slowly enter her.

Janine kept eye contact and nodded as he slowly entered her carefully.

"Yes," she said, "yes, that's it, more now, baby, yes, that's it, yes, that's good, oh god, yes."

Then, as he entered her fully, "Oh god, you fill me, baby, that's good, oh god, now fuck me, slowly at first," so he started to move in and out of her as she urged him on, "Yes, baby, that feels good, yes, faster, oh god, faster, deep, baby," she cried.

He started to fuck her faster until he was building his orgasm. It was erotic for him to see his cock deep in her, her Flower in full view, glistening with wetness from the desire she was experiencing.

He moaned as she cried for more, for deeper, for faster until he tipped and called, "Oh god, baby, I'm cuming, I'm fucking your butt and cuming in your Ani, fuck this is good," and then she tipped, having another orgasm she used to think was not possible with anal sex.

She cried out, "Fill me, baby, fill me with your cock, and cum," as she did.

They slowly disengaged as Steve's cock subsided and slipped back into the bath to soak and bathe in the glow of their erotic act. They drank champagne and later ate cheese and antipasti before fucking once more on the sun bed and finally returning to their room.

They had almost forgotten that it was Christmas when they woke the following day, but as they roused, Steve remembered something and rolled over, kissed Janine on her cheek, and said, "Merry Christmas, sweet pea."

Janine kissed him back and responded, "I assumed because you were Jewish that you would not celebrate Christmas."

Steve smiled and replied, "There are many atheists and agnostics that celebrate Christmas, baby. It's a festive holiday, and you don't have to believe in the Jesus bit to join in the fun. I like the festive nature of Christmas; it is fun, and I love the gift-giving part too."

Janine sat up quickly. "Gift giving, you mean you got me a gift," she asked excitedly.

"Of course I did, sweet pea. Did you think I would not?" he responded with a smile.

He reached under the pillow and pulled out a small wrapped package.

Sweet—it's small, so it must be jewelry, she thought.

Janine jumped out of bed, went to her small suitcase, and pulled out a small wrapped gift.

"Just as well; I got you a small gift, too," she said as she handed it to him.

"You go first," said he, so she carefully unwrapped her gift. It was a small box (*yes, jewelry,* she thought again), and she opened it slowly to extend the time of excitement, but was surprised to see what was inside.

It was a key!

"Oh, I see it's the key to your heart. How sweet," she guessed, trying to hide her disappointment. "Thank you, baby. It's so romantic."

He laughed. "My heart is always open to you, baby. You don't need a key for that.

"This is the key to our new home, just south of Nice in France. It's on the Mediterranean coast and is a renovated cottage with four bedrooms, a huge industrial-style kitchen, and a bathroom en-suite to die for with a black double bath.

"I was finalizing the sale the other day when I lied about the superannuation paperwork at the Israeli office. I was completing the paperwork for the conditional purchase. We take possession just as we finish this trip in Scotland, and we will fly there from Glasgow.

"I hope you are okay with me choosing our home, but I have a deal with the owner. If you don't like it, the sale does not proceed. I pay him three months' rent, and we don't have to proceed with the purchase. So if that happens, we can look for another home together, and either way, we get a holiday in Nice and you get to choose our Australian home."

Janine was speechless and turning the key over in her hand. She felt the weight of the gift beyond its physical presence. This wasn't just property but permanence—a declaration of intent more meaningful than any ring could have been.

He was offering not just a shared space but a shared future, the chance to build something lasting together. The gesture acknowledged both their past connection and future potential, a perfect bridge between what had been lost and what could still be created.

"Oh my god," she said, "I don't know what to say; I'm sure I will love it. Thank you, baby," she said, and then paused, "not for the house, although that is generous beyond measure, but for what it says about us. You want to spend the rest of your life with me; that is the best Christmas present you could have ever given me.

And now I'm embarrassed as I only got you a small trinket," she added.

"You did not have to get me anything, my love; you are my gift; you are the gift of a lifetime," Steve responded as he opened the wrapping on his gift.

He immediately recognized that it was a mezuzah and turned to Janine and said, "You could not have chosen better, sweet pea, because this will complete the house we have just purchased. It would not have been complete without it; it makes the house a home and speaks volumes of your love for me. Thank you, my love."

They kissed and wished each other a Merry Christmas, then made passionate love, had a long bath, and talked about how they would furnish their new home.

They had breakfast in their room before Steve said he wanted to show her something. It was in the hotel basement, so they would have to go downstairs. He took her down to the basement, where they met a porter who led them down a long corridor before stopping at the door. Janine was curious, but he would not tell her where they were going.

As the porter opened the door and the daylight filled the corridor, Steve finally said, "It's just one final present for both of us to make our home a home; I hope you like it."

As they stepped into the light and a small courtyard, another porter stood there; he had a puppy on a leash, a small English bulldog with a Christmas ribbon and bow around her collar.

"I hope you like her," he said, "she has the best pedigree in England, and her name is Emerald."

The puppy jumped up and down with excitement, and Janine looked around. They were in a small area that was the hotel's kennels, a service for their wealthy clients who could not bear to leave their dogs at home.

She ran up to the puppy, saying, "Oh, she is adorable, baby, so cute, and I love her name."

Suddenly she realized something, "But we are heading to Scotland on the yacht; how will the puppy, how will Emerald travel?" she asked.

He explained that he had to buy her in Bath, as this was where the best bulldog breeder in England was, but he had arranged for all her papers so that she could travel to Nice when they left Bristol for Scotland.

A family that lived next door to their new home would care for her. They were professional dog trainers and would continue the puppy's training. It would be less than a week before they were there and reunited with their Emerald. In the meantime, they could take her for walks, take her to Bristol, and help load her on the boat to France just before they left.

Janine turned to Steve and said, "This is the best Christmas ever; I love you!"

They checked out of the hotel later that morning after taking Emerald for a walk to the park, their bath, some particularly passionate sex, and a Christmas lunch at the hotel.

The hotel porter ensured that Emerald was watered, taken to the bathroom, fed, and prepared for their trip to Bristol and their Georgian hotel, which was located opposite a park. The car arrived, and they placed Emerald in the back with Janine and Steve. Janine spent most of the time ensuring Emerald was okay, but Emerald seemed to like travel and just slept in her travel cage most of the way.

They arrived an hour later, checked Emerald into the hotel kennel, and themselves into their room. It was at their usual standard: a large, separate living-dining area, a massive four-poster bed, and a large en-suite with a bath.

They took Emerald for a short romp in the park. She was energetic and loved to chase the small, soft ball that came with her and the traveling case. She was partially house-trained already, as good breeders would not sell the puppies until they were ten weeks old and seemed well settled moving from place to place.

They returned to their room for their afternoon bath, talked about Emerald, and prepared for dinner.

They had a lovely evening in the hotel restaurant, drank too much wine, and returned to their room feeling a little aroused. When they arrived in the room, they were surprised to see that the fire had been set and was now blazing. A large fur rug was on the floor in front of the fire.

They had noticed the fireplace when they checked in, but Janine had dismissed it as decorative (and Steve let her believe it was).

The rug appeared from nowhere (again, Steve feigned surprise), but Janine did not care; she loved the ambience in the room and immediately suggested they had their nightcap in front of the fire.

Their nightcap was hot chocolate, which soon arrived courtesy of room service. It was the perfect Yule time treat. And as they sat, they started to kiss, drawn in by the romantic atmosphere. Finally, they discarded their clothes to be naked on the rug by the glow of the fire.

He was already erect from his passionate kisses and was kissing her back and buttocks as she lay on her stomach, staring at the fire, enjoying the sensations.

Janine was getting increasingly more aroused but wanted to be pampered by his attention.

He produced some massage oil and started to give Janine a slow, sensual massage. He started with her neck and shoulders, slowly moving down her back until he reached her buttocks. He used his arms to massage her buttocks, massaging close to her Flower and her inner thighs now and then.

It was driving Janine wild. She could feel her wetness rising, and while she was enjoying the massage, she needed her lover's thick cock.

The fire spread light and shadow across her body, and he was in awe of her beauty. His massaging of Janine was sensual, and he was becoming harder as he did. He wanted her badly, but she was enjoying the massage, and he did not want to take that away from her.

Finally, she had had enough and sat up on her hands and knees and said, "Are you going to fuck me or what? God, I'm so hot, and I need your hot cock; I need HIM, please."

He was a little surprised by her sudden demand but was more excited by her assertiveness; it was hot, so he moved next to her on all fours. It was reminiscent of the forest.

Pure lust was driving them both.

He knew she wanted him, and he certainly wanted her, but he also understood the power of teasing in building sexual tension in them both. So he played with her, taunting her as he moved around her on the rug.

She had remained on her hands and knees and responded to his game. She would present herself to him and then move away a little; she was so wet now that her passion fluids were starting to dribble down her leg.

He could see this, smell her; he could feel her heat.

They continued to tease each other, each waiting for the other to cave in, her to submit, he to take her, but they both continued.

Then, finally, he started to move in a way that meant she could see his thick, erect cock more. He had taunted her with it before, and eventually, as he moved behind her to breathe her in, he was overcome by her scent.

He could not wait any longer to take her.

He moved to her side and grabbed her, rolled her over, and moved on top of her. He wanted her and to see her face as he finally entered her.

As he mounted her, she feigned resistance.

Janine did not *resist* long, and he quickly had her underneath him in seconds, her legs apart and her Flower centimeters away from penetration. He felt her wetness, probing and watching her eyes as he pushed forward.

Her eyes said it all.

As he penetrated her, she uttered a soft cry but did not take her eyes off his. He could see the desire in her, the pure lust for his cock, and the pure pleasure when he pushed in deep in her cunt.

They started fucking, her with her legs high up and his arms locking her hips in place so this when he thrust his manhood deep within her, she would not move backwards.

This made the depth total, every inch of his cock penetrated her, and the soft pad of his pubis pushed against her Button on each stroke.

He had moved a little higher on her to ensure this happened.

As he picked up the pace, he kept eye contact with Janine.

There was no need for words; her eyes said it all: fuck me deeper, yes, yes, I love that, more, faster, deeper; before finally, her eyes widened, and her pupils dilated, and her expression changed in a way that said: I'm cuming, baby, yes, cuming, god I'm cuming, and she breathed faster as she did, never taking her eyes off his as she exploded in an orgasm that he could not only feel, but could see her experience in the depth of her body through her eyes.

It was so erotic, beautiful, and sensual that he forgot to cum.

It was not long before she had recovered; it was never long, and she was soon kissing Steve on his chest; now and then, she would suck his nipples, hoping to teach them how to respond to her loving stimulation.

He now enjoyed this; it was sensual, but his nipples had not awoken completely, certainly not like hers.

He was still erect, aching for his climax and wanting Janine.

He moved to his knees again and got Janine to do the same.

He wanted something; she did not know what yet, and as he moved toward her, Janine's anticipation mounted. He then moved behind her and asked her to open her legs, and as she did, he moved under them from behind and on his back.

"Lower," he said, encouraging her to spread her legs and lowering her Flower to his face. Janine now lowered her arms and placed her Button on his thick lips, resting her head on her arms, waiting for this new position to bring forth its pleasure.

It did in full measure.

Janine sat on her knees, her legs apart, her head on her hands, and her lover underneath her, his wonderful full lips engulfing her Flower and her Button. She was in sexual heaven. Of course, she loved his mouth and tongue on her Flower and Button, but this was a little different, very sexy, and like her experience against the tree in the forest.

Janine could be alone or with her lover as she chose, a masturbation fantasy with all the benefit of perfect stimulation from his beautiful mouth. She could feel his lips against her and moved a little lower; he responded to her call, repositioned himself closer to her Button, and, using his lips, opened her up so he could caress her Button directly.

It was glorious, so hot, and she could feel herself progressively building.

As she did, she periodically lowered herself more to make the pressure firmer; he always responded in just the right way, and she continued to build and then rest as she teased herself with building and resting from his pleasuring.

She was building up to something good here; she knew it; she was in control and could shift the focus of his attention with a slight movement of her hips. Now she wanted this; she wanted this orgasm that had been tantalizingly close and teased her just below the surface of her body. She dropped her hips and wiggled her butt ever so slightly, then felt the response.

As she lay there completely focused on the sensation, she felt his lips clasp against her now engorged Button; his lips teased it out of her hood and sucked it up into the perfect position for the grand finale.

The anticipation was electric for her.

Then it happened: a slight flick of the tongue first, and then faster, firmer, and followed by such incredible suction she felt it would tear the orgasm out of her.

"Oh yes," she finally cried after being silent for so long, "I'm cuming baby, make me cum, my love, yes, that's it, god, deeper, faster, oh, oh, ooohhh," she cried as she came profoundly and intensely.

He felt her juices dribble on his face as her cunt contracted with her orgasm, and his cock stiffened from the pure lust of her orgasm and the scent of her.

Janine was desperately pushing her Flower in his face as if to pull every little sensation she could get out of her orgasm.

"Oh god," she said, "that was fantastic; we have to put that on the menu from time to time; I so loved that; thank you, my lover, for being so generous with your time and attention."

He was now intensely aroused and glad that he had taken his time with her; it had heightened his arousal, and he knew his orgasm would be as intense as hers.

But how did he want it?

He loved all the positions they tried: behind, on top, sideways, pumping his cock for her, and even oral (though he knew she did not want to tip him over that way often).

Even anal was on the list now.

He no longer had to choose because as he lay there carefully thinking about it, Janine had dismounted her Flower from his face, turned around, and now mounted him.

"Stay there, lover boy," she said. "I'm in charge here."

She grabbed his firm, pulsating cock and used it to probe her wetness before inserting it in her a little.

Janine took a very deep breath and then dropped right down, all the way, right through the resistance, until his firm manhood filled her. She cried out as she did, moaning as his cock slid through and stimulated every nerve fibre in her cunt.

"Oh god, that's fucking amazing," she said, as she looked down to see an expression of such ecstasy on his face.

He loves this, she thought.

It was now her turn to lock eyes with him, and she did not waver. As she rode him faster, she focused entirely on him, his eyes, watching every expression, seeking what it was that took him closer to his climax. She could see it; every time she moved a different way, she could tell what brought him close and what made his passion subside.

She liked the control.

She could tease him a bit and heighten his final climax.

She rode him in short drops, meeting his trusting hips as she did. She raised herself high and slid his cock full length into her cunt slowly and deep.

That's it, she thought, *that's the right move*, and she repeated this move for confirmation.

He groaned.

I have him now, she thought; *I control his orgasm, I can make him cum at my will*, so she started to move this way slowly at first, watching his climax build.

It was intense and very sexy as she pumped his cock with her Flower, bringing his climax ever so close. She was so focused on tipping him over the edge that when she finally took him over in an intense orgasm, she was surprised to feel herself spill over.

She had not sensed her rising orgasm.

They both moaned and breathed deeply as they came together, Steve pushing every last drop of his cum into her, and Janine squeezing her cunt to extract every last bit of his cum from him.

Finally, they both collapsed, exhausted.

They slowly fell asleep by the fire, waking at three a.m. and crawling into bed to be more comfortable.

Steve remembered their last act of passion, which renewed his arousal, and took Janine from behind as he spooned her on his side. Again, it was quick, passionate, and lustful, and although she was still half asleep, they both came again before finally falling asleep with Steve inside her.

The next morning was very sunny, and Steve had a special day planned for Janine. He would not say what, and resisted revealing anything despite her urges to take Emerald with them. It would not be appropriate for a puppy, and the quarantine regulations meant Emerald could not be in a rural area for three months before she traveled to France.

After breakfast, a driver picked them up and drove them to the countryside outside Bristol.

The country was comprised of lush green hills, mostly dairy farms, with periodic wooded areas that typified this area of England. Now and then, they drove through small hamlets, and she urged them to stop so she could look at the small village shops and markets. She purchased several small items that she thought would suit their new house, even though she had yet to see their new home.

After two hours, they arrived at a huge stately manor and were greeted at the door by a distinguished butler dressed in a period butler's suit.

"Very please to have you here, sir, madam," he said very formally, and as if recognizing them both.

Janine was now very curious.

"I'll take you into the drawing room for tea so you can refresh yourself from your journey; I will serve lunch at two o'clock, then your afternoon is your own. The valet will show you to the changing rooms after your tea so you can ready yourself for lunch.

"I have arranged for the driver to collect you at five o'clock this afternoon," he finished as he sat them down in a splendid room reminiscent of a Victorian home.

Janine was now so curious.

"Well, aren't you going to tell me what's happening?" she asked.

"In good time, Janine. I will tell you as we change," he replied sheepishly.

They had a delightful cup of Earl Grey tea served in a silver teapot by a maid dressed as if she had walked out of an early English novel.

Janine was slowly starting to understand.

Steve began the explanation as the valet took them to the changing room.

The manor was the home of Lord Butterworth: He inherited the large estate from his father, and it had been in his family for over 400 years. He was relatively cash poor (for a Lord, that is) and had to resort to renting his home out for 'Victorian Experiences' to help pay for the high maintenance costs.

Their experience was lunch and the opportunity to spend an afternoon walking the manor and its magnificent grounds with as much discretion as they required.

After the valet left them in the dressing room, Janine thought that he must have planned this all along, for on the chair was a full Victorian costume, including underwear, all in her size. They even had period shoes in her size.

They each dressed behind a dressing screen, so the impact was better when they emerged. It took a little while as Janine struggled with the corset and underwear provided.

When they finally came out from behind the screens, they were both stunned; before each stood a Victorian Lady of some standing and the Lord of the Manor.

"Why, My Darcy," Janine started, "You look particularly handsome today."

Good you have the right idea, Steve thought.

"Good afternoon, Lady Janine; what brings you to Duckworth Manor today? Should we walk in the gardens to discuss your business here?"

"Why certainly, Mr. Darcy," she responded with a smile that almost made her break character.

She enjoyed this game.

They walked around the gardens, chit-chatting about Janine's (character) aunt, that had the vapors and had to be rushed by carriage to see the local village doctor, only to find that she had been drinking a little too much that morning.

Mr. Darcy talked about the farm and the trouble he was having finding reliable laborers who were hard-working and honest, but it was clear that both were skirting around the real reason for the visit.

Mr. Darcy had heard the rumors already.

They were nearing the stables when she broke the news.

"Mr. Darcy, I must inform you that I am to marry Mr. Pemblebrook in spring; my father has insisted; he is worried that my delay in getting married may send the wrong signals to potential suitors. Moreover, he thinks I am headstrong and wants an heir."

Even though he had already heard the rumors, Mr. Darcy seemed shocked as he heard it from her lips.

"I guess that means you will be moving to London," he replied, trying desperately not to reveal his true feelings.

"I guess so, for most of the year, he has a country house not far from here though," Lady Janine replied. "I will try to visit now and then," she added hurriedly and then realizing she had been too bold, added, "with my husband of course."

These words hit Mr. Darcy hard; *husband, no,* he thought, *it cannot be, I cannot let this happen, I must, I must tell her.*

He failed, and like the shy coward he was, he could only muster a polite observation that belied the passion beneath the surface.

"Lady Janine, I had thought that one day in the future, the nature of our relationship may have changed, but now I see I must have been mistaken."

"Mr. Darcy," Lady Janine said as they were walking through the deserted stables, "I had no idea you would even consider such an arrangement; I would not have agreed to marry another if I had only known."

She spilled the words from her heart without a thought for their consequences.

It was too late, like Pandora escaping from the box; it had released hope and passion for them both.

It was a force so intense there was no stopping it now.

"Oh, Lady Janine, how could you have not known my heart beats every second for you? I spend every moment thinking of you; my love for you has burdened me, for I believed it unreciprocated. Until now, I assumed you saw me no more than a companion friend. How could I have been such a fool?"

Mr Darcy swept her into his arms and kissed her passionately.

Lady Janine swooned as he embraced her; she surrendered completely.

This man, the love of her life, had been her only desire for so many years as she had visited her friend from boarding school since she was sixteen.

He was her older brother, and she had loved him from the moment she first saw him.

It was unspoken love, her secret desire hidden because of the times, their age, and his clear disinterest in her in any way other than as a friend.

He was now passionately kissing her.

She did not care; she thought, *this was all she ever wanted and dreamed about and could not let it go.*

As he kissed her, Lady Janine felt strange sensations in her loins.

They were familiar; she had felt something like this while washing her private parts in her bath.

Lady Janine felt wet '*down there*', and even though she was scared, she did not care; it felt good, exciting, and a portent of something more. She had heard the stories about these feelings and sometimes played with herself in bed to see what would happen, but she only felt shame and abandoned the effort.

Now it was different, this feeling was different.

She did not care about anything other than this moment.

"Oh, Mr Darcy," she cried, "I have always loved you. I have never wanted anyone else but you. Kiss me, love me; I cannot marry another now I know you truly love me."

Her confession moved Mr Darcy.

"You have always been on my mind, Lady Janine, but I could never reveal my love for you as I feared you would reject me, and that would ruin our friendship," he said, as he felt his manhood rising.

Mr Darcy had always prided himself on his self-control. He had these feelings before but had always managed to suppress them as a gentleman had to exercise restraint, but the floodgates of passion were open now, and he desired her more than anything in the world.

Mr Darcy moved her to the haystack in the barn, and they fell onto the soft hay locked in their embrace. He was wild with passion now and ripped open her dress, popping all the buttons on the front, releasing her bosoms from their tight cage.

He held her breast with one hand and started to suck it with his mouth. It was instinctive, passionate, and lustful.

Years of secret love poured out of him and into her, and he moved his leg over hers and started to press his manhood against her.

She submitted willingly; she was his.

As Mr Darcy pulled up her dress and ripped at her panties, she did not stop him; she wanted him; she wanted to submit to his will, his love.

He had her pants off in seconds and undid his pants in equal time.

His manhood burst out as he did. It was large and thick, and when she saw it, she gasped.

She immediately understood where this was headed, which slightly frightened her.

It was so large, but she wanted him completely.

Darcy mounted her and felt her womanhood with his hand. She was wet, very wet, and that excited him even more. He guided his cock toward her wet entry, and as he did, he kissed her.

She moaned under his kiss, and as he pushed forward, he felt resistance.

Her hymen, he thought; he had heard stories at university. He remembered the stories: *push firmly, and it will break.*

So he did.

Lady Janine screamed and shuddered with delight, then cried, "Oh god, My Darcy, take me, take me completely, this feels so good."

She moaned in a way that he understood was pleasure.

He also felt intense pleasure, a sensation he had never had before. It drove him to push firmly and move faster inside her, and fucked her deep as she moaned and called out, "Yes, yes, oh god, yes, more, faster," until she screamed in ecstasy and she shuddered and shook just as he did likewise, and he spilled his seed deep inside her.

The sensation was beautiful, and he wanted more; she wanted more, but his manhood soon subsided.

Lady Janine was lying there now, touching herself, trying to find the sensations that came as she lost her virginity.

Darcy was likewise trying to make his cock harder; he, too, had not only lost his virginity but had cum for the first time in his life.

They both looked at each other; they did not break character. "Mr. Darcy," she cried, "that was wonderful, more please," she added, looking forlornly at his limp cock. "Can you make it work again, please?"

Mr Darcy looked at her still-exposed womanhood, and instinctively, he was drawn to her, bending over to kiss her wet and inviting lady parts.

"Oh, Mr Darcy, what are you doing? You can't... oh god, what are you doing?" she cried as his lips and tongue caressed her Flower.

"What are you doing to me?" she said, rhetorically as the sensations started to rise again in her.

Mr Darcy was unsure what he was doing, but some instinct drove him; he felt her parts with his lips and tongue, she tasted good, and she smelled even better, and as he moved his tongue, he began to understand her reaction and learnt what she enjoyed the most.

He found the spot, this button-like part of her Flower, and started to suck on it and flick it with his tongue. She moaned louder, and he moved his tongue faster and firmer as she increased her breathing before finally screaming again, "Oh god, that's magnificent, ooohhh," and she shuddered again.

They fucked again after he recovered. Then Lady Janine reciprocated and took his cock into her mouth; they kissed passionately and finally rose, adjusted their dresses as best they could, and strolled back to the manor, still in character.

"I will call on your father in the morrow," said Mr Darcy, "and demand your hand in marriage. If he refuses, I will have no option but to challenge Pemblebrook to a duel."

He would have no choice given what we have just done. But," he added, "if I don't survive, please remember me fondly."

It was at this point that Janine burst out laughing.

"That was fun, Steve, very sexy, and I have never done anything like that before. So sexy."

"I thought you would, my love, and I certainly did. It was so hot taking you as a virgin."

As they returned to reality, shedding their Victorian personas, Janine felt a lingering disorientation. The boundaries between play and truth had blurred in surprising ways. In pretending to be other people, discovering each other for the first time, they had somehow revealed new facets of themselves. Perhaps that was the true gift of their connection—the freedom to explore, to be multiple versions of themselves without fear of judgment or abandonment.

They were driven back to the hotel just in time to take their Emerald for a final walk, place her in her travel cage, and take her to the dock where the berth of the Bristol to Nice cargo ship was.

Janine spent some time saying farewell to Emerald. She had grown very fond of her in the few days since she had been in their life.

A tear rolled down each cheek as she left Emerald behind for the short walk to their yacht.

As they made their way back to the hotel, Steve comforted her with his arms. When they returned to their suite, they took a bath and had passionate sex.

Later that night, Janine woke to find his side of the bed empty. Through the balcony doors, she could see him on the phone, his silhouette tense in the moonlight. While she could not hear the conversation, the word 'Damascus' carried faintly on the night air. When he returned, he slipped into bed as if he'd never left.

"Everything okay?" she murmured, feigning grogginess.

"Fine," he said, too quickly. "Go back to sleep."

But his arms, when they wrapped around her, held her too tightly to believe him.

voyeurs

They set sail at first light the following morning; it would take two days to get to Glasgow. The sea between England and Ireland was known for its strong winds, but generally, they went north to south, and this wind would be no exception.

The yacht would have to tack up the English coast to Scotland, doubling the typical time it would take if the winds were southerly. They settled in for some serious sailing.

The crew were fantastic, the best in their class, and the yacht cruised through the seas effortlessly. They were now taking shifts with three on deck to manage the sails and tacking and two below. One rested, and the other would tend to their's needs. Each would only have four hours of sleep as they rotated through this pattern for the two days it would take.

It was pretty smooth sailing for the first day; Steve and Janine kept below most of the time, only emerging periodically to get some fresh air. The crew were always busy, and they did not wish to distract them or get in their way.

They did not mind.

Between their baths and intimate conversations, and passionate sex, the time passed quickly.

They often talked about their sexual experiences with each other, re-living each experience, getting aroused and hotter as each explained how they felt before satisfying their passion with another bout of passionate sex, masturbation, or oral sex.

During one of these sessions, she decided she would give Steve something she had never liked doing. He had just finished giving her a particularly erotic special, breathing her in deeply at first, teasing her and getting her particularly wet. Then, he spent some time inside her Flower with his tongue tasting her juices before sending her wild with the sucking and flicking of his tongue.

It was deep and satisfying, and she felt particularly grateful to her lover.

As was often the case, they followed this with some deep fucking with Janine on the soft chair in the corner and Steve on his knees. She was close to cuming, and Steve wanted to cum with her, but as he was close, she told him, "Not yet, baby. I want your cock hard for more after this," before she shuddered with another deep orgasm. When she recovered, she told him to swap places and sit on the chair. Janine dropped to her knees. She started to kiss him, then kissed his nipples, slowly working her way down to his cock.

Janine teased him, kissing him all over for a while before using her tongue to stimulate his shaft, balls, and Ani. He was aroused more than she had seen him before. He had not cum since the morning, and it was late at night. They had fucked and played around at least six times since then, and his tension was explosive.

Finally, she grabbed his thick, erect cock in her hand and started to pump it, slowly at first and then faster, as she leaned forward and took him into her mouth.

She lingered at first around the tip before plunging the entire length down her throat. Then, she started to suck him, taking his cock in and out of her mouth.

He groaned; he was close. *It was time for her to mount me*, he thought, *mount my cock, and fuck me on the chair*.

But she kept going.

He tried to stop her, to show he was close to cuming, but she pushed his hand away and just kept sucking and pumping his cock with her mouth until he could no longer hold back.

He shuddered and cried out as he did, 'oh god, baby. I'm cuming, move away,' trying to grab his cock and pump the now-committed orgasm out of him.

She stopped him and kept pumping his cock and sucking until he came, bursting his warm and slightly salty semen into her mouth.

She could feel his cock pulsing in her mouth; she could feel the semen rise, and she could feel it enter her.

Janine had done this in the past. She did not like the taste and braced herself for the inevitable.

It was different.

Steve's semen tasted different; it was not as salty or unpleasant as she had expected. Was it because men tasted different, or was it because she loved this man, and that had changed her perception? She did not know but was pleased to give him this at least once. *Who knows,* she thought, *maybe more than once,* as she kissed his now receding cock as he lay back, somewhat surprised at what had just happened.

A satisfied smile moved across his face.

The next day was not so pleasant as the winds picked up considerably, and the yacht lurched across the five-meter waves they faced when tacking into the wind. It was all they could do to stay in bed or sit in chairs—their bath was impossible as it would have simply emptied itself of water along with them had they tried.

They had managed a special in the morning and a passionate fuck in bed with Steve on top of Janine and her lying face down, but as the winds picked up, that made any form of other sexual activity nearly impossible.

By lunchtime, it was even more impossible as Janine returned her lunch to the sea via the toilet bowl as she heaved from sea sickness that even the most seasoned sailor could not avoid in this weather.

He comforted her and managed to get some intra-muscular Maxalon into her (he almost stabbed himself as the boat lurched just as he was about to jab her in the buttock with the needle), and slowly the anti-nausea drug helped settle her.

The yacht had an excellent first aid kit, and it carried plenty of Maxalon.

And so went the rest of the afternoon with Janine recovering for several hours, finally throwing up again, and Steve giving her more Maxalon. They could not eat, and it was all they could do to drink a little water to keep them hydrated until finally, he could no longer take it and heaved into the toilet.

This time Janine had to play nurse and give him a shot of Maxalon.

She laughed quietly to herself as she did; she did not like that he had seen her so seasick, and this evened the ledger somewhat.

It was midnight before the yacht turned into the large bay off the Irish Sea and the protection of the large and hilly islands of Kintyre and Arran, shielding the bitter northerly wind and rain from the sea and yacht.

The winds dropped considerably, and the waves tossing their large yacht subsided to smaller one-meter waves. It would still take them all night to sail up the coast from here, into Wemyss Bay, and finally down the Clyde River to Glasgow, but it would be sheltered sailing, and they and the crew could get some well-overdue sleep.

It was the first night they had slept together and did not make love.

They were too tired and queasy to contemplate any passionate or romantic activity.

They made up for it in the morning, spending the first hours of daylight in various erotic positions before taking their morning bath and finishing with an intense special as the yacht sailed slowly down the Clyde River.

The river banks became increasingly dense with housing, industry, and fishing wharves.

It would have been clear to all on the banks what was going down on the yacht as it passed their shores, as Janine's vocal response to his pleasuring was particularly loud and profane that morning. The crew were in no doubt.

They docked five kilometers from the center of Glasgow at the yacht's home marina. There were others from Jessie's homeport staff to greet them, and they soon swarmed over the boat, taking their bags, cleaning, and relieving the crew from their yachting duties.

Finally, they all met in the marina's clubhouse for final farewells.

Steve and Janine went one by one to each of the crew and thanked them, giving them each a big hug as they did.

They left Angie to last, and Janine hugged Angie, giving her a lingering kiss goodbye.

As she hugged Angie, she placed a piece of paper in her hand and whispered into her ear, "This is my mobile number and our new address in Nice; if you are ever in the area or simply want to visit, just call. We would both love to have you visit sometime."

Their driver took them to their hotel just out of Glasgow.

'Hotel' was not the right word to describe this place's magnificent buildings. It was centered on a 700-year-old Scottish castle with a modern accommodation wing tastefully built on the side wing.

The traditional castle was open for the guests to see what life was like in early Scotland.

On the weekends, they served traditional Scottish meals in the large dining room and staffed the castle with fully costumed Lords, Ladies, and servants.

To make the experience even more authentic, the guests could roam around pretending to be part of the household on the weekend. It was a Thursday, so they would have to wait till Friday night to get that experience.

The room in their accommodation was grand, an adequate en-suite with a standard bath that would serve their purposes, and they walked the grounds once they settled in.

The grounds were beautiful and circled the old castle part of the hotel. It was quiet in the castle as it was closed to the public until the Friday dinner. The cost of staffing to the level of the olden days was prohibitive, so they could only open on the weekend when the modern hotel was at full capacity with high-income guests willing to pay handsomely for the experience.

They decided to get a driver and visit downtown Glasgow.

They first visited the famous Willow Tea Rooms and had beautiful cakes and tea as a treat following their somewhat nauseating experience up the Irish Sea.

Steve kept checking his phone frequently, although he was doing his best to be discreet and pay attention to her.

"Another message?" Janine asked.

"I am sorry," he put the phone away.

"I was trying not to worry you, but I guess the secrecy does not help. I was following up on the issue with Leila. There is nothing to worry about now. I have been calling in favors from former colleagues to ensure we can all put the incident behind us."

"Let's move on and see more of Glasgow," he said reassuringly.

After that, they visited the Glasgow School of Art. It had one of the top university-level art schools in Europe, and Steve had heard that among its collections were the early works of potentially some of the best up-and-coming contemporary artists in the world.

Some of these works could be purchased reasonably before these artists became widely known.

The collections included art from across the spectrum, including paintings, drawings, photography, and even artistic furniture.

They spent three hours there, casually walking through the exhibition center and the student rooms where the artists worked. Even though it was the term break and almost New Year, many young artists were busy creating their various artworks. Such dedication to their craft demonstrated the high standard of students that the school attracted.

They purchased a large nude of a woman and a man painted by a young woman whose talent was evident from the first moment they looked at it.

It was erotic but captured something else as the couple embraced.

If you could paint love, she had managed to do it.

They both loved that painting and had paid $5000 plus another $200 to have it packed and shipped to Nice.

The Gallery Director explained that the artist would be able to continue their study and feed themselves for twelve more months by selling her painting to them, and Janine and Steve thought it was good that they had managed both a good deal on the painting and supported a talented artist.

Janine purchased several ceramic pieces she wanted to use in their new home.

These were works of art, but she would use them as functional pieces. She thought they would hold salt and fruit or work as holders for her collection of peacock feathers.

They returned to the hotel, had dinner in the modern dining room, and returned to their rooms for a bath and a fun night.

They had their bath and fooled around a little there as a prelude to their usual passionate lovemaking.

Steve stopped dead as they stepped into the lush dressing gowns provided by the hotel and walked into the bedroom.

'Something's wrong,' he said.

Janine was startled and looked around the room.

"What, my love?" she implored. "I can't see anything wrong."

"That's just it. We can't see anything. Here we are in Scotland and sitting in a modern hotel. We could be anywhere: New York, Sydney, anywhere. Where is the Scottish experience? Where is the excitement in this room?" he asked.

"Apart from us," he added as he realized what he might have just inferred.

Then an idea hit him.

Janine always knew that look when it came; generally, it spelt trouble, a fantastic time, or both. But, whichever it was, she was always up for it.

"What is it?" she asked, "out with it before I get cold feet."

"Let's sneak into the old castle and up to the bedrooms, have a little illicit hanky-panky in olden-day Scotland, and sneak back again. As the whole castle is closed during the week," he suggested, "no one would know."

"What about the security and lights?" she responded. "And the locked doors and alarms?" she added. "And we don't have a key!"

"As good as," he responded.

"You don't think I worked for Israeli intelligence and did not get trained to pick locks and disable alarms, did you? I still have my little kit in my suitcase. Let's go; I saw an entry door at the end of our corridor; they must take the linen through when they clean the old castle and change the demonstration beds. I'll wager that will take us through to the bedroom level."

They snuck down the corridor in their dressing gowns, figuring they could say they were looking for the spa and sauna if anyone asked.

Janine stood to watch while Steve ably picked the door lock, and they slipped through and closed it behind them.

They kept it unlocked for a quick getaway should they need it.

Steve had explained that if they had an alarm, it would be directed to the inside corridor of the castle from the door, and once in, they would be undetected as long as they stood close to the door while he disabled it.

He pointed to the wires going to the detector above them, gave Janine a small pair of wire cutters, and lifted her to snip them.

Janine was scared but also excited. This was unlike anything she had ever done.

Once the alarm was disabled, they could walk around this floor and look at a few rooms, hoping to find a large bed they could christen.

There was a full moon, and they could see quite clearly. Finally, they found what looked like the main bedroom.

Perfect, he thought.

They entered, closed the door behind them, moved across to the bed, and were about to take off their gowns when they heard a noise in the corridor.

"Quick," Steve said, "behind the dressing screen over there."

They both hurried behind a large four-paneled dressing screen that hid them from view.

It was just as well because the bedroom door opened, and a man entered. They could see clearly through the gap in the screen's panels. It was one of the hotel staff; Steve had seen him before.

Perhaps he was security; they just might be caught, he thought.

Then suddenly, another figure came through the door. This one was a woman, about thirty years old.

He recognized her from the reception desk.

They shut the door and started whispering, then embraced and kissed passionately.

Steve and Janine looked at each other, smiled, and continued to watch the show.

The couple were having an illicit affair and had chosen the safety of this room to conduct it.

Steve thought about declaring their presence but noticed Janine was intently watching, so he let the scene play out.

They kept kissing with an urgency that suggested this was a new affair.

The man's hands explored her blouse while she felt for his emerging erection through his trousers. Soon, clothes began to fall away—her top, his shirt—leaving them both exposed from the waist up. He leaned down to suck on her ample breasts, their firmness and large areolae visible even from Steve and Janine's hiding place.

Steve felt himself stirring beneath his dressing gown while Janine remained transfixed by the scene.

When the couple moved to the bed, they were only 1.5 meters away. Steve held his breath before realizing they were far too absorbed to notice anything around them. The woman knelt to remove his trousers, then reached into his underpants to free his erection. Steve felt a flicker of relief that while ample, it wasn't as thick as his own.

Janine couldn't tear her eyes away as the woman took the man in her mouth. The secret voyeurism heightened everything—she reached under her dressing gown to find herself already wet with arousal. When she glanced at Steve, she noticed him watching her and the prominent bulge beneath his robe.

With a smile, she reached over to undo Steve's design gown and release his erection. With one hand on Steve's cock, the other on her Flower, Janine turned back to the unfolding scene.

The woman seemed satisfied she had her secret lover hard and stopped sucking his cock; she stood up and undid her skirt, dropping it to the floor.

She allowed the man to remove her panties, and he fell to his knees to help her take her feet out and kiss her vulva. Finally, she rolled back onto the edge of the bed, allowing him access to her cunt as she lifted her legs in the air.

Steve and Janine could hear his sucking and licking clearly, and from what they could see and hear, it was clear he was inexperienced and had no idea of what he was doing because she had to reach down and masturbate her clitoris until she came with his mouth and tongue firmly focused on her cunt.

Her secret lover clearly did not understand what a clitoris was for or even if it existed.

Still the same, the sound of the woman cuming made both Steve and Janine very aroused.

Janine was now half pumping Steve's cock and masturbating as the woman came.

The couple moved.

This time, her secret lover tried to mount her on the bed in the traditional style, but she was not having any of that.

This woman was in control and more experienced than he. She made him lie on his back, and as if she knew they were there watching, she pushed him to lie across the bed and mounted him, giving them a prime view of his entry.

They could see both her, her cunt, cropped but not shaven, and his cock in her hand as she guided it lustfully into her.

Her secret lover groaned; and as he did, the woman muttered something that Janine thought was, *'You dare cum too fast!'* She started to ride him, slowly at first, then faster as she built her orgasm.

Steve moved closer to Janine and now placed his hand on her Flower, scooped an ample amount of her juices, and used it to pump his cock as Janine rubbed her Button.

They knew just what they were going to do.

They had to.

As the woman built her orgasm, Steve and Janine did too.

It was like they were in one sexual act, except the secret lover's presence seemed to be merely a prop for the combined pleasure for the three of them.

The woman was close but not satisfied with the cock inside her.

*Bet you wish you could have my man's cock in you right now, J*anine thought as the woman reached down and started the most rigorous masturbation they had ever witnessed.

The woman appeared to have forgotten, or chose to ignore, the man that was still under her, or at least it looked that way, and she rubbed her Button until she was screaming with lust.

She was coming, loud and completely. The man was starting too, and Steve and Janine tipped over.

Steve came onto Janine's breasts.

They both moaned a little, in muffled sounds, drowned out by the woman's screaming.

She was a vocal woman who had to proclaim to the world that she had climaxed.

It was hot, sexy, and very illicit.

They were fortunate that this woman was using this man for her pleasure only because no sooner than she had satisfied her desires, she was getting up and dressed, encouraging him to do likewise. "I have to get back to work," she snapped as he attempted to kiss her affectionately.

So sad, thought Janine. *Hot sex is great, but hot sex with love is much better,* as she thought of her and Steve.

After they left, Steve gave Janine a special, and they slipped out of the room and back to their suite unnoticed.

Back in their room, Janine found herself reflecting on the stark difference between what they'd witnessed and what she shared with Steve. The couple's encounter had been furtive, functional—a transaction lacking the fundamental recognition she felt in Steve's arms.

It wasn't just the physical pleasure that made their connection powerful, but the gradual unveiling of souls that accompanied it, the safety in which both could reveal their deepest selves.

On Friday evening, New Year's Eve, the castle welcomed the public; they dined in the large dining hall with about forty others, engaged in polite conversation, and took part in the after-dinner Scottish dancing lessons and the general festivities.

They slipped out quietly at ten p.m., bored with the American tourists who assumed the 'Mc' name in their family from 200 years ago gave them ancestral rights to do as they please in Scotland.

En route to their room, they passed the reception area. The girl on the desk looked at them with what Janine read as envy.

It was her, the girl from the night before; she was on duty, at least for now; who knows where she would end up later in the night.

She was not so attractive in full light but still sported the ample breasts that would ensure she would never lack for lustful suitors to fuck in the chambers above.

They returned to their room as planned to have a long bath so they could fuck from the end of the year until the next.

While everyone else would politely kiss those next to them at midnight, they would moan with the pleasure of their mutual orgasm.

They laughed about the poor hotel man, so dominated by the reception girl and the titillation of the voyeur experience.

toys

They moved to their bed around ten thirty and started to kiss.

"Wait," she said, "First, I have to give you a little New Year's Eve present. I know it is not traditional, but I could not resist.

"I purchased these in France and have saved them for this night."

Steve was curious as she pulled a wrapped package from under the pillow. "And before you protest, don't worry, it's a New Year present for the both of us."

There was one wrapped present, and whatever it was, it was for the both of them.

He racked his brains about this clue but had no idea what it could be.

He tore open the wrapping, excited to find out what she had given them.

It was two sex toys; one was a long pink anal dildo. It was not as thick as Steve's cock, but was about where he thought it should be for their anal pleasure and comfort.

The other was a strange shape, large on one end, curved up and curved back on the other. The box said it was a vibrator with a rechargeable battery for anal prostate stimulation for him, anal stimulation for her, or G-Spot stimulation for her.

"Thank you, baby," he said. "Now we have another set of twins. It's the perfect gift for us, and this is perfect timing. We could be a bit adventurous tonight if you are up for a bit of fun."

"Oh, I am," said Janine.

"I've been waiting patiently for this and cannot wait any longer. I want that curved one in Flower first, then we experiment with the anal stimulation the other will provide."

They began with his special technique. Janine was already wet with anticipation, and her orgasm shuddered intensely through her body. She loved the view from her position—her lover between her legs, his face reflecting pure desire as he pleasured her.

He moved to his knees and prepared the curved vibrator with a generous amount of lube. It slid in easily, curving upward to her G-spot. He started with manual movements, watching her reactions closely until her eyes told him he'd found the right spot. As he worked, she felt the familiar pressure building.

When he activated the vibration without warning, she nearly jumped from the sudden sensation. Within seconds, she was bearing down, squeezing out a deep, shuddering orgasm that left her smiling with satisfaction.

He was visibly aroused by her response. As he withdrew the toy, she pulled him toward her with her legs, guiding his hardness to her entrance.

"The vibrators are nice," she breathed, "but I need you to fill me."

She moaned as he pushed deep inside. The fit was perfect—she enveloped him completely, tightening around him and stimulating every nerve. Janine lifted her legs higher, urging him deeper and faster as her excitement built. Though Steve responded eagerly, he held back his own release, wanting to build the tension to something extraordinary.

He feigned his build because he knew that she would hold back so he could cum with her, and he wanted her to have that added excitement as she tipped over.

"Yes, baby, yes, I'm close, baby, I'm nearly there, cum, baby, cum," he said, but he did not lie.

He was nearly there, but it was enough to bring her to climax as he thrust his thick cock deep and fast into her cunt.

Janine shuddered, Steve moaned, and she moaned and writhed as she came, closing her eyes to focus on the sensation coursing through her body.

Janine instantly knew what he had done, or had not, to be precise, as the lack of semen pulsating into her was obvious. She smiled as she reflected on his sexual generosity.

They took a short break as they ran the bath, opened a bottle of Verve, so it was ready for midnight, and moved to the full bath.

They took their new toys with them.

Janine was so excited to try her new toy on him.

She was curious about the stories about the male G-Spot (sometimes referred to as the P-Spot) as it was the prostate that, when stimulated internally, could cause intense sexual arousal and, in some men, could even cause them to orgasm.

She wanted to see if this would work with him.

They lubed up the curved vibrator, and Steve sat on the edge of the bath with his back on the wall and legs up on the bath, so his Ani was exposed completely.

Janine twinged as she looked at him in this position, mainly as his cock was erect from anticipation.

She used play lube to stimulate him around his Ani first, teasing him as she did.

He pumped his cock as she did this because it felt good, but also because he knew she found that very sexy.

Next, she inserted her finger into his Ani slowly.

Janine liked the sensation of his Ani contracting against her finger, and the sight of her finger deep inside him excited her; she felt herself getting wetter. Finally, she picked up the vibrator and slowly inserted it deep inside him, turning it upwards so that its end rested on his prostate.

She moved it manually first, experimenting with different movements to see his reaction.

Steve reveled in the sensation, and he pumped his cock harder. Janine then turned on the vibrator on the slow vibration.

Steve's eyes lit up.

"Now that's interesting," he said.

"I've not felt anything like that before; it feels good," he added, still pumping his cock.

"Let's experiment with the different settings," she said, not waiting for a response before turning on a faster vibration.

"Oh yes," said Steve, "I like that one," but before he could settle into it, she switched again.

The fourth change did the trick: a fast vibration with a short pulse.

He came almost immediately, even though he was hardly pumping his cock.

"Oh god," he said, "that's like flicking a switch to make me cum, very interesting.

Very nice," he added.

The unexpected orgasm had them both surprised and pleasantly so.

Suddenly, they heard fireworks and realized it was midnight; the New Year had arrived. They had almost forgotten.

They kissed passionately, wished each other a happy New Year, and then toasted with their Verve.

"May 2014 bring love and passion into our new life together," said Steve as he raised his glass.

"May we never take our love for granted and ensure that in the years to come, we make up for the thirty-three years we lost," she responded.

It was now Steve's turn to experiment.

Janine leaned over the edge of the bath as he lubed up the long pink dildo that had waited patiently on the sidelines.

He loved her presenting her rear to him; it was very erotic, and he thought he would cum as he felt deep twinges inside him.

He could not resist trying their new toy inside her Flower as he probed her with the dildo.

Janine moaned a little "nice," then: "Not as thick as you, baby, but it's erotic having you use this on me."

She asked him to move it deeper and then faster as she used her hand to masturbate her Button. "Yes, baby, that's it, oh this is good, faster, oh god yes, I'm cuming baby, yes, yes, yes, ooohhh," she cried as she came.

He applied some more lube and now started to probe her Ani. He took it slow at first so she could get used to the sensation.

"Oh, that is erotic," said Janine. "Yes, I like that, it's very sexy," she pushed back a little, signaling she wanted this a little deeper and was enjoying the sensation when he started to insert their now clean curved vibrator into her Flower.

"Oh god, yes," she said, "I had not thought of that, both at the same time, god that's good; I feel so full of cock, turn it on baby, give me vibration, fuck that's nice, yes baby, more, faster, fuck, more, fuck me up the butt baby, yes, yes, yes, oh god, faster baby, make me cum, yes baby, fuck my cunt, fuck my arse, fill me baby, oh god, yes, yes, yes, ooohhh," she moaned as she tipped over into an intense and different deep orgasm.

"My god, that was good," she said, as she settled back into the bath to soak.

"Looks like we have found another thing to add to the menu, my love; that was very erotic."

"Yeah, it was pretty erotic for me too, doing that to you, watching you respond, seeing those two vibrators deep inside you from behind, it was so sexy," he said.

Then, they cleaned up their toys and talked in the bath for a little while.

Once back in bed, they kissed passionately.

They snuggled together afterward, while Janine traced lazy patterns on Steve's chest. Their exploration tonight had been about more than physical sensation—it represented their willingness to be vulnerable, to communicate desires without judgment. Each such experience built another layer of trust between them, another confirmation that they could grow together rather than apart.

This was their last night in Glasgow, and they would fly to Nice and their new home in the early afternoon.

Steve had arranged delivery of a new bed, an extra-large king bed, to their new home. It would be their only furniture for the first week, but they did not need much more. The rest of their combined furniture and belongings were being professionally packed and shipped and would arrive later.

They fell asleep locked in an embrace and dreamed of each other and their new life together.

They woke at six a.m., had breakfast in bed, fucked again, and had their bath.

After Steve gave Janine her morning special, they packed and checked out for the drive to the airport. They waited for their flight in the airport executive lounge.

Janine was thinking about the night before, the erotic time they had, and was getting wet again. She excused herself and went to the bathroom.

She was only gone about a minute (again too short for a wee), returned, took him by the hand, and dragged him to the lounge's shower room.

This time he knew what she wanted. He loved that she was always hot, he had a strong sex drive, and few women had ever satisfied his constant need for sex.

She was his equal in this respect.

There was a comfortable chair in this lounge, and they were soon fucking each other frantically as she straddled him while he sat in the chair.

Janine was moaning a little too loudly, but they did not care as she rode his manhood up and down.

The sight was too much for him as he sat back and watched his cock disappear inside her as she sat on him, only to reemerge as she lifted again and again and again as he tipped over from pure lust at this erotic view.

He rarely came before her, but he could not control himself; it was too erotic.

Janine was not disappointed; she liked that she could make him lose control.

She knew her orgasm would always be available one way or the other, and she was not disappointed as he gave her a special she would never forget.

Whether it was because they were in a public place, or the thought that he was giving her oral while she was full of his semen, or because she was so happy, or all of the above, his oral that morning was particularly good, as she had an intense and long-lasting orgasm (or was it two one after the other).

She was delighted with her lover, and she was happy.

sanctuary

The flight took four hours; they flew business class in the small jet that flew this boutique route and landed in Nice around three thirty p.m.

Their driver was there to take them to their new home. It was only thirty minutes from the airport, a short drive to a small coastal village outside Nice.

Janine had breathtaking views of the Mediterranean coast and sea as they drove toward their new home; *perfect*, she thought.

They pulled up to a driveway of a house, their house, and the driver opened their doors and started to retrieve their luggage.

Janine had the key ready.

The house was black and had a black roof, not typical of the Mediterranean style in the area, but it was a stunning and sat discretely in the landscape. It was a sizable modernized cottage-style house of two stories with lovely front gardens.

She was so excited as she put the key into the door and walked through the entry hall into a vast open-plan area with bi-folded panel glass doors looking out to a patio with what would have to be the most beautiful beach in the area and an azure Mediterranean sea.

It was stunning.

"Oh my God," she said, "you did not tell me it was right on the beach; it's beautiful."

Janine turned to look at the expansive kitchen with a double oven, a large island bench, heaps of cupboards, and the largest two-door fridge she had ever seen. She opened the fridge doors; one side was full of Verve and the other food.

"I had them stock the fridge; I figured we might need some food and some champagne; we are in France, after all," he said.

Janine opened the door next to the fridge, a large walk-in pantry with a wine cellar stocked with red and white wine.

The house's interior was painted white and was a blank canvas on which they could paint their taste, their décor. Two bedrooms were downstairs, a guest room with a lovely en-suite, and a shower and change room off the patio.

Janine was going from room to room like an excited child.

Steve followed behind, equally enthusiastic as he had only seen the photos and a detailed video and was not disappointed in his choice.

Janine ran up the short spiral staircase, another bedroom, and then a study with views across the ocean. It had wall-to-wall shelving and a built-in desk large enough for two.

There was room for two large armchairs near the door, which opened onto a balcony. Janine wanted to go out and see, but she was more eager to find their bedroom.

She ran down the hall and opened the door.

It was breathtaking.

The bedroom was huge, even with their new extra-large king bed already set up in it. *Nice bed,* she thought momentarily.

The bed faced the large folding glass doors with an even better sea view and opened onto the same balcony as the study.

There was a central wall against which the bed was situated, and behind it, on both sides, there was a spacious dressing room. There were doors on each side of the dressing room (*his and hers*, she thought). As she walked over to open one of the doors, she realized this must be the en-suite.

It was spectacular and had large windows on two walls, ceiling to floor, that took in the sea view on one side and the hills and city view of Nice on the other. There was a large double black freestanding bath right at the windows.

"Not very private," she said, thinking about their bath-time sexual activity. She did not mind being nude in public but not if it involved their passion.

"The glass is one way," he said. "no one can see in, and if you want to close the view from inside, you just press that button next to the bath," he added.

As he pressed the button to demonstrate, the windows suddenly went opaque, leaving enough light to make the bathroom romantic.

There was a separate shower room and a separate toilet. There was a bidet, as in the case in most modern French homes.

Janine turned to him and said, "It's perfect; I could not have chosen better myself. We can walk on the beach, entertain as we like, relax reading books together, and my god, we will have fun decorating this home. I hope you love shopping, my love?"

The driver had taken their cases upstairs and placed them in their dressing room.

They went back downstairs, and Janine went onto the patio to take in the sea views and air as Steve went to get two glasses of Verve from the fridge.

Standing on the patio, the Mediterranean stretching before her, Janine felt something settle in her chest—a recognition that had been building since their first meeting on the train. This wasn't just a beautiful house but the physical manifestation of their connection—a space where they could continue discovering each other, creating memories to replace the years lost. The path ahead wasn't certain, but for the first time in decades, it felt right.

Steve broke into her thoughts as he handed her a glass of champagne and raised his glass.

"To our new life together, sweet pea, may it always be as exciting as this," he said.

"To a perfect life, this could not possibly get better," she responded.

As she said this, a voice called out.

"Hello, Mr. Steve, are you there?" The voice called, and a woman walked through the door with Emerald bounding behind her.

"Oh, my god," she said. "I had almost forgotten; I was wrong; our life just got better," she added and ran to greet their puppy in their new home…

shadows

Emerald was first to notice, her puppy ears perking up at a sound too faint for them to hear. She trotted to the patio doors, tail wagging expectantly.

"What is it, girl?" Janine said as she peered into the gathering dusk. "See something?"

Steve joined her, champagne in hand. "Probably just a neighbor," he said to reassure her. But he scanned the beach with careful eyes.

Later, after they'd gone to bed, Janine rose for a glass of water. The kitchen was dark, moonlight streaming through the windows. As she reached for a glass, something on the counter caught her eye—an envelope that hadn't been there before.

She opened the envelope slowly, thinking it was a surprise card to celebrate their life in their new home.

It was not. Instead, it was a single photograph: Steve and Leila in what appeared to be Damascus – the infamous 'Operation Mirage' that had haunted him – arms around each other, laughing. Leila's piercing eyes cut through time as they appeared to reach through and stare threateningly at Janine. On the back, a message in elegant script:"*The past is never really behind us, is it? See you soon.—L*"

Janine stood frozen, the implications washing over her. Their perfect sanctuary wasn't as private as they'd thought. And whatever had happened in Damascus; work or romance related, it clearly wasn't finished or resolved.

She slipped the photograph into her robe pocket. Steve had been through enough.

Tomorrow would be soon enough to shatter their hard-won peace.

For tonight, she just wanted to feel his arms around her, before whatever storm Leila was bringing reached their shores.

To be continued in book two of the trilogy

D & V Lovers - love and life

Love the book?

Enjoyed this book? Please consider leaving a review on Amazon!
Reviews help authors and readers discover new books.

About the Author

After an extensive nursing and human resources career, Steve Dover is now retired in Tasmania, Australia.His private passion was to write - never dreaming that one day he would pick up a 'pen' and write paragraph after paragraph to his newfound love when in a long-distance relationship. But, before he knew it, he had written three erotic romance adventure novels!

Books by this author

D & V Lovers - with love and passion - (May 2025)

D & V Lovers - love and life - (September 2025)

D & V Lovers - and so it is - (December 2025)